Connections : short stories by
outstanding writers for

Lexile Value: 82OL

CONNECTIONS

Also edited by Donald R. Gallo

SIXTEEN: Short Stories by Outstanding Writers
for Young Adults

VISIONS: Nineteen Short Stories
by Outstanding Writers for Young Adults

CONNECTIONS

Short Stories
by
Outstanding Writers
for Young Adults

Edited by
DONALD R. GALLO

Delacorte
Press

2490

Published by
Delacorte Press
Bantam Doubleday Dell Publishing Group, Inc.
666 Fifth Avenue
New York, New York 10103

A portion of this book's royalties, earmarked for research in young adult literature, will go to the Assembly on Literature for Adolescents of the National Council of Teachers of English (ALAN).

Library of Congress Cataloging in Publication Data

Connections : short stories by outstanding writers for young adults / edited by Donald R. Gallo.
    p. cm.
    Summary: A collection of seventeen short stories by such noted writers for young adults as Gordon Korman, Chris Crutcher, T. Ernesto Bethancourt, Richard Peck, and M. E. Kerr, spanning subjects that include penpals, the first day of high school, computers, and family life.
    ISBN 0-385-29815-3
    1. Children's stories, American. [1. Short stories.]   I. Gallo, Donald R.
PZ5.C746   1989
[Fic]—dc19   89-1126
                                                                                CIP
                                                                                 AC

Manufactured in the United States of America
November 1989
10 9 8 7 6 5 4 3 2 1
BG

For my son
who, through excessive conflicts and sorrow,
has finally gained significant insights
in his painful struggle to connect

ACKNOWLEDGMENTS

As I compiled this collection and its predecessors, several authors have thanked me for giving them the chance to write something different and to be included in such good company. But it is I who am thankful to each of them for taking the chance on writing something for which there was no promise of acceptance. Of course, because the seventeen stories in this collection were judged to be the best from all those submitted, there are several other outstanding authors whose stories have not been included. Those writers are also owed thanks for their contributions.

Thanks are also due to three young people—Jeremy Goldberg, Cindy Romano, and Alison Trumbull—who read and commented candidly on a variety of stories submitted for this volume.

In addition, a special thank-you must go to the thousands of students, teachers, parents, librarians, and young adult literature specialists whose enthusiasm for *Sixteen* and *Visions* has encouraged the production of this third volume.

Don Gallo

CONTENTS

Introduction   xi

ENCOUNTERS

Dear Marsha   2
JUDIE ANGELL

Moonbeam Dawson and the Killer Bear   15
JEAN DAVIES OKIMOTO

Life's a Beach   27
SUE ELLEN BRIDGERS

A Reasonable Sum   45
GORDON KORMAN

A Brief Moment in the Life of Angus Bethune   54
CHRIS CRUTCHER

CLASHES

As It Is with Strangers   74
SUSAN BETH PFEFFER

White Chocolate   84
ROBIN F. BRANCATO

Mildred   95
COLBY RODOWSKY

SURPRISES

User Friendly 108
T. ERNESTO BETHANCOURT

Fairy Tale 123
TODD STRASSER

The Inn of Lost Time 138
LENSEY NAMIOKA

Love Potion 159
CIN FORSHAY-LUNSFORD

School Spirit 170
JERRY SPINELLI

INSIGHTS

I Go Along 184
RICHARD PECK

Tree House 192
ALDEN R. CARTER

After the Wedding 206
OUIDA SEBESTYEN

Sunny Days and Sunny Nights 218
M. E. KERR

INTRODUCTION

When *Sixteen* and *Visions,* predecessors to this volume, were first published, readers asked, "Where did you find all these great stories?" They found it difficult to believe that none of the stories had appeared in print before. That's probably because almost all other anthologies of short stories that teenagers have access to in schools and libraries consist of stories reprinted from other sources.

The seventeen short stories in this book, like their predecessors, were all written just for this collection. They were chosen from among more than two dozen stories submitted by some of the country's best and most famous writers of fiction for young adults. Stories by some of these authors—for example, M. E. Kerr, Richard Peck, Susan Beth Pfeffer, and Ouida Sebestyen—have appeared in earlier volumes in this series. Other writers appear here for the first time—T. Ernesto Bethancourt, Alden Carter, Chris Crutcher, Gordon Korman, and Jerry Spinelli.

The addition of those authors is significant to note: the two previous volumes had a predominance of female authors; this volume contains a better representation of male writers. There is also another important difference in this volume: none of the stories is about death. For some unknown reason, in more than half of the stories submitted for *Visions,* somebody was dying or had just died. So potential authors for this collection were asked to avoid death in their stories, if they could. All of them made a point of doing so. Instead, a different theme dominated the submissions for this collection: romance. More than half of the stories contain some boy-girl relationship. The seriousness of that relationship ranges from a casual attraction in "Life's a Beach," to the search for a marriage partner in "Sunny Days and Sunny Nights," and from a humorous attachment in "Fairy Tale," to a seriously sexual involvement in "After the Wedding."

But there are other themes and issues in most of those stories: self-image, conflicts with parents, relationships with peers, and interactions with teachers. Those issues and others—some realistic, some fantastic and supernatural—are the focus of the other stories in this volume. Together these stories are about Encounters, Clashes, Surprises, and Insights. In each story teenage characters gain perspective on their world, mature, and come to terms with peers, adults, and most importantly themselves. In short, they make connections.

We hope you as a reader will establish your own connections with some of these stories, that most of these stories will entertain you, that you will recognize yourself in some of them, and that you will learn from others.

If you've read *Sixteen* or *Visions,* you are already familiar with other stories by several of the authors in this collection. As a student, you may have previously read several novels written by some of these authors. Other writers included here may be new to you. In any case, you will find at the end of each story some biographical information about each author, along with a description of some of his or her most important novels. If you have enjoyed an author's short story, you may want to try reading one of his or her novels.

Read on!

ENCOUNTERS

Writing to a pen pal can be fun. It can even be helpful when you need someone to share your problems with. But for Marsha, it has an unexpected outcome. . . .

DEAR MARSHA

JUDIE ANGELL

July 13

Dear Anne Marie,

I guess this letter is probably a big surprise to you . . . I mean, you probably looked at the return address and sign-off and all and saw that it's from nobody you ever heard of, right? Well, here's the reason I'm writing.

Maybe you remember this assignment that the kids in our English class got back in February. Our teacher (Ms. Bernardi, maybe that rings a bell) wrote to your English teacher and she asked him if he'd like to do this experiment: He would send a list of all the kids in your class with their names and addresses and we would pick those names out of a hat and write a letter to the name we picked. See, you all lived far away and the idea was to see if we could form a "relationship" (Ms. Bernardi grew up in the sixties) with a perfect stranger, using only pen and paper. (Or typewriter, I mean, *you* know.) Anyway, Ms. Bernardi said she wasn't going to grade the assignment, or even see it or anything because this assignment was personal, just for ourselves. You know, to "express ourselves" with a perfect stranger. Whatever. So naturally, if it didn't mean a grade or anything, I didn't do it.

But the thing is—I picked your name out of the hat and I just sort of kept it, you know, and now it's summer and hot and practically all of my friends are away, so . . . Here's a letter. You're a stranger even if you may not be perfect (or maybe you are perfect, I don't know), but here I am, trying to form this "relationship" using only two fingers on the typewriter (please excuse the mistakes, I'm taking Business Typing next semester) and you're the one I'm supposed to try it with.

Well, I'm not going to say anything more until I hear back from you—Hope you turn out to be cool.

　　　　　　　　　　　　Your new pen pal (maybe)
　　　　　　　　　　　　Marsha

　　　　　　　　　　　　　　　　　　July 18
Dear Marsha,

Your letter was great! It really picked up a slow summer for me.

I remember that assignment. Some of the kids really got into it when they got letters from your class and they're still writing back and forth. The friendships are terrific because everybody feels safe with them, you know? I mean, because we're so far away no one knows anyone the pen pal knows. And since you never have to meet, you feel freer to say whatever you want with no one coming down on you or whatever, you know.

So I'm glad you wrote and I'm also glad it's now instead of then, because back in Feb. I was really *wiped*, I mean really. See, my dad died, it wasn't sudden or anything, he was sick a long time, but still it was very hard on everybody as you can probably figure out. So now it's just my mom and my sister and me and . . . we miss Dad, so sometimes we get on each other's nerves.

I guess if you wanted me to be the first one to give out personal stuff I guess there's that. Plus . . . let's see. . . . If you're thinking about "m-e-n," I don't go out a whole lot, but there's one guy I like at school. The thing is, he's *younger* than I am and I get embarrassed about that and since he doesn't even know I like him . . . I guess you can't count it as a "relationship." (That word bugs me too.)

I hope this is enough for you to think that maybe we could be friends, and I like the idea of a pen pal.

From
Anne Marie

July 21

Dear Anne Marie,

You are *definitely* the coolest person! I couldn't wait to hear back from you so I'm writing you the same day I got your letter.

I'm sorry about your dad. That must be tough to deal with. I mean, I have both of my parents and it never occurred to me that one of them could die. I know that sounds stupid, but I just never thought about it. They're okay most of the time, but really, I guess I just take them for granted, to be honest about it.

So now I'll tell you more about myself.

I'm a senior in high school, or at least I will be starting September. Which is okay, because the sooner I graduate the sooner I can start My Life. My dad says I could go to college if I want *(he's* the one who really wants me to go), but I'm not sure I could stand all that much school. I'm thinking about it more this summer, though, because I have this job at our local five-and-ten as a checkout girl and if anything is bor-ing, that is *it!* Here's what you get: "Mar-sha, last week you had green grosgrain in the sewing department and now it isn't there, why *not?*" And—"Mar-sha, you took ten minutes extra for lunch yesterday and it came off *my* time, so you better come back ten minutes early today." That kind of stuff. Borrrrr-ing.

Okay, well—I'm five feet five inches tall, which is about average, I guess, and I have black hair which in this weather

I wear either in a chignon (sp.?) or in a ponytail. It's pretty long and straight and I guess it's my nicest feature. I'm a cheerleader and I think my hair looks good flopping up and down when I jump. (I'm not really as conceited as that sounds!) Also I have brown eyes and no-more-BRACES. I'm pretty thin, which isn't too great when you wear a bathing suit. What do you look like? I picture Anne Marie as a blonde.

I don't have a boyfriend right now, although there's a very nice guy who works in the stockroom at the five-and-ten. Hmmm . . . maybe. . . .

Most of my friends got jobs at resorts and hotels in the mountains. I should have applied to one of them but as usual I was late and lazy, so here I am, bored at the five-and-ten. Write soon.

> Your friend,
> Marsha

July 25

Dear Marsha,

Boy, do I know what you mean about boredom! I'm working part time at my school—office stuff, and the rest of the time I'm at home because my mom and sister really need for us all to be together. Your town sounds like the same kind of hick burg mine is. You have one movie house and it's just got around to showing talkies, right? And: one Laundromat, a drugstore (NO BARE FEET, THIS MEANS YOU), a post office, and if you're real lucky, one of those no-alcohol bars for kids to hang out in on weekends.

One nice thing here, though—there is a lake we can go to. In fact, our family has always had a cabin there. It's called Lake Michigan, which was someone's idea of a joke because it's more of a pond than a lake and it has a lot more brambly woods than pond. But this summer no one in my house seems to have the energy for going up there a lot.

I'm a little shorter than you—five two exactly—and I do have blondish-brownish hair that's short and curly. I always wanted long black hair like yours. You sound really pretty and I bet that guy in the stockroom notices you pretty soon! I used to wear glasses but I got contacts finally and I think I look better now. Wish I had more to write but I don't, so let's hope things start to get more exciting for both of us!

Love,
Anne Marie

August 2

Dear Anne Marie,

It took me a while before I could write again. It's not that I didn't want to, but some stuff happened and I've been kind of scared and depressed ever since.

What happened was, this girl at work—she's the one I was kidding about in my last letter, the one who bitches about my coming back late from lunch. Her name is Claudia and we alternate shifts. Anyway, when I realized she was actually counting every one of my lunchtime minutes, I started coming back really on time, you know? Sometimes, even early. Well, last week when I relieved her, I counted up the receipts and the money in the register and stuff and it seemed to me that I was coming up short. The receipts and the money didn't check out, you know? But I figured it was me, I must've done something wrong. I mean, my math is hardly the greatest. So I let it go and when Claudia came back at four o'clock, I told her to check it out. So she did and said I was wrong and dumb and everything was okay and blah, blah, blah. But the next thing I know, Mrs. Handy, the manager, started checking everything between shifts because she said we were losing some money.

Listen, I won't drag this on, but accusations were thrown around and Claudia accused me of stealing. That was when I caught on that she was the one who was stealing and I knew that one time I got back too early for her to be able to hide it.

Well, of course she said I was the one and since it was her word against mine and she's a full-time worker and I'm only part time and no one noticed any shortage before I got there—naturally I got blamed. I wasn't arrested or anything because no one could prove I did it, but I did get fired. And as you put it so well, this *is* a hick burg, and I stand about as much chance of getting another job as I have of spreading wings and flying away. Which I'd sure like to do. I really didn't steal, Anne Marie. I hope you believe me. The cute boy in the stockroom sure doesn't. You should have seen the look he gave me.

So . . . things got exciting for a while, anyway.

Love,
Marsha

August 5

Dear Marsha,

I got your letter and broke into tears, I swear I did. Of course I believe you didn't steal anything. But they will find out eventually. Claudia won't stop stealing and I bet she does the same thing with the next person they hire and they will all catch on.

I feel so bad for you, I don't know what to say. After I read your letter I told my mom and sister that I just had to get away for a while, so I took the bus up to our cabin and that's where I am now. I'm sitting on the porch and looking out at (ha-ha) Lake Michigan and thinking about you. People can be so mean. But I bet there are lots of people in the town who know you well enough to know it was all a lie and will be glad to hire you.

It's so peaceful up here, really. Just about an hour and fifteen minutes north of my house, but it feels like another world. Wait a minute, Marsha. . . .

You won't believe it! I'm back now, but I had to go inside and close the windows and doors and spray everything with Lysol! While I was sitting there describing all the peace and quiet, this SKUNK marches right up on the porch and lets me have some of what skunks do best! YUUUUCH! This is just AWFUL, did you ever get a whiff of skunk? They say tomato juice takes the smell away, but I don't have any and what are you supposed to do, bathe in it or what? PEEEEW!

So I'm sitting here in this locked cabin wondering which smells worse, the Lysol or the skunk or the mixture of both, and thinking of you.

Love,
Anne Marie

August 10
Dear Anne Marie,

Your letter gave me the first good laugh I've had in a while! I'm still laughing because I think I can smell that combination of stuff you mentioned on the pages of the letter! You can't even imagine how much I wish I had a place to go like Lake Michigan (without the skunk!) but we're pretty far from any quiet place with water and woods. I mean, there's a pool at the town recreation center, but that's not exactly what I had in mind. The closest I can get to coolness and peace and quiet is my basement, but *that* smells of cat litter and Clorox, *almost* as bad as your place!

Well, my mom and dad believe I didn't take any money or anything else, but it's hard for them because everyone they know heard about what happened. And so when people say, "Oh, Marsha, wasn't that awful, we just *know* you'd never" and all that, I somehow get the feeling they're really thinking Maybe she did, you know these kids today. . . .

Anyway, tell me something good to cheer me up. Your

letters are the only nice thing to happen this whole stinking summer—NO PUN INTENDED!

Love,
Marsha

August 16

Dear Marsha,

I hope by the time this gets to you that you're feeling better. I want you to know I really do think about you all the time.

Maybe this will cheer you up a little. . . . Did you ever have a carnival come to your town? Our firehouse sits on a tract of land of about twelve acres and every year they put on a really terrific carnival. Picture this: There's a high booth on wheels with a glass window where you can watch a boy spin pink cotton candy around and around. Close your eyes now, and you can smell it, all sickly sweet and gorgeous, and you can make mustaches and beards and eye brows and earrings all over your face with it, you know? And they also have this huge plastic bubble, all different colors, with a foam bottom and you can go in there and jump your heart out. You fall over a lot, of course, but you don't get hurt even if you fall on your face because it's so soft. And there are these booths where you can throw baseballs at little Indian tepees and win neat stuff like plush polar bear dolls and clock radios and blow-dryers with three speeds and makeup mirrors and everything. And best of all is the Ferris wheel, because they stop it for a few minutes when you get to the top, and it's like you really are on top of the world. So picture yourself on top of the world and that's where you'll be.

That's where I was last night. And when I got to the top I thought about you and made a wish, so I know things will get better soon for you.

And also, guess what? At the shooting gallery, guess who

I met? That younger guy I told you about. And we went on the Whip together. And I'm going back tonight, so . . . who knows?

Love,
Anne Marie

August 20

Dear Anne Marie,

I have read your letter about eight hundred times. Where you live sounds so great. I pictured the carnival. I really tasted the cotton candy. I won a stuffed bear. I rode on the Ferris wheel with you and I think the "younger man" is cute. I liked being on top of the world, even if it was only for a few minutes.

Things here only seem to be getting worse. One of my girlfriends is back from her hotel job and you wouldn't believe how she sounded on the phone when I called her up. I feel like everyone's looking at me whenever I walk down the street.

Now I'm seriously starting to think about college, if only to get away from here. My dad says he's sorry it took something like this to get me thinking about it, but he's glad I am, he says. A blessing in disguise, he says. Ha, some blessing! But even if I do go to college, I still have a year of high school left and I honestly don't know how I'm going to stand it.

Tell me something else to smell and taste and ride on.

Love,
Marsha

August 25

Dear Marsha,

I think it's neat you're thinking about college. If you're lucky enough to be able to go, I really think that's what you should do. It's just my opinion, but that's what I think.

Marsha, did you ever see kittens being born? You have *never* seen anything so incredible in your whole life! My Y-M (younger man) works at his dad's carpentry shop in the summer and they have this mama cat who was about to give birth and he asked me if I'd like to watch. Well, it took from six o'clock to around ten. The mama had a litter of seven kittens, and they came out two, two, one and two, over all those four hours. They each came out wrapped in a shiny silver cover, which the mama licked up and ate. I know it sounds really gross, but it was honestly beautiful. Their teeny eyes were shut tight and they made these little squeaky noises and they looked at first as if they had no fur, but they do. Y-M says I can have one.

Keep thinking about college and you'll see how quickly the year will go.

Love,
Anne Marie

September 1

Dear Anne Marie,

It's Labor Day weekend and I'm spending it crying. The cheerleading squad is meeting Tuesday, the day before school starts and I'm "not welcome" on it anymore. I got the word straight from the captain herself. "Oh, I don't believe any of it, Marsha," she says, "but you know how people think of cheerleaders, they're supposed to represent the school's highest standards" and blah, blah, blah! "I know you'll sacrifice," she says, "for the good of the school." Right. Can you *believe* it? Anne Marie, it's *so* not fair!

Well, I can't handle it, Anne Marie, I really can't. I just can't spend an entire year at school like this. So I've made this decision, and I just know being the kind of person you are and with the kind of family you say you have, that you might be happy about it. This decision, I mean.

I know my mom and dad are on my side, but they're not, you know, the same as a *friend* or anything. And this summer, I guess you know that you became my very best friend.

I want to be where I can sit on top of the world on a Ferris wheel and watch little kittens being born and chase skunks away from a cabin porch. And spend all my time with a true friend, who's sensitive and caring and growing up with the same kinds of feelings I have. That stupid school assignment was the best thing that ever happened to me, Anne Marie, and I know I'm dragging this out, but here's my idea:

Could I spend the year with you? I swear on my own life I won't be any trouble, in fact, I'll be a help. With your dad gone, I can help make up for the work he did around the house. I'm very handy, I really am, I can do all kinds of things.

And best of all, we could go to school together, and do our homework together, and sit up nights and talk, and bake stuff and double date and go to the prom and make Senior Year everything it's supposed to be! And I'll bring my tapes—I bet I have the best rock and roll tape collection you ever heard!

Don't you think it would be great? Don't you? School's starting next week, Anne Marie. . . . Please let me know. . . .

Love,
Marsha

WESTERN UNION NIGHT LETTER TUES SEPT 5

DEAR MARSHA—YOU MUST STAY IN SCHOOL, RIGHT THERE IN YOUR OWN TOWN—IT WILL BE HARD, VERY HARD, BUT YOU MUST DO IT—REMEMBER, YOU DIDN'T DO ANYTHING WRONG AND THEREFORE YOU MUST NOT RUN AWAY—YOU MUST NEVER LET STUPID AND CRUEL PEOPLE GET THE BEST OF YOU—I AM SURE YOUR MOM AND DAD HAVE TOLD YOU THE SAME—HOLD

YOUR HEAD UP AS HIGH AS YOU CAN AND GIVE THAT CHEER-
LEADING SQUAD A GOOD RASPBERRY—

MARSHA, I CANNOT TELL YOU HOW SORRY I AM FOR THIS—MY
NAME WAS NOT SUPPOSED TO BE INCLUDED IN THAT LIST YOUR
TEACHER RECEIVED FROM OUR TEACHER—SOMEONE MUST
HAVE PUT IT IN AS A JOKE—BUT I DIDN'T MIND BECAUSE YOUR
FIRST LETTERS WERE SUCH A JOY THAT I SIMPLY HAD TO AN-
SWER THEM IN KIND—THEN WHEN YOUR TROUBLE BEGAN, ALL I
WANTED WAS TO MAKE YOU FEEL BETTER—MARSHA, I HOPE
YOU WON'T MIND THIS—I HOPE IT DOESN'T MAKE ANY DIFFER-
ENCE TO YOU—I HOPE WE CAN CONTINUE TO WRITE AND BE
FRIENDS—

DEAR MARSHA, MY DAD DID DIE LAST WINTER AND I DO LIVE
WITH MY MOTHER AND SISTER—THEY ARE EIGHTY-THREE AND
SIXTY-THREE, RESPECTIVELY—I'M THE PRINCIPAL OF OUR
SCHOOL AND I'M SIXTY-ONE YEARS OLD—

> ALL MY BEST LOVE,
> ANNE MARIE

JUDIE ANGELL

Judie Angell is the author of *In Summertime It's Tuffy; Tina Gogo; Ronnie and Rosey; A Word from Our Sponsor or My Friend Alfred; Secret Selves; Dear Lola or How to Build Your Own Family; What's Best for You; The Buffalo Nickel Blues Band; Suds; First the Good News; A Home Is to Share . . . and Share . . . and Share; The Weird Disappearance of Jordan Hall;* and *One Way to Ansonia,* a novel based on her immigrant grandmother's life from 1891 to 1899 on the Lower East Side of New York City when she first came to America. She is currently working on a sequel to that book for adults.

Under the name of Fran Arrick she has written highly praised novels that deal with the harsher aspects of teenage lives. *Steffie Can't Come Out to Play* tells the story of a runaway teenager who is led into prostitution in New York City. It was named an Outstanding Book for Young Adults by the American Library Association in 1978 and was followed by *Tunnel Vision,* which was listed among ALA's "Best of the Best" books in 1983. In *Tunnel Vision* several characters—adults as well as teenagers—examine their past relationship with Anthony, a bright, well-liked fifteen-year-old who has committed suicide.

In *Chernowitz!* a teenager in a small community has to confront anti-Semitism spread by a vicious bully in his school. Religious extremism is the subject of *God's Radar,* another ALA Best Book for Young Adults. *Nice Girl from Good Home* explores the destructive reactions of a girl whose father has lost his job and whose mother cannot cope with the loss of their comfortable existence.

The author lives with her musician husband and two sons in South Salem, New York.

Moonbeam Dawson had never even owned a toy gun, but to impress beautiful Michelle Lamont, he promises to take her hunting. . . .

MOONBEAM DAWSON AND THE KILLER BEAR

JEAN DAVIES OKIMOTO

Moonbeam Dawson got sick of explaining about his name. The problem was at its worst during the height of salmon season when the lodge was loaded with guests. Once he'd thought of making a tape. He'd have a miniature electronic gadget, like James Bond might have, and he'd casually flick a tiny switch hidden on his pants, in the pocket or something. Maybe on his belt. So when some guest said, "Moonbeam? You're kidding! Moonbeam! How'd a guy get a name like Moonbeam?!" he'd flick the switch, the tape would come on, and he'd go about his business, busing tables, or pouring water. He wouldn't even have to look up. The tape would play and say the whole thing:

When I was born my mother lived with a group of people on Vancouver Island in a commune. They called themselves the Happy Children of the Good Earth. All the people named their kids things like Rainbow, Meadow, Starlight, things like that. She named me Moonbeam. Then the Happy Children of the Good Earth got all pissed off with each other. They had a fight about weeding the vegetables. Some people yelled at other people for not doing enough of the

work, then one of the Happy Children of the Good
Earth bashed another one over the head with a rake
and the whole place fell apart. Then my mother got a
job as the cook here at the Pine Tree Lodge and we've
been here ever since.

Moonbeam especially wished he had a tape like that this
weekend, since the lodge was full up with a lot of first-
timers. The repeats knew about his name, so he didn't have
to go into it. Bound to be a busy weekend, he thought, as he
leapt off the bus and trotted down to the dock where the
school boat was waiting. It was a clear September day, crisp
and cold. The few trees that weren't evergreens were turning gold and the water of Barclay Sound was a fierce, deep
blue.

Jumping on the dock, he took one step—and then got
stuck. His legs just stopped moving. He saw a girl sitting on
the school boat, no one he had ever seen before. And not
just a regular girl. Probably just about the best-looking girl
he'd ever seen who wasn't in a magazine or in the movies,
but who was in real life. What was she doing there? He
couldn't stop staring. And why was she on his school boat?
Sitting next to her was a silver-haired guy who looked like
the guy from reruns of *Mission: Impossible*. Must be her father. Looked like a rich guy, too, not like anyone from
around there.

Moonbeam couldn't figure it out, the *Lady Rose* always
took the tourists down the channel. The only people who
rode the school boat were the handful of high-school kids
from Bamfield who went to Port Alberni High. They
boarded out with families in Port Alberni and went home
on weekends, since Bamfield didn't have a high school.
With a town of only two hundred you couldn't have much
of a high school. The boat, which took two hours, was the
fastest way to get to Port Alberni from Bamfield because
the only roads into Bamfield were logging roads; just rutty

dirt, dotted with boulders and pitiful. If you took them, it'd be at least five hours before you got there. Bamfield wasn't exactly the hub of Canada.

Moonbeam realized he must look ridiculous standing on the dock staring like that. So he threw his jacket over his shoulder, held it loosely with one hand, slid his other hand into his jeans pocket, and strolled slowly down the dock toward the boat. A cool breeze ruffled his hair. He took a deep breath as he reached the boat and casually swung his foot over the side.

"Ooops!" His foot slipped on the deck. "Oh sh—!" His right leg buckled under him and he crashed half in her lap and then rolled against the rail, banging his head. As he grabbed the rail to steady himself, his letter jacket flew in the water.

He couldn't believe it. Just when he was trying to make such a nice first impression, he practically squished her. "Sorry," he mumbled to the girl. Damn. Now his jacket was about to drown.

"Chester!" Moonbeam leaned over the side and called to the Coast Guard skipper who was loading the mail sack. "Can you grab my jacket?"

Chester fished out the jacket and lifted it up to Moonbeam on the boat hook. "Thanks, Chester." He leaned over the side and wrung it out. "Sorry," he mumbled again to the girl.

"Hi." She smiled, and Moonbeam thought she had the whitest teeth he had ever seen. He actually wasn't that much of a teeth man, but this girl's teeth were awesome. He was sure they just grew that way. Probably she'd never had braces. Moonbeam picked his teeth with his little finger while three other kids from Bamfield got on the boat. He couldn't decide if he should sit next to her or across from her. He didn't want to get her wet with his jacket. So he just stood in the middle of the boat wadding it up into a ball.

David McGraff decided for him when he shoved Moonbeam into the seat across from her.

"Watch it, will you?" Moonbeam growled.

"You're blocking traffic, Dawson." David looked up at Chester, who was starting the engine. "Where's the *Lady Rose?*"

"In dry dock for repairs." Chester headed the boat away from the dock.

Moonbeam looked at the deck, at the mailbag, at the dock fading from sight behind them, and at Chester. He looked everywhere but at the girl. David McGraff was already buried in a rifle magazine and the other kids started to nod off the minute they got in the channel. Most people slept on the way home. By the time they passed the fish farm five miles out of Port Alberni, David McGraff was asleep too.

"Do you always go to school on this boat?" she asked in a soft voice.

"Yeah. Well, just on the weekends. I board out in Port Alberni during the week."

"We're from Vancouver." She smiled.

"We'd planned to take the *Lady Rose* down but they booked us on this boat instead," her father chimed in. "We're staying at the Pine Tree Lodge. One of my law partners stayed there—he highly recommended the place. Know anything about it?"

"I live there." Moonbeam smiled. "Work there too. I'm a busboy for the dining room and I do odd jobs around the place. My mom's the cook."

"My partner raved about the food."

"She's a good cook. She grows all the vegetables."

"How's the fishing?" the man asked eagerly.

"Great. Some guy caught a forty-one-pound tyee last weekend." Moonbeam crossed his legs and settled back in the seat, enjoying being the authority.

"I'm Dexter Lamont and this is my daughter, Michelle."

"I'm Moonbeam Dawson." Moonbeam decided to head them off at the pass. He went right into it. "My mother used to live in this commune in the west side of the island and all the people there named their kids things like Rainbow, Meadow, Starlight—things like that."

"Oh." Mr. Lamont nodded.

David McGraff snored and the rifle magazine he had on his lap slipped to the deck. Moonbeam picked it up and put it back on the seat next to him.

"Do you hunt around here?" Michelle looked up at Moonbeam with her huge dark eyes.

"Yeah. All the time." He pointed to the right of the bow of the boat. "See that island? There was a bear there, just sunning himself on that rock when the school boat came down last Monday. Looked like a killer. A big black one."

"Do you hunt bear?"

"Yeah. All the time." Moonbeam grinned.

"Would you take me?" Michelle asked.

"Huh?"

"I get seasick. So I don't go out fishing. I was just going to do homework while Dad was out fishing. But I'd sure love to go hunting."

"It'd be fine with me if you'd take her along, son. A kid like you, who's spent your whole life here, I'm sure you know what you're doing."

"Yeah."

"Could you take me tomorrow?"

"Well—yeah, guess so."

Moonbeam closed his eyes and pretended to sleep the rest of the way to Bamfield. He couldn't believe what he had gotten himself into. What a jerk. How had this happened! He'd never held a gun in his life, much less gone hunting for animals. The only true thing was that there had been a big black bear on the rock last Monday. The rest of the truth was that his mother was completely against guns; she had never let him have one, not even a toy gun. Not even a water pistol. She thought killing animals was immoral. She was a vegetarian even though she cooked other stuff for the people at the lodge, but she still felt the same way about most things as when they had lived with the Happy Children of the Good Earth. And one of the things she felt the strongest about was guns. She hated them.

As soon as they got to Bamfield, Moonbeam ran through the woods to Harvey's house. Harvey Hattenbach was a very intelligent person. He'd think of something. Harvey liked Moonbeam's mother quite a bit, too, and he was always willing to get in good with her by helping Moonbeam with one thing or another. The story was that Harvey used to be a big shot in banking in Toronto who got sick of the rat race. After he'd come to Bamfield to go fishing one season he just ended up staying. No one in town was too sure of what Harvey did besides hunting, fishing, writing poetry, and eating a lot of brown rice.

All Moonbeam knew was that he would be grateful to Harvey his whole life for the time Harvey had figured out how to get Moonbeam's mother to sign the permission slip so he could play hockey at Port Alberni High. She had been totally against it. Too violent, she said. So Harvey told her that the reason there was so much violence in the world was because of the surplus of testosterone. He said testosterone, the male hormone, was needed when primitive man had to go out and whomp lions in order to survive, but in our modern high-tech society only a minimal amount of the stuff was needed and we have this testosterone surplus which means that there's tons of useless testosterone which causes a dangerous buildup of aggression which could cause war. Then he said that if she was interested in world peace, she could do her part by allowing Moonbeam to discharge aggression with other males by gliding around on ice skates and bashing each other with wooden sticks. His mother thought Harvey had a point and in the interest of world peace she signed the slip.

Moonbeam was sure Harvey could come up with some plan to get him out of the mess with Michelle Lamont. "Harv!" Moonbeam banged on the back door. "It's Moonbeam. I gotta talk to ya!"

In a few minutes Harvey opened the door, rubbing his eyes. "Hi, Moonbeam. What's up?"

"Did I wake you up?"

"Just taking a little snooze."

"Harv—I gotta problem."

"Come on in." Harvey yawned as he motioned for Moonbeam to follow him inside.

Moonbeam slumped down in the big easy chair in front of the fire and told him what had happened with Michelle Lamont. "She's really something. Now she'll think I'm a jerk. And a liar too. A liar *and* a jerk."

Harvey poked the fire and leaned against the mantel. "Just take my .303."

"Huh?"

"Look. It's simple. You can borrow my boat and we'll just put the .303 in under the tarp the night before. Out of consideration for your mother. So she won't see you carrying it."

"I don't know how to hold the damn thing. Much less shoot it."

"You don't have to. It won't be loaded. Look, Moonbeam, you can just have the gun in the boat. You get to the island where that bear was. Walk around a little carrying the gun, then come on back home."

"What if the bear comes?"

"That bear is more scared of you than you are of it. They aren't like those park bears that people feed—the bears on those little islands are extremely shy bears. I guarantee it."

Moonbeam wasn't so sure. But Harvey hadn't failed him before and he decided he didn't have a choice, since he had no other brilliant plan of his own other than to pretend he was sick, which was a dumb plan. His mom needed him to work dinners this weekend and he didn't want to cop out on her. Besides, he wanted to be with Michelle Lamont. He wanted that a lot.

At dinner when Moonbeam was pouring water and got to the Lamonts' table, Michelle looked up at him and smiled. On the boat her hair had been in some kind of fancy braid. Now it was down around her shoulders, dark and shiny. She was wearing a BC Lions sweatshirt. He looked at her eyes, her smile, and the BC part of the shirt. Then he poured water on the edge of the glass and it went on the table.

"Oops. Sorry." He blotted up the water with the edge of the tablecloth.

"Can we go hunting tomorrow, Moonbeam?"

"Yeah. Okay." He poured the water in her father's glass, trying hard to concentrate.

"I'll be up at the crack of dawn to get out fishing and get those chinooks."

"Do you have to go early to hunt too?" Michelle asked.

"Uh-huh."

"What time?"

"Dawn. The bear's more likely to be moving around then."

"Oh. Well, where should I meet you?"

"Down at the dock."

Moonbeam walked back to the kitchen hoping that bears slept late in the mornings. He didn't have a clue about what bears did, except hibernate. And it would certainly be nice if the bear might have decided to get an early start this year and was asleep for the winter in some cave, even though it was fall.

That night after everyone was asleep, Moonbeam went to Harvey's and got the gun. He took it to the boat and hid it under the tarp just like they'd planned. Just carrying the thing made him feel terrible. A person can't be told that something is that evil his whole life and then be calm about it.

At four-thirty when the alarm went off, he dressed quickly, then slipped out the side door of the lodge. Down at the dock, after he pulled the tarp off Harvey's boat, he leaned against the pilings and waited for Michelle. Through the trees against the blue-gray of the early morning sky, he could see lights coming on at the lodge as the guests were getting up to go fishing. Then a small figure emerged from the trees and his heart fired like a machine gun as he watched Michelle come toward him.

"Have you been waiting long?"

"No. Just got here." Moonbeam climbed in the boat and held out his hand for her and helped her in. Her hand seemed very small in his. He started the motor, then asked Michelle to hold the dock while he untied the stern, then the bow. "Okay. You can let go now." He steered the boat carefully away from the dock and headed around the point. As he got the motor up to speed the sun was starting to come up and everything was pink and purple and silvery blue. Michelle said something but he couldn't hear over the motor. He slowed the boat down.

"Couldn't hear ya."

"It's so beautiful!" She leaned against him and seemed to glow, like the world around them. "How long does it take to get to the island?"

"About twenty minutes, if we go full speed."

She glanced at the rifle under the bow. "If we get the bear, how do we get him back to the lodge?"

"The *Lady Rose* always comes for the big ones, and it'll take a couple of guys to haul it out."

Michelle's eyes got wide and Moonbeam thrust the throttle hard and the boat shot across the waves. He was glad they wouldn't be able to talk over the motor. He'd probably just end up making up more stupid crap about hunting. As he spotted the tiny speck down the channel which was the island, he wondered how hunters actually did haul out those big bears.

Circling the island, he looked for a good place to beach the boat and slowed down until the motor was so low they were hardly moving. The island was empty except for some sea gulls hanging out on the rocks. So far so good.

Michelle's eyes scanned the trees. "Can you imagine just living here and having this whole place all to yourself?"

"It'd be kinda nice I guess."

"Especially if there was a honey tree like Pooh had," she said, and huddled next to him. "My little sister loves bears. She has Care Bears."

"They didn't have those when I was little."

"Me either. I had a book about Paddington."

"I liked Smokey the Bear a lot."

"I thought Yogi Bear was great." She smiled.

Slowly, Moonbeam steered the boat around the east side of the island. The rocks jutted out into the water and he hoped he wasn't in too close. The last thing he'd need would be to shear a pin.

"Oh!" Michelle shrieked and clutched the side of the boat.

He thought he'd lose his load when he saw it. A huge black bear ambled toward the water's edge, stopped, turned, and stared at them. Terrified, Moonbeam glanced under the bow at the .303.

"Moonbeam!" Michelle grabbed his arm. "Don't! I can't let you. Think of Pooh-and-Paddington—and Smokey—" She leaned against him and looked up at him. Her dark eyes were pleading. "Don't do it, Moonbeam. Please!"

Moonbeam reached his arm around her. "Okay, I won't shoot him," he gasped, and he hit the throttle. As the boat lunged forward, the bear dived into the bushes.

Moonbeam held Michelle next to him all the way back to Bamfield. The morning sun sparkled on the water and the forest was a deep green against the bright sky. They passed a barge pulling logs to the mill at Port Alberni; it rippled the water and the boat bounced over the waves.

When they got to the dock, he tied the lines and jumped out, holding out his hand and pulling her out of the boat. "Thank you for letting him live, Moonbeam," she said softly and lifted her face up close to his.

"Think nothing of it." He swallowed hard, then grinned. Michelle's face was still there so close to his, it seemed like she wanted him to kiss her. So he did.

JEAN DAVIES OKIMOTO

After tutoring remedial readers in a high school and then serving as an assistant to the director of a Youth Services Bureau, Jean Davies Okimoto is now both an author of books for young adults and a psychotherapist in private practice in Seattle.

Her novels include *My Mother Is Not Married to My Father,* the story of an eleven-year-old girl's anger, confusion, and eventual acceptance of her parents' divorce. In its sequel, *It's Just Too Much,* the girl, Cynthia, has to deal with her mother's remarriage, two stepbrothers, and the onset of puberty. That book won the Washington Governor's Writers' Award in 1982.

Norman Schnurman, Average Person, her third book, also focuses on family problems, but this time from the point of view of a sixth-grade boy whose father wants him to play football when his own greatest interests are video games and garage sales.

Both suspense and humor fill *Who Did It, Jenny Lake?* Sixteen-year-old Jenny and her friend solve a murder mystery that disrupts their vacation in Hawaii.

In *Jason's Women,* an American Library Association Best Book for Young Adults, Jason Kovak seeks excitement in his lonely life by fantasizing about women whose ads he reads in the personal column of his local newspaper. His life takes an unexpected turn when he responds to a job ad and meets an eighty-year-old lady and a young Vietnamese refugee girl.

Jeanie Okimoto has also coauthored *Boomerang Kids,* a nonfiction book for adults about the relationships between parents and their adult children who return home, and has written a picture book about a cat that lives in a country inn with eighteen other cats. She is currently completing a novel about a romance that an eighty-year-old man is having while his twelve-year-old granddaughter is having one of her own.

Besides getting a tan, what else can the beach offer to Roseanne and Melissa? Boys, of course. At the top of the list is Scott. . . .

LIFE'S A BEACH

SUE ELLEN BRIDGERS

The only reason I'm here is that Cousin Roy got married. Mama was heartsick over it. Cousin Jessie's memory is as fresh in her mind as this morning's news, and she puts her hand on her chest like she's clutching at her heart and lets out this little moaning sigh every time she thinks about Roy getting married so quick, on Valentine's Day just six months after Jessie's funeral. We hear her groaning but neither of us says anything to comfort her, it's gotten so tiresome to Daddy and me. My own opinion is that Mama is just going to have to accept how things are the same way she tells me to.

When Craig Watkins stopped coming around and I actually saw him at the movies with Cindy Craddock, Mama told me to accept how things were and then went on to tell me it was my fault anyway. If I'd been halfway encouraging to Craig, I'd be the one seeing *Crocodile Dundee II* with him, was what she actually said and went back to stirring her custard as if that was the end of it.

If Cousin Roy was going to get married to somebody, I'd like to tell Mama, at least he picked a woman of means. Right away he and Melissa moved into her brick ranch-style house in the nicest suburb I've ever seen and now here we are at her place on the coast.

That's what Roy said when he called Mama about my

coming down here—Lillis has this little place on the coast
—and it turns out to be a great big gray shingled house with
enough bedrooms for an army and a picnic table in the
dining room that seats twelve. Right on the beach! I can
look out my bedroom window and there's the ocean. The
waves are clicking in, but beyond the breakers it's as calm as
a lake, and where the water meets the sky, there's a sailboat
like in a picture. I am having the time of my life.

To begin with, for once I've got a tan. In Lillis's bathroom she has an entire shelf of suntan preparations. I
promise you, there are twenty strengths and brands, all
smelling fresh or fruity. I put several different kinds on at
the same time so anytime I want to, I can sniff my arm and
smell coconut or press my nose to my knees and whiff this
perfect combination of baby soap and pineapple. Melissa
had a tan when she got here so she doesn't have to be so
careful. She's coconut from head to toe and the oil glistens
on her shoulders and pools in that dip above her bikini
bottom when she arches her back. Her hair is so blond, it's
painful to look at in the sunlight when she leans over to
read. She can read on the beach all day with the book
between her elbows and shaded by her face. I can't read a
word in the hot sunshine. Besides, there are other things to
look at.

For example, yesterday afternoon I spent time on the
porch watching some guys who were messing around down
by the water. One of them had the sexiest walk I've ever
seen—the kind that lifts on his toes a little like he's got
energy he's holding on to. Anyway, Lillis came up behind
me and dangled the binoculars over my shoulder. It is the
strangest thing—examining a person up close like that.
First I focused on his face and then on his shoulders. All of
a sudden he put his hand up and made a little circle on his
chest in a protective sort of way. I think he might have
known he was being watched but didn't want to seem startled by it. I know that kind of uneasy feeling so I stopped

looking. His face wasn't all that handsome but at least now I know where the binoculars are.

Well, besides lying on the beach and watching boys, Melissa and I go to the grocery store. Lillis doesn't like to shop and most nights she and Roy go out. This is vacation, she keeps saying, but I think they eat out at home, too, or order Chinese. Lillis has a real-estate business with five agents working for her so cooking is not the first thing on her mind.

She doesn't care what we buy and we can charge it too. There's only one grocery store on the island and it's busy all the time, full of feverish sunburned people who just got here, and dark wrinkled folks who live on the beach all year or at least for the three hottest months. Lillis has air conditioning, else I would have had to go back home the first night there wasn't a good breeze. When the wind stops, the beach is like a frying pan and even the sound of all that cool water crashing doesn't help any.

Every day Melissa buys a package of raspberries, and when they're good and cold, she takes them out on the porch and eats them one at a time as slow and careful as she can, but still her fingers turn red and there's juice on her lips and chin. We also get Doritos and frozen yogurt and cans of squirt cheese and deli fried chicken. If a person ate like this all the time, they would probably die from it.

We go to the grocery store every day because Melissa is in lust with one of the bag boys. She's the one who says "in lust"—I would call it "in love" whether it's the truth or not, just because it sounds better. She says Jamie Fletcher, her boyfriend last summer, is the only person she's ever been in love with. She has to say that because I know she took her shirt off. But two months after he went to college in the fall he all but stopped writing to her and at Christmas he didn't bring her a gift although she had one for him that stayed under the tree all by its lonesome until they took the decorations down and he'd gone back to school. It wasn't a present she could give to just anybody—a silver-plated monogrammed belt buckle, the preppiest thing I've ever seen to go with those pastel Argyle socks he wears—so now she has it in her panty drawer, waiting to fall in love with another boy whose initials are JF. This boy in the grocery store's name is Scott.

I must say I saw him first and pointed him out to Melissa. Well, I figured I might as well get it over with because if Melissa wanted him, she'd get him and I'd know to look elsewhere although he's my type more than hers. Maybe five nine. Dark hair with just that hint of curl that wouldn't show at all in a cold, dry climate. Thick hair that lies down everywhere. That was one thing about Craig Watkins, he had cowlicks all over his head so bad, he carried a little hairbrush around with him. The bulge it made in his pocket was positively gnarly.

This Scott person has a wonderful wet-looking tan, like his skin would be moist and quivery under your hand. I can imagine him right now in his wet suit—a yellow one—with his surfboard rope wrapped around his ankle. There is something enticing about a man attached to his surfboard that not everybody sees. The best thing about him is his smile, though. It starts out embarrassed and he tries to hold on to it, but then it just plain bursts out on his face and he is so beautiful you just want to eat him with a spoon.

I doubt Melissa sees it. What she sees are biceps and a weight lifter's neck. Melissa always sees body because she's such a physical person herself. She stretches all the time real slow so you can't help but notice her and she doesn't mind touching people. I mean, she hugs Lillis all the time, just like she's been her mama all her life, and sometimes she comes up behind Cousin Roy and wraps her arms around him so her face is over his shoulder and her breasts are pressed tight to his back and just kisses his cheek and neck and ear a hundred times.

Daddy would be mortified if I did something like that.

When he hugged me good-bye at the bus station last week, he didn't even touch me except with his arms when what I must have wanted was a bear hug, because after the bus pulled out and I was stuck there with all those dreary, nasty people, I felt so lonesome I thought I'd die. In a few minutes it passed, though, and I slept till Durham, where I had to change.

What with all the hugging Melissa does, you could think she's forgotten Cousin Jessie, but she hasn't. Her mama's picture from her room at home is here at the beach and every night Melissa stares at it hard before she shuts off the light. The first time I saw that, I got tears in my eyes, but now I'm used to it. The picture is of Cousin Jessie young, probably about the time she had Melissa, and looking at it makes me think of Mama and Jessie growing up together. Mama is forty-two this year and I know that is not old, but Mama acts ancient sometimes, not like Lillis, who is full of life and interested in everything. Maybe that's because she and Roy are so recently married. Or maybe because she has all this money. Money can probably keep a person as young as anything.

At the grocery store Melissa and I wait around—linger over the spaghetti-sauce jars and the pasta display—to make sure we get Scott's checkout lane. We never buy enough to need a bag boy so Melissa has taken to buying a bag of ice which he has to go outside to the freezer to get. Since he's already out there getting ice we don't need since Lillis has an ice maker, he goes ahead and takes our stuff to the car, which is usually Lillis's BMW. Melissa flits around opening the car door so he can put the bags on the back floorboard, but she talks to me all the while, giving Scott information. "I think I'll go down to the Pavilion tonight," she says. So far this week she's given him her taste in music and the length of our stay. He knows she's a senior in high school and head cheerleader for both football and basketball. He's heard that she's dying to go sailing and considers

Judith Krantz trashy reading. It's truly incredible how she gets all this across while I just stand there.

Across the car roof Scott winks at me and that smile just bursts forth. "You going to the Pavilion too?" he asks, the first words he's uttered in the six days we've been shopping.

"I guess so," I mumble.

"There's a better place, ya know," he says. This to Melissa although his eyes, dark and squinting in the bright sunlight, dart between us. My hand is burning on the door handle and there's a heavy trickle of sweat down my spine that's going to show along the back seam of my best shorts.

"Where?" I croak.

"Two miles down that way," he waves to the left of the intersection. "Spinner's."

"Exactly what takes place there?" Melissa asks, suddenly the demure one.

"Shagging mostly," Scott says. His voice makes shagging sound like it's the only thing left in the world worth doing. "There's a live band on weekends."

All afternoon we practice.

"No way, José," Cousin Roy says, trying to charm us.

"Oh, Daddy." Melissa pouts, frowning with her lip poked up like she's playing too.

"I mean it, Melissa," Roy says, and I see that this time he intends to put his foot down. "You girls are not going off to some beer joint to do anything." And to make sure, he pockets the keys to the BMW because he and Lillis are going to the Beaufort waterfront to meet some friends for dinner and they're taking the Lincoln.

"Don't you want to come with us, girls?" Lillis asks, looking like she's as disappointed as we are. Her daughter's married and her one son just graduated from college and is walking around Europe, so she misses what young people are up to.

All afternoon she's been bopping around, keeping time to our music with these funny little double-time steps she does. I can tell you it's very strange being with a grown-up person who wants to go to a Bruce Springsteen concert and who rented *Dirty Dancing* for us and then watched it three times. She's a serious person, for sure, but she enjoys herself too. Mama and Daddy haven't been to a movie since *Terms of Endearment* and Mama says she's never going again unless there's a revival of Ginger Rogers–Fred Astaire movies where nobody dies or even kisses each other.

Tonight Lillis is wearing white slacks and a yellow knit top that bares her tight, tanned middle when she reaches above her head and snaps her fingers, dancing. Mama wouldn't be caught dead in such an outfit, but Lillis looks super in it.

"We'll be out late," she says, now that we've refused to go with them. "Why don't you walk down to the video store and rent a couple of movies? Or you could go to the Pavilion. That's all right, isn't it, Roy?" Sometimes she remembers Melissa is his daughter alone—you can see it in her face, this cloudy, hesitant look like she's just embarrassed herself a little.

"I suppose," Cousin Roy says sternly. He's looking at Melissa, who I can promise you is planning to punish him forever for this. Melissa is used to getting her way. From day one she's been spoiled.

But they are hardly out of the driveway before Melissa is up the steps and into their room, scrounging through the dresser until she comes up with a key ring heavy with keys. It's the alternate to everything Lillis owns, so naturally there's the BMW key among them.

"You wouldn't," I say. I'm uncomfortable just being in their room. I know they're married and all, but I get this illicit feeling when I think about their being in bed together. I mean, do they do things just the way Jessie and Roy used to? I just shut my eyes to it. My imagination is big enough for several people and sometimes I wish it wasn't, although Daddy says someday I'll turn it to good use.

"They'll never know the difference," Melissa says, twirling the key ring on her finger.

Of course I know there's all sorts of ways they can know. Maybe Cousin Roy checked the mileage on the car before he left. Maybe they'll come home earlier than us or phone to make sure we're there. Maybe a neighbor-lady Lillis knows real well has been persuaded to spy on us.

We don't even bother to eat anything, just touch up our makeup and go.

Spinner's is set between a service station and a dilapidated duplex on the sound side of the island. Cars are nosed in all along the road because the parking lot is small. The building is small, too, and the music booms out of it so loud that the neon trim darts like it's getting little shocks.

We walk up there, sand sliding into our sandals. Melissa is in front and she's putting on this beach walk she's got. The balls of her feet turn a little in the sand, which sets her hips to twisting just a bit more than necessary. Anybody else might think this is just her normal way of walking, but I know better.

We get in line at the door and Melissa gets out her money. (Roy told Mama if I could come I wouldn't need a cent of money, and I haven't. They pay for everything.) At the door Melissa holds out the ten and the man looks at it, then at us. "ID's, ladies," he says.

Now, I do believe that Melissa, who purports to know everything, ought to know that two high school girls seventeen and sixteen respectively can't get into a dance place at the beach without pretending to be at least eighteen. At home you have to be twenty-one, and I couldn't look twenty-one if my life depended on it. My driver's license picture makes me look twelve.

"We're meeting somebody," Melissa purrs. I can see

she's flustered, but to the rest of the world she's pure cool. "If we could just step inside and see if he's here . . ."

"Not without an ID, honey," the man says nicely, although the line behind us is easing up on our heels, impatient to get in. Inside, the band is playing "Sixty Minute Man" and the dance floor is loose with easy shuffling bodies. "Sorry," he says, looking to the next customer.

It takes all my strength to pull Melissa away, because she's got her feet planted and her hips set like she's in there for the long haul. "It doesn't matter," I whisper to her. "It wouldn't be all that much fun, anyway. See, they're all older than us."

"It does too matter," Melissa spits at me. I can see she doesn't intend to leave.

"Hey, there," a voice says in the dark beyond the building lights. It's Scott coming toward us. "Whatcha doing out here?"

"We aren't old enough," I blurt out before Melissa can make up some lie. She would too.

"Well, what do you know?" Scott chuckles. He starts past, then holds up. "You mean you don't even have a fake ID?"

"Of course not," I say, since he seems to be talking to me. "We've never needed one."

"I don't guess so," Scott says. I think he's laughing at us, but he seems disappointed too. "If you hadn't already let them know you're underage, I could have borrowed from some girls inside. We do it all the time. On band nights they stamp your hand so you can't order from the bar and let you in if you're eighteen."

"Well, too late now," I say. I have to admit I'm relieved. Have you ever noticed things are rarely as exciting as you think they're going to be? I mean, here's this Scott who's acting more interested in me than in Melissa and instead of feeling excited, I'm wishing we were home eating guacamole and watching *The Way We Were.*

Melissa is pouting just a little bit. She's learned she can't push that little-girl act too far with guys. I mean, eventually they're bound to say "What the hay" and go on to somebody who's perky and a lot less trouble.

"We could go back to the Pavilion," I say. "We could play putt-putt."

"Well, I wanted to dance," Melissa says. She can make three syllables out of "dance" and does.

"I tell you what," Scott says, talking to Melissa now. "Let's go down on the beach and have our own little party."

We don't know this boy from Adam.

"I'll go next door and get some beer. I've got a blanket and a radio in my trunk. We'll get that and forget all about this joint."

There are two of us and one of him, but he's strong looking and for all I know he pulls stuff like this all the time. I mean, what if it's a trick and he's got buddies waiting on this particular deserted stretch of beach, all planned out?

"I think we ought to go home," I say to Melissa, but I can tell by looking at her that she's gone with the wind.

Scott gets his blanket, his radio, and a six-pack and follows us to the BMW. "Great car," he says, climbing in the backseat without any sort of invitation. "I'm saving my summer money to get a Porsche. It's secondhand, of course, but this man I know over in New Bern has it and he's kept it nice. He's just waiting for me to get the down payment because he knows I'll take good care of it."

He gives Melissa directions and we drive farther down the road that separates the beach side of the island from the sound side. There's not much empty beach down here anymore, but Scott knows a place. "Where do you go to school?" Melissa asks. She's happy now and her voice kind of sings at him out of the dark.

"UT," he says. "What about you? Where're you planning to go?"

She asked him just so she could tell this: Melissa is suddenly going to Hollins or Sweet Briar or Mary Baldwin, one of those girls' schools that's been trying for a hundred years to be Ivy League but can't because they're located in the South. Lillis is responsible for all these goings-on, Mama said when she heard about it, because Lillis went to Agnes Scott, for heaven's sake. Daddy says, what's wrong with that? At least it's southern! Mama says the state university system has been good enough for everybody in our family until now. I know she says that because I'll be going to one of them, sure as the world. I don't mind, either, no matter what Mama thinks. Maybe it's Mama who minds, come to think of it.

Melissa pulls over where Scott tells her to, deep off the road into the sand. There're dunes between us and the ocean but Scott knows, even in the dark, where a trail between them lies. There's a little moonlight and a wealth of stars when we actually reach the beach.

The beer tastes like the water Mama's just boiled corn in, warm and sweet and a little rancid like that. I sip at it anyway. You know, Mrs. Reagan's just-say-no business has got a lot of holes in it. To begin with, the "just" part aggravates me no end. It sounds like not drinking or taking drugs is an easy thing to do, even if that's not the way they mean it. The other thing is, pride gets all mixed up in it. Like, at home if one of my friends offered me something I would tell them off good. I mean, I've known those people all my life and I haven't got to impress them or anything. It's new people who catch me up—like this Scott, who so far hasn't jumped us and is handsome in a major way. For some reason I want him to think I'm used to drinking beer even though he knows already I don't go to places like Spinner's. Now, why is that?

Scott squats in the sand to find a clear station on the radio. It's quiet stuff, but that's okay because I just want to lie back and listen to the waves and look at the stars. I don't, of course. I sit on this scratchy old blanket with my arms

locking my knees. Melissa is on the other end of the blanket
with room for Scott in the middle. That's the kind of thing
Melissa would think through. She's drinking her beer and
humming with the radio. Scott comes over and sits down,
but not in the middle like Melissa arranged for but on the
other side of me!

Melissa notices but she doesn't say anything, just keeps
drinking her beer like she's used to it, when I know for a
fact she is not.

"So you go to UT," I say because the silence is killing me.

"Yeah. Knoxville's a great town," Scott says. He's rubbing his beer can up and down his bare shin.

"I know," I say. "I live just this side of the Smokies from
there. I had a great time at the World's Fair."

"You did?" He seems real excited.

"Yeah," I say, because that's really all I know about
Knoxville and I don't want to tell him what actually happened at the World's Fair. After waiting in line half the day,
Buddy, who was five at the time, got lost in China and we
spent the other half of the day looking for him. Mama said
she was never taking him anywhere again until he was
twenty-one years old and could halfway take care of himself.

Melissa pops another beer. She's singing along with the
music now just like Scott and I don't exist and she's got to
entertain herself.

"So what are you studying?" I ask him.

"Business," he says, getting his second beer. "But I plan
to go to law school later on."

"It must be great knowing what you want to do with your
life," I say. I don't think I should tell him that I've been
thinking about studying journalism and not just because
Daddy runs the newspaper. I want to work for *People* magazine and go jetting around interviewing movie stars and
famous authors beside their swimming pools.

"I'm going to Sweet Briar and major in music," Melissa

says. This is not true. Melissa has taken nine years of piano and she still cannot play "Moonlight Sonata" by heart. "Then I'm headed straight to New York City." She tosses her beer can into the sand and gets another one.

"Melissa," I say to warn her but she pretends not to hear me so I ignore her, too, and keep on talking to Scott. "I hope we didn't mess up your night. I mean, we could have found something to do by ourselves."

Now I wish I hadn't said that about putt-putt. He probably thinks he's rescuing us from major boredom.

"This is okay," Scott says. "I can go to Spinner's anytime. I live down here, you know."

"That must be really neat, living at the beach in the wintertime."

"Boring," Melissa says. She strings out "boring" on her tongue.

"Not really," Scott says. "I love the beach in winter. In the summer we natives feel invaded."

"If we didn't come, you wouldn't have a living," Melissa says. I can see now she's determined to be hateful.

I say, "Melissa, I think you've had enough to drink," in my mama's voice.

"It's my family who has the cottage down here," Melissa says. "Roseanne's just here because my daddy invited her."

"Well, if you didn't want me to come you should have said so," I say. Melissa's high horse can really gall me.

"I don't care what you do," Melissa says, trying to get up. She has to get on her knees and push herself into a standing position. She stands there, swaying above us, beer sloshing over her hand. "I think I'll take a little walk," she says.

"We'll come with you," I say because she's wobbling with her feet tight together when she steps. She's kicked off her shoes but she can't manage that silky walk she's been practicing since the beginning of time.

"Three's company and all," she says, waving me down.

We watch her meandering toward the water. She goes slow, like there's a path she has to follow.

"I think she drank too much too fast," Scott says while we're watching her.

She's almost to the surf when we see her doubling over, her knees locked, feet spraddled. Her blond hair and white shorts glow but the rest of her is dark like only parts of her are there. "Good grief, I think she's throwing up," I say.

By the time I reach her, the retching is over and she's leaning forward like there's a wall she's resting on. "Come on," I say, stepping around the mess. I practically have to pull her with me.

"We didn't eat dinner," I say to Scott. "That's all it is." Melissa is trembling under my hand like she's having a chill. "I'm going to take her home."

Scott starts collecting his stuff. He doesn't act mad or anything. I guess he'll go back to Spinner's and have a good time.

I get behind the wheel. Scott offers but I know he's had two beers and I've only taken a few sips. Melissa is lying down in the backseat although we sat her up. I just hope I can get her in the house and in bed before Cousin Roy gets there. I start the car and go in reverse. The car doesn't move, just churns and growls, throwing sand.

"The emergency brake," Scott says in the dark, but it's off.

I hit the gas again and feel the front tires spin under us.

"Holy hell," Scott says, "she drove us into a sand sink."

"She parked right where you told her to," I say. Who does he think he is blaming Melissa, when all of this was his own idea?

"Roseanne, I'm sick," Melissa moans, and Scott gets her head out the door just in time. There's not much breeze here behind the dunes and the hot beery smell of puke hangs around us. I, for one, am sweating.

"What are we going to do?" I ask Scott. I don't even

know where we are exactly. This is what happens when you put your life in somebody else's hands.

"I'll walk back to Spinner's," Scott says finally. "It's only a couple of miles."

"A couple of miles! That'll take hours!" It occurs to me he might not come back at all.

"Thirty minutes or less," Scott says. "I'll get my car and a couple of buddies and we'll pull you out." He seems satisfied with the plan and I don't have a better one, so what can I do?

After he's gone, I get Melissa out and sit her on the blanket beside the car. We can see the narrow road from here but no cars come by. I guess I'm glad. I'd be scared to death if somebody stopped. At least I know who Scott is. I kick sand over Melissa's up-chuck and walk around the car just because I'm too nervous to sit down. Mama says I can't stand not being in control and it's the truth. I want to just lift the stupid car out of the sand and be gone, leave Melissa and this beach forever. Since I can't do that, I just walk around and around the car, passing Melissa every time although she doesn't even notice.

It's the beach patrol who comes roaring between the dunes from the beach like something out of a science fiction movie.

"What's the trouble, little lady?" one of the men says just like in the movies. He swings himself out of the Jeep and stands there with his hand on his weapon. He's tall and thin and has this interested look on his face, like he's been bored all evening and this is the first thing that's turned up worth bothering with.

"We parked here to go for a walk on the beach," I say as pathetic as I can sound. It's a shame Melissa is a zombie because she's the one who can put on pathetic with a capital *P*.

"What's the matter with her?" he wants to know.

"She's not feeling good," I say. I put my hand on her

head which she's bobbing like somebody with a genetic illness. "I think we had some bad coleslaw at supper, because I'm feeling sickish myself."

"Well, I reckon we'd better get this fancy car out of here, then," the policeman says. "Won't take but a jiffy and you'll be on your way. You got a license, don't you?"

"Yes, sir," I say and start for my purse in the car.

"I believe you, honey," he says, and motions for his buddy to pull the Jeep up behind us so their lights are shining through the BMW. "Let's see here," he says, bending down to look under the car. "These here fancy cars don't pull easy. Looks like nobody expects them to be anywhere but flying down the road." He feels under there until he's satisfied, then releases the winch in front of the Jeep so the chain rolls off.

"You all get in," he says to Melissa and me. "And you, Missy"—this is to me—"you do the driving. Just put her in reverse and hold on to the wheel till she's free."

Melissa's head is wagging, but she gets in the car like she's told and so do I. I feel the Jeep revving up behind us, the quick jerk as the chain goes taut, then the churning wheels beneath until the tread takes hold and we're suddenly on the pavement. The policeman unlatches us and comes around to the driver's side. "You ladies get on home now," he says patting the roof while he talks. "And don't be pulling off the road in the dark anymore tonight. I'm on duty several more hours and I don't want to have to do this again."

I start the car and move slowly away, hardly going five miles an hour until I see in my rearview mirror that the Jeep has disappeared back down onto the beach.

My heart is racing faster than the car but gradually I pick up speed and get us home in a hurry. Nobody's there. The house is dark and quiet just like I prayed it would be. I get Melissa up two flights of steps, one on the outside and then the inside steps to the second-floor bedrooms. There are four bedrooms in this house so Melissa and I could have separate ones but we're sleeping together like we used to when she'd come stay with me in the summer. It was her idea to do that.

I know that Melissa didn't mean what she said tonight about her daddy being the only one who wanted me here. Melissa wanted me to come, too, and just me—not her friends at home she's always competing with no matter how chummy they act. She wanted somebody she could be herself with, somebody she didn't have to feel jealous of. And that person has always been me.

I get her smelly face and hands washed and put her to bed in her panties and bra. Her sleeping face is hidden in a tangle of hair across her cheek so I brush the damp hair away before I put out the light. Downstairs in the dark house I turn on a few lights and the television, just so Lillis and Roy will think we've been around all evening. I know I'm going to tell them a lie. I can feel it figuring in my head but I don't know exactly what it is yet. Like always I'm going to protect Melissa, but I don't mind doing it.

Tonight there was a boy who liked me better than her and she's not accustomed to that. Neither am I, for that matter. But I know for certain that somewhere some other time, a man is going to look at both of us and choose me. Now Melissa knows it, too.

I bet you anything tomorrow we don't go to the beach market. We'll probably go across the bridge into town and find a grocery store there. That's all right too. Scott who-ever-he-is doesn't know our last names or where we live and Melissa intends to keep it that way. I don't mind that either. I've got plenty of time.

SUE ELLEN BRIDGERS

Sue Ellen Bridgers lives with her husband in the Blue Ridge Mountain town of Sylva, but she grew up in a small town in eastern North Carolina, surrounded by relatives. Thus, the lives of farmers and rural people figure prominently in her novels for young people. Families, too, are very important to Bridgers and her novels contain important adult characters with whom her teenage characters interact. Her stories are also hopeful ones. They deal, as she says, "more with head and heart than with adventure and intrigue."

Her books have another element in common: they are all prizewinners. All five of her novels have been named a Best Book for Young Adults by the American Library Association. In addition, *Home Before Dark* was named a *New York Times* Outstanding Book of the Year, *All Together Now* received the Christopher Medal, *Permanent Connections* won the Parents' Choice award in 1987, and both *All Together Now* and *Notes for Another Life* were nominated for the American Book Award.

Home Before Dark explores the feelings of Stella, the daughter of migrant farm workers who finally finds a place where she can *belong*. In *All Together Now* motherless Casey grows up in a big house in a small town with a wonderful great aunt and a retarded man named Dwayne. Grandparents are also central figures in *Notes for Another Life* and *Permanent Connections*. But *Notes* is also about Wren's mother's leaving the family, and their father's mental illness, while *Connections* deals with a troubled teenage boy, his senile grandfather, and his great aunt, who suffers from agoraphobia.

Sara Will is an adult novel which older teenagers will appreciate. Sara is a middle-aged spinster whose solitary life is disrupted by her sister Swanee, her dead sister's brother-in-law Fate Jessop, his unwed teenage niece Eva, her baby, and Eva's "boyfriend." In 1985 Sue Ellen Bridgers received the ALAN Award for her "outstanding contribution to the field of young adult literature."

Today is your first day in high school. Where are you supposed to be?
Where's your locker? Where's your homeroom? Where's the cafeteria?
How will you survive? . . .

A REASONABLE SUM

GORDON KORMAN

Well, you stayed up all night, but today came anyway. Your head aches, your stomach groans, and your palms are sweaty. In short, you're nervous. You are starting high school today even though you are far too ill to be out of bed.

There is no point in hoping the bus won't show. You can see it in the distance, surer than death and taxes. The yawning doors swallow you up and you pay your fare. On the way to school you make a pact with heaven that you will be good forever—at least, fairly good—in exchange for divine intervention in the horrors to come. Maybe high school can't be avoided, but with help from above, surely some of the blows can be softened.

You arrive at school to find that all those cutthroats who are seven feet tall are your fellow students. The only people who don't have beards are the girls, and even one of them has managed a creditable mustache. You wonder if the school crest depicts a lead pipe on a field of blood red.

Your first assignment is to find your locker, in which will be kept all your worldly possessions. This is far more difficult than it may seem, as all secondary school halls have been laid out as a maze. It's part of a biological experiment designed to discover if high school freshmen are as intelligent as white mice. If you learn to negotiate the halls, you have triumphed over the experiment; if you do not, a shoe box containing your remains will be sent home by third-class mail. It is not a place for the timid or the stupid, and since the most strenuous or intellectually challenging activity of your summer was heating up a TV dinner when the folks were at the country club, you are not in shape for a life-and-death struggle.

Once your locker has been located, you can concern yourself with the intricacies of the combination lock. Since you have a faulty memory for numbers, you have cleverly written your combination, along with all other vital information, on the waistband of your underwear. This system has one serious drawback: it is impossible to maintain your dignity while consulting your notes. Nevertheless, rooting around under your belt in public is infinitely preferable to being found sobbing in front of your unopened locker. 24–26–28. No, that is not your locker combination; that is your underwear size. Finally, the lock opens, and you stow your coat. You are the only one in sight with this particular style of coat. You wonder if, while you were hibernating in front of the television set all summer, fashion changed radically, leaving you a museum piece. Your hair is too short, or maybe a little too long, and—you look down. Your shoes are absurd! Why, there is nothing a peer group sinks its claws into faster than absurd shoes!

Taking a wrong turn on your way to your first class, you are very nearly recruited into a spirited touch football game, but you manage to escape to English class just a little late. The only vacant seat is located right under the teacher's nose, and her hot breath and windmill arm motions begin to take the curl out of your hair. As she rambles on about the joyous learning experiences she has planned for this semester, you muse on something that has been bothering you subconsciously for some time—why is the school office so concerned with obtaining the name, address, and telephone number of your next of kin? Any well-rounded

TV addict knows that next of kin are the people notified when the body washes up on the beach. Do they expect you to *die*? Exactly what is the mortality rate in this place?

The teacher then issues a textbook complete with dire warnings of what will happen to you if this book is lost and/ or mutilated. She says that you will be charged "a reasonable sum of money" for replacement. The book weighs roughly thirty pounds and has an expensive look about it. You picture yourself washing dishes in the cafeteria for the rest of your life trying to raise the reasonable sum of money.

As you leave the class, it is your misfortune to stumble between two wild-eyed students who are having a ketchup fight. Red slop is flying everywhere. Your first impulse is to save the textbook at all costs. Dropping it to the floor, you fall upon it, shielding its precious pages with your body. Your left shoe is splashed, rendering it even more absurd than before.

Because of a short but perilous trip to the bathroom to clean up, you are late for your next class, which is instrumental music. You rush into the music room, your heart set on a saxophone. They are taken. Your second choice, trumpets, are all in other hands. Ditto, trombones and clarinets. Okay, sacrifice the macho and go for the flute or piccolo. All taken. As a matter of fact, there is only one vacant chair, one instrument at rest. Face it, you are stuck with the tuba.

As you strain to pick it up, you feel your innards drop. You make a mental note to ask your next of kin if your health insurance extends to hernia. The teacher explains how to blow into a tuba. You draw a mighty breath, put your mouth to the mouthpiece (did the guy in period one have pellagra?), and blow until you start to black out. Not a sound. A big cheer goes up from the class as you and the tuba clatter to the floor. The teacher then informs you that, for destruction of an instrument, you will be charged a reasonable sum—in the case of a tuba, about eight hundred dollars. He explains that the instruments may be borrowed for additional practice at home. You have a giddy vision of yourself hauling this brass behemoth onto the bus and being charged another fare for it. Does a tuba qualify for the student discount? Idly, you wonder how your next of kin will take to an evening of oom-pah-pah.

Your French class is right across the hall. Your teacher, who is Madame Something-or-other, hands you a textbook and probably tells you about the reasonable sum. You're not certain, however, because she says it in French. She might have been saying almost anything. Her stream of gibberish virtually uninterrupted, she strolls through the class, stopping directly in front of your desk—the one you had selected as the least noticeable spot in the room. You look up in alarm. Her monologue has ended on a questioning note, and she is looking at you expectantly. You decide to take a stab at it.

"Oui."

She beams, thanks you profusely, and moves on.

A voice comes from behind you. "Psst. Do you know that you just volunteered to make the decorations for our first French party?"

French party? What's a French party? How would you decorate one? When? Where?

You are then excmpted from the homework because you have so much to do. As the period ends, you are confronted with a choice. You can stay and find out exactly what is going on, or you can obey your every instinct, which is to run for your life. Retreat wins out. After all, you should get a head start searching for the cafeteria.

You make for your locker but abort that plan to follow an intelligent-looking student who is walking purposefully down the hall carrying a paper bag. In this way you end up in the biology lab where your man rips open the bag, pulls out a dead frog, and begins to dissect it enthusiastically. You stagger out of the lab, no longer hungry.

At length you locate the cafeteria and stare in horror at the chalk board which displays today's menu. Could anyone here know that your mother spearheaded the parents'-group campaign for more nutrition in the school lunches? That your mother, the formerly beloved fairer half of your next of kin, was responsible for today's entree, the alfalfa sloppy joe? You look at all the innocent people in the line behind you and feel a terrible guilt. As you pay the cashier, you notice that there is a big puddle of split-pea soup on the cover of your French book. Oh, no. Is this mutilation? Will you be charged a reasonable sum?

You eat a miserable lunch in the company of a few friends from elementary school. Everything is going along beautifully for them. They are waxing eloquent over the joys of high school, the freedom, the challenge. They don't have to make French decorations. They don't have to play the tuba. They don't already owe a reasonable sum. It's obvious that they are survivors and you are a casualty. What happened to your pact with heaven? Haven't they been paying attention up there? Your friends have obviously been graced with help from above. Why are you the odd man out?

You check the timetable on your underwear and discover to your dismay that your next class is swimming. This is particularly disquieting, since the larger part of your lunch is still lodged in your upper digestive tract. You imagine the coroner's certificate: *Cause of death—sloppy joe.* Well, at least you know where to find the pool.

The water temperature is kept slightly below the tolerance level. This, the instructor informs you, is to keep you active. The only thing that is active, however, is your lunch, which is rising. You know a brief moment of panic as you realize that your clothes are unguarded in the change room. If you lose your underwear, and with it your locker combination and all other vital data, you will never see home again.

"Ten lengths!" As you thrash wretchedly along, fighting

off a paralyzing cramp, you wonder if anyone will pull you out if you go under. Probably not. Who would risk hypothermia to save the life of a guy whose mother is a PTA activist responsible for fifteen hundred counts of first-degree heartburn? You sincerely hope that, if you die here, your next of kin will charge the school a reasonable sum.

As the class ends, you are just alive enough to listen as the instructor tells you that your crawl is pitiful and that you tread water like a Hovercraft. You would like to explain the extenuating circumstances, but you are hyperventilating.

Soggy but dressed, you move on to your science class, where you are immediately informed that you are far too wet to work with any electrical equipment. You look around the lab. There is the emergency eyewash and the emergency extinguisher for chemical fires. The radioactive material is kept in that locked cabinet. Everywhere there are signs and instructions on what to do until the doctor comes. This place is obviously a death trap.

A reasonable sum of money will be charged for the loss of an experiment booklet or the destruction of equipment. This is where you learn your first natural law of physics—glass beakers shatter when dropped on the floor. You are standing in the ruins of a whole tray of them. Your socks sparkle with glass slivers, forming regal crowns for your absurd shoes. The debt is mounting.

You decide to stash your books for safety's sake, and find your locker without too much wandering around. You are just about to pat yourself on the back for your powers of navigation when you see it. Someone has scratched an obscene word into the paint of your locker door. It is not just any obscene word, but one of that elite group of obscenities guaranteed to grow hair on the palm of your hand, rarefy the atmosphere, and make a lumberjack blush. Where are you going to find paint to cover up this crime against society before the principal or the morality squad sees it? Everyone knows school lockers are painted in a gray-beige so drab that it can never again be matched. How will you explain your innocence? And why you in the first place? There are rows of lockers in both directions as far as the eye can see, all of them immaculate, and yours is the only one that says————. This is going to cost you.

You are a good ten minutes late for your last class of the day, Industrial Arts. As you slip into the wood shop and slink toward the nearest vacant seat, the voice of the teacher cuts the air like a razor:

"How considerate of you, young man, to take the time and trouble to appear before us in this humble classroom and gild our wretched selves with your exalted presence. Do sit down and add your genius to our unworthy efforts."

Well, this is the cherry on the bitter ice cream sundae. Heaven, which has seen fit to catapult you from disaster to catastrophe all day, has decided to top your afternoon with the meanest man in the world.

As he lectures on the various pieces of equipment in the shop, with an uncomfortable stress on the damage potential of each, you find it difficult to draw your attention from the razor-sharp stiletto which he is absently using to pare his fingernails. It seems like only yesterday that your teacher marched the class two by two to the local shopping center to visit Santa Claus. Now you are trapped in a wood shop with a maniac with a knife. How time flies.

You are selected for the class demonstration of the wood lathe. The Maniac hands you a partially finished salad bowl, which you fit onto the spindle as per instructions. You flick the switch. The bowl begins to spin, picking up speed. There is an unpleasant screech, and the salad bowl, now a lethal projectile, shoots from the lathe, whistles past the instructor's ear, and sails out the open window into the parking lot. The class breaks into admiring applause.

"You missed me," says the Maniac, following this up with a barrage of abuse and sarcasm aimed directly at you. The class laughs harder with each barb until you sink into your absurd shoes and contemplate a course change. Maybe a history of Teflon manufacturing in Sweden. It might be boring, but at least the teacher won't carry a knife.

As you make your weary way to the bus stop, you notice that the vice-principal's new car has a broken windshield and a salad bowl in the front seat. There is a faint chance that this will be blamed on equipment malfunction and not you, depending on whether the school can charge a reasonable sum for damages occurring outside the building. What if the damage starts inside the building and then leaves, say, by a window? Forget it. Go home. You are ill.

Your next of kin is at the door waiting for you. She asks, "How was your first day at high school, dear?"

A long, elaborate sob story forms in your mind. "Fine," you reply. Next of kin wouldn't understand such things.

GORDON KORMAN

Although he now lives in New York City, Gordon Korman was born in Montreal and was raised in Toronto, Canada, where many of his novels take place. As a seventh grade student he started writing his first novel, a story about two fun-loving "troublemakers" in a boarding school. By the time he graduated from high school, Korman had already published three novels and had completed two more. Bruno and Boots, the two main characters in *This Can't Be Happening at Macdonald Hall!*, continue their zany adventures in *Go Jump in the Pool!*, *Beware the Fish!*, *The War with Mr. Wizzle*, and, most recently, *The Zucchini Warriors*.

Korman's humor comes through in several other books for middle-school readers. Among them are *I Want to Go Home*, about an unhappy camper who intends to make life so miserable for everyone that they'll send him home; *Who Is Bugs Potter?*, the story of a high school student who becomes an overnight rock music star; *Our Man Weston*, a madcap spy story featuring twin bellboys at a summer resort hotel; and, more recently, *Radio Fifth Grade*, about a group of students who produce a weekend radio show sponsored by the town pet shop.

For older teenagers there is *Don't Care High*, in which a Canadian teenager is appalled by the apathy he finds in the high school he attends when he moves to New York City. With his help, the situation is soon totally out of control.

In *Son of Interflux*, Simon Irving and his fellow students take control when they learn that a gigantic corporation, led by Simon's father, is going to build a factory in the green space adjoining their school.

Raymond Jardine is a friendless, unfortunate student whose plans to win a summer trip to Greece result in more than he bargained for in *A Semester in the Life of a Garbage Bag*, the most recent of Gordon Korman's fun-filled YA novels.

Angus is a big guy. Some would say big fat *guy. Fortunately Angus is very agile for someone his size. He needs all the agility he can find. . . .*

A BRIEF MOMENT
IN THE LIFE OF
ANGUS BETHUNE

CHRIS CRUTCHER

Sometimes, when I stand back and take a good look, I think my parents are Ambassadors from Hell. Two of them, at least; the biological ones; the *big* ones.

Four parents are what I have all together, not unlike a whole lot of other kids. But quite unlike a whole lot of other kids, there ain't a hetero among 'em. My dad's divorced and remarried and my mom's divorced and remarried, so my mathematical account of my family suggests simply another confused teenager from a broken home. But my dads aren't married to my moms. They're married to *each other.* Same with my moms.

However, that's not the principle reason I sometimes see my so-called "real" parents as emissaries from Way Down Under. As a matter of fact, that frightening little off-season trade took place prior to—though not *much* prior to—my birth, so until I began collecting expert feedback from friends at school, somewhere along about fourth grade, I perceived my situation as relatively normal.

No, what really hacks me off is that they didn't conceive me in some high-tech fashion that would have allowed them to dip into an alternative gene pool for my physical goodies. See, when people the size of my parents decide to reproduce, they usually dig a pit and crawl down in there together for several days. Really, I'm surprised someone in this family doesn't have a trunk. Or a blowhole. I swear my gestation period was three years and seven months.

You don't survive a genetic history like that unscathed. While farsighted parents of other infants my age were preenrolling their kids four years ahead into elite preschools, my dad was hounding the World Professional Wrestling Association to hold a spot for me sometime in the early nineteen nineties. I mean, my mom had to go to the husky section of Safeway to buy me Pampers.

I'm a big kid.

And they named me Angus. God, a name like Angus Bethune would tumble *Robert Redford* from a nine-and-a-half to a four, and I ain't no Robert Redford.

"Angus is a cow," I complained to my stepmother, Bella, the day in first grade I came home from school early for punching the bearer of that sad information in the stomach.

"Your mother must have had a good reason for naming you that," she said.

"For naming me after a cow?"

"You can't go around punching everyone who says that to you," she warned.

"Yes, I can," I said.

"Angus is a cow," I said to my mother when she got home from her job at Westhead Trucking firm. "You guys named me after a cow."

"Your father's uncle was named Angus," she said, stripping off her outer shirt with a loud sigh, then plopping into her easy chair with a beer, wearing nothing but her bra; a bra, I might add, that could well have floated an ejected fighter pilot to safety.

"So my father's uncle was named after a cow too," I said. "What did *he* think of that?"

"Actually," Mom said, "I think he was kind of proud. Angus was quite a farmer, you know."

"Jesus help me," I said, and went to my room.

As Angus, the Fat Kid with Perverted Parents, I've had my share of adjustment problems, though it isn't as bad as it sounds. My parent's gene pool wasn't a *total* sump. Dad's family has all kinds of high-school shot-put record holders and hammer throwers and even a gridiron hero or two, and my mom's sister almost made it to the Olympic trials in speed-skating, so I was handed a fair-sized cache of athletic ability. I am *incredibly* quick for a fat kid and I have world-class reflexes. It is nearly impossible for the defensive lineman across from me to shake me, such are my anticipatory skills, and when I'm on defense, I need only to lock in on a running back's hips to zero in on the tackle. I cannot be shaken free. Plus, you don't have to dig *too* deep in our ancestoral remains to find an IQ safely into three digits, so grades come pretty easy to me. But I'd sure be willing to go into the winter trade meetings and swap reflexes, biceps, and brain cells, lock, stock, and barrel, for a little physical beauty.

Which brings me to tonight. I don't want you to think I spend *all* my life bitching about being short-changed in the Tom Cruise department, or about having parents a shade to the left of middle on your normal bell-shaped sexual curve, but tonight is a big night and I don't want the blubbery boogeymen or the phantoms of sexual perversity, who usually pop up to point me out for public mockery, mucking it up for me. I want *normal.* I want *socially acceptable.* See, I was elected Senior Winter Ball King, which means for about one minute I'll be featured gliding across the floor beneath the crimson and gold crepe paper streamers at Lake Michigan High School with Melissa Lefevre, the girl of my dreams—and only my dreams—who was elected Senior Winter Ball Queen. For that minute we'll be out there alone.

Alone with Melissa Lefevre.

Now, I don't want to go into the tomfoolery that must have gone on behind the scenes to get me elected to such a highly regarded post, because to tell you the truth I can't even imagine. I mean, it's a joke, I know that. I just don't know whose. It's a hell of a good one, though, because someone had to coax a plurality of more than five hundred seniors to forgo casting their ballots for any of a number of bona fide Adonises to write in the name of a cow. At first I tried to turn it down, but Grandad let me know right quick I'd draw a lot more attention if I made a fuss than if I acted as if I were the logical choice—indeed, the only choice— and went right along. Grandad is the man who taught me to be a dignified fat kid. "Always remember these words, and live by 'em," he said after my third suspension from kindergarten for fighting. "*Screw 'em.* Anybody doesn't like the way you look, screw 'em."

And that's just what I've done, because my grandfather— on my dad's side—is one righteous dude, and as smart as they come in an extra-large wide body sport coat. Sometimes I've screwed 'em by punching them in the nose, and sometimes by walking away. And sometimes by joining them—you know, laughing at myself. That's the one that works best. But when my temper is quick, it likes to speak first, and often as not someone's lying on the floor in a pool of nose fluids before I remember what a hoot it is to have the names of my mother and father dragged through the mud or my body compared to the Michelin tire man.

So you see, slowly but surely I'm getting all this under control. I don't mind that my detractors—who are legion— will wonder aloud tonight whether it is Melissa or I who is the Winter Ball Queen, a playful reference to my folks' quirky preferences, and I don't mind that I'll likely hear, "Why do they just swim up on the beach like that?" at least three times. What I mind is that during those few seconds when Melissa and I have the floor to ourselves, all those kids, friend and foe, will be watching me *dance*. Now, I've chronicled the majority of my maladies here, but none remotely approaches my altogether bankrupt sense of rhythm. When it comes to clapping his hands or stomping his feet to the beat, Angus Bethune is completely, absolutely, and most of all irreversibly, brain dead.

I've known about the dance for three weeks now; I even know the name of the song, though I don't recognize it, and I went out and spent hard-earned money on dance lessons; dance lessons that sent not one, but two petite, anorexic-looking rookie Arthur Murray girls off sharpening their typing skills to apply at Kelly Services. Those girls had some sore pods.

I've been planning for Melissa Lefevre for a long time. I fell in love with her in kindergarten when she dared a kid named Alex Immergluck to stick his tongue on a car bumper in minus thirty-five degree weather for calling her a "big fat snot-nosed deadbeat," a term I'm sure now was diagnostic of his homelife, but which at the time served only to call up Melissa's anger and indignation. Being a fat kid, I was interested in all the creative retaliatory methods I could get to store in the old computer for later use, and when I saw the patch of Alex's tongue stuck tight to the bumper as he screamed down the street holding his bleeding mouth, I knew I was in the company of genius. And such lovely genius it was. God, from kindergarten on, Melissa was that tan, sinewy-legged blond girl with the brown eyes that just make you ache. You ache a lot more when you're a fat kid, though, because you know she was only put on the earth, out of your reach, to make you feel bad. You have no business trying to touch her.

But at the same time my grandfather—a huge silver-haired Rolls-Royce of a grandfather—kept telling me over and over I could have any damn thing I wanted. He told me that down under that sleeping bag of globules I wore under my skin beat the heart of a lion and the body of Jack LaLanne. In fact, in the fifth grade, Grandad took me down to San Francisco on Jack's sixty-fifth birthday to let me watch him swim to Alcatraz with his hands cuffed behind him, towing a boat on a line with his teeth. He did it, he really did. He still does.

Grandad also took me to San Francisco to see some gay people, but we went to a place called Polk Street and it didn't help much. I mean, my parents are working folks who are with only the person they're with, and Polk Street was filled with people looking like they were headed for a Tandy-leather swap meet. Maybe it helped, though. At least my parents looked more normal to me, although my mother could pass for Bruiser of the Week about fifty-two times in any given year, so "normal" is a relative term.

The bottom line, though, no matter how my grandfather tried to convince me otherwise, was that Melissa Lefevre would remain a Fig Newton of my imagination throughout my school years, and no matter how hard Grandad primed me, I would never have the opportunity for any conversation with Melissa other than one in my head. Until tonight. Tonight I'll *have* to talk to her. If I don't, she'll have only my dancing by which to remember me, which is like Mrs. Fudd remembering Elmer for his hair. It'd be a damn shame.

All I really want is my moment with her. I have no illusions, no thoughts of her being struck blind and asking me to take her home. When you're different, on the down side, you learn to live from one scarce rich moment to the next, no matter the distance between. You become like a camel in a vast, scorched desert dotted with precious few oases, storing those cool watery moments in your hump, assuring survival until you stumble upon the next.

All I want is my moment.

So here I sit, my rented burgundy tux lying across my

bed like a drop cloth waiting to be unfolded on the floor of
the Sistine Chapel, digging deep into my reserves for the
courage not to crumble, hoping for the power to call up the
vision of the decent guy I know I am rather than the short-
fused, round clown-jock so many people see. What can
Melissa be thinking? She'll be there with someone else, of
course, so her winter Nightmare on Elm Street will last but
a few minutes at most. She's probably telling herself as I sit
here that it's like a trip to the dentist. No matter how badly
he's going to hurt you, no matter how many bare nerves he
drills or how many syringes of Novocain he explodes into
the roof of your mouth, in an hour you'll walk out of there.
And you'll still be alive.

Of course, Melissa hasn't seen me dance.

My dad was in an hour ago, looking sadly at me sitting
here on the side of my bed in my underwear next to this
glorious tuxedo, which, once on, will undoubtedly cast me
as a giant plum. Dad's the one who escorted me to Roland's
Big and Tall to have me fitted, and to make sure I got
something that would be comfortable. He's a sensitive guy,
one who has always scouted uncharted waters for me in an
attempt to clear away at least the huge logs, to render those
waters a *little* more navigable.

He wore his Kissbusters T-shirt, with the universal stop
sign—a circle with a slash through it—over huge red lips. I
gave one to each of my four parents back in junior high
when I negotiated the No Kissing Contract. ("I don't care
who's with who or what you do in the sack at night," I
screamed out of exasperation during one of our bimonthly
"absence of malice get-togethers," designed by my parents
to cement our extended family solidarity. "Just don't *kiss* in
front of me! I'm in junior high now! Look! Under here!" I
said, raising my arms, pointing to the budding tufts of hair,
"I got a bouquet of flowering pubiscus under each arm!
And the jury's in: I like girls! The only people I want to see

kissing are boys and girls! Not boys kissing boys. Not girls kissing girls! I want to see boys kissing girls! Understand? Hairy lips on smooth lips! Read mine! Boys . . . kissing . . . girls!'' I started to walk out of the room, then whirled. "You know what I need? You ask me that all the time! 'Angus, are you suffering emotional harm because we're different? Angus, are you feeling angst? Angus, do you need help adjusting? Angus, do you want to see a therapist?' I'm not having trouble adjusting! I don't even know what angst is! I don't want to see a therapist! I just don't want to see you *kissing*! You want to know what I need? I'll tell you! Role models! Someone to show me how things are done! Don't you guys ever watch Oprah? Or Donahue?'') It was a marvelous tantrum, and effective in that it resulted in the now famous, ironclad No Kissing contract, which I have since, for my part, dissolved but to which they adhere as if it were the Kama Sutra itself. You will not hear the smacking, sucking reverberations of lips parting in passion from lips in either of *my* happy homes.

"The cummerbund is good," Dad says. "It changes your lines; acts almost as a girdle. Don't keep the jacket buttoned for long; unbutton it early in the name of being casual; that way it won't pull tight where you bulge." Dad is the person most responsible for teaching me to dress a body ignored by the sensibilities of the world's clothiers. It was he who taught me to buy pants with a high waist, and to go ahead through the embarrassment of giving the salesman my full waist size—instead of cheating a few inches to save face—so I could always get *all* of myself into my pants and leave nothing hanging over. He also drilled into me that it is a mortal sin for a fat man to buy a shirt which tucks in. In short, my father is most responsible for teaching me to dress like a Big Top.

As he stands staring at the tuxedo, his brain grinding out camouflage intelligence, I read his mind.

"Don't worry, Dad," I say. "I can handle this."

"You've had this girl on your mind a long time," he says sadly. "I don't want you to be hurt."

I say, "I'm not going to be hurt, Dad," thinking *Please don't make me take care of you too.*

Alexander, my stepdad, walks through the bedroom door, places a hand on Dad's shoulder, and guides him out of the room, reappearing in seconds. "Your father's a pain in the butt sometimes, huh?" he says, "—worrying about things you wouldn't even think about."

I say, "Yeah, he is. Only this time *I'm* thinking of them. How am I going to get through this night without looking like Moby Melon with a stick in his butt?"

Alexander nods and looks at my near naked carcass. He is like an arrow, sleek and angular, the antithesis of my father. It is as if minor gods were given exactly enough clay to make two human forms, but divided it up in a remedial math class. Alexander is also sensible—though somewhat obscure—where my father is a romantic. "Superman's not brave," he says.

I look up. "What?"

"Superman. He's not brave."

"I'll send him a card."

Alexander smiles. "You don't understand. Superman's not brave. He's smart. He's handsome. He's even decent. But he's not brave."

I look at the tux, spread beside me, waiting. "Alexander, have I ever said it's hard to follow you sometimes?"

"He's indestructible," Alexander says. "You can't be brave when you're indestructible. It's guys like you and me that are brave, Angus. Guys who are different and can be crushed—and know it—but go out there anyway."

I looked at the tux. "I guess he wouldn't wear such an outrageous suit if he knew he looked like a blue-and-red Oldsmobile in it, would he?"

Alexander put his hand on my shoulder. "The tux looks fine, Angus." He left.

* * *

So now I stand at the door to the gym. The temperature is near zero, but I wear no coat because, once inside, I want to stay cool as long as possible, to reduce the risk of the dike-bursting perspiration that has become my trademark. No pun intended. Melissa—along with almost everyone, I would guess—is inside, waiting to be crowned Queen of the Winter Ball before suffering the humiliation of being jerked across the dance floor by an escort who should have GOODYEAR tattooed the length of both sides. My fear is nearly paralyzing, to tell the truth, but I've faced this monster down before—though, admittedly, he gets more fierce each time—and I'll face him down again. When he beats me, I'm done.

Heads turn as I move through the door. I simulate drying my butt with a towel, hoping for a casual twist-and-shout move. Your king is here. Rejoice. Marsha Stanwick stands behind the ticket table and I casually hand her mine, eyes straight ahead on the band, walking lightly on the balls of my feet, like Raymond Burr through a field of dog-poop sundaes. I pause to let my eyes adjust, hoping to God an empty table will appear, allowing me to drop out of the collective line of sight. Miraculously, one does and I squat, eyes still glued to the band, looking for all the world like the rock and roll critic from the *Trib.* If my fans are watching, they're seeing a man who *cares* about music. I lightly tap my fingers to what I perceive to be the beat, blowing my cover to smithereens. I see Melissa on the dance floor with her boyfriend—a real jerk in my book, Rick Sanford—and my heart bursts against the walls of my chest, like in *Alien.* I order it back. A sophomore server leaves a glass of punch on the table and I sip it slowly through the next song, after which the lead singer announces that the "royal couple" and their court are due behind the stage curtain in five minutes.

Tributaries of perspiration join at my rib cage to form a

raging torrent of sweat rushing toward my shoes as I silently hyperventilate, listening for my grandfather's voice, telling me to screw 'em, telling me once again I can do anything I want. I want my moment.

I rise to head for the stage and look up to see Melissa on her boyfriend's arm, coming toward me through the crowd parting on the dance floor. Sanford wears that cocky look, the one I remember from football; the one he wore continually until the day I wiped it off his face on the sideline during our first full-pad scrimmage. Golden Rick Sanford —Rick Running Back—danced his famous jig around end and turned upfield, thought he could juke me with a couple of cheap high-school hip fakes, not realizing that *this* blimp was equipped with tracking radar. It took him almost fifteen seconds to get his wind back. Hacked him off big time, me being so fat and ugly. But now the look is back; we're in his element. He's country club, I'm country; a part of his crowd on the field only.

As they approach, I panic. The king has no clothes. I want to run. What am I doing here? What was I thinking of? Suddenly I'd give up my moment in a heartbeat for the right to disappear. What a fool, to even think . . .

They stand before me. "Angus, my man," Rick slurs, and I realize it's not a change of underwear he's carrying in that paper bag. "I'm turning this lovely thing over to you for a while. Give her a chance to make a comparison. You know, be a bit more humble."

Melissa drops his arm and smiles. She says, "Hi. Don't pay any attention to him. He's drunk. And even without that, he's rude."

I smile and nod, any words far, far from my throat.

Melissa says, "Why don't we go on up?" and she takes my arm, leaving Rick's to hang limply at his side.

"Yeah," he says, squinting down at the paper sack in his hand, "why don't you go on up. You go right on up behind that curtain with my girl, Snowball King."

Melissa drops my arm and grips his elbow. "Shut up," she hisses. "I'm warning you, Rick. Shut up."

Rick tears his arm away. "Enjoy yourself," he says to me, ignoring her. "Your campaign cost me a lot of money, probably close to two bucks a pound." He looks me up and down as couples at the nearest tables turn to stare. The heat of humiliation floods up through my collar, and I fear the worst will follow. I fear I'll cry. If I do, Rick's in danger because it's a Bethunian Law that rage follows my tears as surely as baby chicks trail after their mama. "Don't you go be puttin' your puffy meat-hooks on my girl," he says, and starts to poke me in the chest, but I look at his finger and he thinks better.

Melissa takes my arm again and says, "Let's go."

We move two steps toward the stage and Rick says, loud, "Got your rubber gloves, honey?"

I turn, feeling Melissa's urgent tug, pulling me toward the stage.

"What do you mean by that?" I ask quietly, knowing full well what he means by that.

"I wasn't talking to you, Bigfoot," Rick says, looking past me to his girl. "I'm asking if my sweetie's got her rubber gloves."

Melissa says, "I hate you, Rick. I really do."

Rick ignores her. "Bigfoot comes from a high-risk home," he says. "Best wear your rubber gloves, honey, in case he has a cut."

In that instant I sweep his feet with mine and he lands hard on the floor. He moves to get up, but I'm over him, crowding. When he tries to push himself up, I kick his hands out, following his next movements like a cow dog, mirroring him perfectly, trapping him there on the floor. No chaperone is in view so it isn't totally out of hand yet. When he sees he can't rise, I kneel, sweat pouring off my forehead like rain. Softly, very softly, I say, "You may not like how my parents live. But they've been together since nineteen seventy-one—monogamous as the day is long. That's a low-risk group, Rick. The only person at high risk right now is you."

He looks into my eyes and he knows I mean it, knows I'm past caring about my embarrassment. "Okay, man," he says, raising his hands in surrender, "just having a little fun."

I'm apologizing to Melissa all the way up the backstage stairs, but she's not having any. "You should have stomped on his throat," she says, and I involuntarily visualize Alex Immergluck clutching at his bleeding mouth in the freezing cold next to the car bumper. "If you ever get another chance, I'll pay you money."

At the side door to the stage I say, "Speaking of embarrassment, there's something you need to know."

She waits.

"I can't dance."

Melissa smiles. "Not everyone's Nureyev," she says. "We'll survive."

I say, "Yeah, well, not everyone's Quasimodo either. I didn't say I can't dance *well*, I said I can't dance. Good people have been badly hurt trying to dance with me."

We're near the risers on the stage now, and our "court," made up of juniors and sophomores, stands below the spot at the top where we are to be crowned. Melissa hushes me as we receive instructions from the senior class adviser. There will be trumpeting, the crowning by last year's royalty, followed by a slow march down the portable steps to the gym floor to begin the royal dance.

We take our places. The darkness of the stage and the silence are excruciating. "What did he mean, my campaign cost him a lot of money?" I whisper.

"Never mind."

I snort a laugh and say, "I can take it."

"He's rich and he's rude," she says. "I'm embarrassed

I'm with him." She pauses, and slides her arm in mine. "I'm *not* with him. It was supposed to be a lesson for me. . . ."
The curtains part as the trumpets blare.

I gaze out into the spotlights, smiling like a giant "Have a Nice Day" grape. The introduction of last year's king and queen begin and they move toward us from stage left and right to relinquish their crowns to us. It would all be unbelievably ridiculous even if they weren't crowning King Angus the Fat. Without moving her lips Melissa says, "I picked a slow song. We don't have to move much. Dance close to me. When you feel me lean, you lean. Whatever you do, don't listen to the music. It'll just mess you up. Trust me. My brother's like you. Just follow."

She grips my arm as the royal march starts and leads me down the risers to the portable steps leading to the dance floor. I have surrendered. If I am to survive this, it will be through the will of Melissa Lefevre.

Somehow I remember to hand her the traditional single long-stemmed red rose and she takes it in her hand, smiling, then pulls me tight. She says, "Shadow me."

A part of me stays to concentrate, but another part goes to heaven. In my wildest dreams I could never have imagined Melissa Lefevre being *nice* to me in my moment, would never have *dared* to imagine holding her tight without feeling pushy and ugly and *way* out of line. She whispers, "Relax," into my ear and I follow mechanically through a song I'd never heard, not that it would make a difference. When I'm finally relaxed enough and know I'm going to live, the words to "Limelight" filter into my head, and I realize I'm *in* it. Like the songwriter, I fear it yet am drawn to it like a shark to a dangling toe.

"Alan Parsons," she whispers in my ear. "Good lyrics. I love 'em. And I hate 'em. That's what makes a song *good.*"

I wouldn't know a good song from a hot rock; I'm just hoping it's a *long* song. Feeling greedy now, I want my moment to last.

"Angus?"

"Yeah?"

"Do you ever get tired of who you are?"

I pull back a second, but it's like Lois Lane releasing Superman's hand twenty thousand feet in the air. She falls. I pull close again. "Do you know who you're talking to?"

I feel her smile. "Yeah," she says, "I thought so. I know it's not the same, but it's not always so great looking the way I do either. I pay too."

She's right: I think it's not the same.

"Want to know something about me?" she asks and I think, *I'd like to know* anything *about you.*

I say, "Sure."

"I'm bulemic. Do you know what that is?"

I smile. "I'm a fat kid with faggot parents who's been in therapy on and off for eighteen years," I say. "Yes, I know what that is. It means when you eat too much, you chuck it up so you don't turn out to look like me."

"Close enough for discussion purposes. Don't worry, I'm in therapy for it," she says, noticing my concern. "A *lot* of pretty girls are."

"Actually," I say, "I even tried it once, but when I stuck my finger down my throat I was still hungry and I almost ate my arm."

Melissa laughs and holds me tighter. "You're the only person I've ever told except for the people in my therapy group; I just wanted you to know things aren't always as they appear. Would you do me a favor?"

"If it doesn't involve more than giving up my life," I say, feeling wonderful because Melissa isn't a goddess anymore; and because that doesn't change a thing about the way I feel about her.

"Would you leave with me?"

My foot clomps onto her delicate toe.

"Concentrate," she says. Then, "Would you?"

"You mean leave this dance? Leave this dance with you?"

I feel her nod.

I consider. "At least I don't turn into a pumpkin at midnight, I'm a pumpkin already."

"I like how you stood up for your family. It must be hard. Defending them all the time, I mean."

"Compared to me a boy named Sue had it made," I say.

The music ends; all dancers stop and clap politely. "I want to dance one more," Melissa says. "A fast one."

"I'll wait over by the table."

"No. I want to dance it with you."

"You don't understand," I say. "When I dance to the beat of rock and roll decent folks across this great land quake in their boots."

She holds my hand tightly. "Listen. Do what you did when you wouldn't let Rick up. Don't listen to the music, just follow me the way you followed him."

I try to protest, but the band breaks into "Bad Moon Rising" and the dance floor erupts. Melissa pushes me back gently and, out of panic, I zero in, locking on her hips as I would a running back's. I back away as she comes at me, mirroring her every move, top to bottom. She cuts to the sideline and I meet her, dancing upfield nose to nose. As the band heats up I remain locked in; though her steps become more and more intricate, she cannot shake me. A crowd gathers and I'm trapped inside a cheering circle, actually performing the unheard of: I'm Angus Bethune, Fat Man Extraordinaire, dancing in the limelight with Melissa Lefevre, stepping outside the oppressive prison of my body to fly to the beat of Creedence Clearwater Revival.

When the drummer bangs the last beat, the circle erupts in celebration and I take a long, low bow. Melissa is clapping wildly. She reaches across and wipes a drop of sweat from my brow with her finger. When she touches the finger to her tongue, I tell God he can take me now.

"You bitch!" Rick yells at the door as I help Melissa into her coat. "You bitch! You practiced with this tub of lard! You guys been getting together dancing. You bitch. You set me up." He turns to me. "I oughta take you out, fat boy," he says, but his unimaginative description can't touch my glory.

I put up a finger and wag it side to side in front of his nose. "You know the difference between you and me, Sanford?"

He says, "There's a *lot* of differences between us, Lardo. You couldn't count the differences between us."

"That's probably true," I say, closing my fist under his nose. "But the one that matters right now is that I can make *you* ugly."

He stares silently at my fist.

I say, "Don't even think it. Next to dancing, that's my strong suit."

CHRIS CRUTCHER

All four of Chris Crutcher's highly praised novels have been named Best Books for Young Adults by the American Library Association. Each one is a compelling, hard-hitting, yet compassionate and often humorous examination of a courageous male teenager's struggle for identity and responsible independence.

In *Running Loose* senior Louie Banks rebels against an immoral football coach and then has to deal with the sudden death of his supportive girlfriend, Becky. In taking a stand against adult authorities Louie discovers consequences he did not anticipate.

The authority figure in *Stotan!* is a wise, nurturing swim coach who, through one grueling week of endurance training, challenges four male friends to become champion swimmers, equipped to face whatever challenges may arise in their unpredictable lives.

When a freak accident leaves sixteen-year-old baseball star Willie Weaver partially paralyzed, he runs away from home in *The Crazy Horse Electric Game*. On the tough streets of inner-city Oakland, California, he begins to find a place for himself in a special school for problem kids.

In his most recent novel, *Chinese Handcuffs*, Dillon Hemingway is forced to deal with his brother's suicide, his brother's girlfriend, a single-minded school principal, a vicious cycling gang, and a female basketball star whose home problems are too horrifying to talk about.

For several years Chris Crutcher was the director of an alternative school in Oakland, California, that became the model for Last Chance High School in *The Crazy Horse Electric Game*. The setting for *Running Loose* is based on the small logging town of Cascade, Idaho, where he grew up. He currently lives in Spokane, Washington, where he is a child and family therapist specializing in child abuse.

CLASHES

Tiffany thinks she understands her mother. But Jack's arrival adds a new dimension. . . .

AS IT IS WITH STRANGERS

SUSAN BETH PFEFFER

For S.

It wasn't until right before I went to bed on Thursday that Mom bothered to tell me the son she'd given up for adoption twenty years earlier was coming over for supper the next day.

"What son?" I asked.

"I'm sure I've told you about him," Mom said. "You must have forgotten."

I figured I probably had. I'm always forgetting little things like my homework assignments and being elected President of the United States. Having an older brother must have just slipped my mind. "How'd you two find each other?" I asked. Presumably Mom had never told me that.

"I registered with an agency," she said. "Put my name and address in a book, so if he ever wanted to find me, he could. I guess he did. Don't be late for supper tomorrow."

"I won't be," I promised. This was one reunion I had no intention of missing.

School the next day really dragged on. School never goes fast on Fridays, but when your mind is on some newly acquired half brother, it's real hard to care about Julius Caesar. I didn't tell anybody, though. It seemed to me it was Mom's story, not mine, and besides, my friends all think she's crazy anyway. Probably from things I've said over the years.

I went straight home from school, and was surprised, first to find the place spotless, and then to see Mom in the kitchen cooking away.

"I took a sick day," she informed me. "So I could prepare better."

"Everything looks great," I told her. It was true. I hadn't seen the place look so good since Great-Aunt Trudy came with the goat, but that's another story. "You look very pretty too."

"I got my nails done," Mom said, showing them off for me. They were coral colored. "And my hair."

I nodded. Mom had taught me that nothing was unbearable if your hair looked nice.

"Is that what you're planning to wear tonight?" she asked.

"I thought I'd shower and change into my dress," I said. I own a grand total of one dress, but this seemed to be the right kind of occasion for it.

Mom gave me a smile like I'd just been canonized. "Thank you," she said. "Tonight's kind of important for me."

I nodded. I wasn't sure just what to say anymore. Mom and I have been alone for eight years, and you'd figure by now I'd know how to handle her under any circumstances, but this one had me stumped. "What's for supper?" I finally asked.

"Southern fried chicken," Mom said. "At first I thought I'd make a roast, but then what if he doesn't like his meat rare? And turkey seemed too Thanksgivingish, if you know what I mean. Everybody likes fried chicken. And I made mashed potatoes and biscuits and a spinach salad."

"Spinach salad?" I asked. I could picture Mom pouring the spinach out of a can and dousing it with Wishbone.

"From scratch," Mom informed me. "Everything's from

scratch. And I baked an apple pie too. The ice cream is store bought, but I got one of those expensive brands. What do you think?"

I thought that there obviously was something to that Prodigal Son story, since Mom never made anything more elaborate for me than scrambled eggs. "It smells great," I said. It did, too, the way you picture a house in a commercial smelling, all homey and warm. "I'm sure everything will go fine."

"I want it to," Mom said, as though I'd suggested that maybe she didn't.

There were a few things I knew I'd better clear up before Big Brother showed up. "What's his name?" I asked, for starters.

"Jack," Mom said. "That's not what I would have named him. I would have named him Ronald."

"You would have?" I asked. I personally am named Tiffany, and Ronald would not have been my first guess.

"That was my boyfriend's name," Mom said. "Ronny."

"Your boyfriend," I said. "You mean his father?"

Mom nodded. "You think of them as boyfriends, not fathers, when you're sixteen," she said.

Well that answered question number two. It had seemed unlikely to me that my father was responsible, but who knew? I wasn't there. Maybe he and Mom had decided they wanted a girl, and chucked out any boys that came along first.

Speaking of which. "There aren't any other brothers I've forgotten about?" I asked. "Is this going to be the first of many such dinners?"

"Jack's the only one," Mom replied. "I wanted to keep him, but Ronny wasn't about to get married, and Dad said if I gave him up for adoption then I could still go to college. I did the right thing, for him and for me. And I would have gone to college if I hadn't met your father. I don't know.

Maybe because I gave up the baby, I was too eager to get married. I never really thought about it."

"Did Dad know?" I asked.

"I told him," Mom said. "He said it didn't matter to him. And it didn't. Whatever else was wrong in our marriage, he never threw the baby in my face."

I found myself picturing a baby being thrown in Mom's face, and decided I should take my shower fast. So I sniffed the kitchen appreciatively and scurried out. In the shower I tried to imagine what this Jack would look like, but he kept resembling Dad's high-school graduation picture, which made no sense biologically at all. So I stopped imagining.

When I went to my bedroom to change, though, I was really shocked. Mom had extended her cleaning ways to include my room. All my carefully laid out messes were gone. It would probably take me months to reassemble things. I considered screaming at Mom about the sanctity of one's bedroom, but I decided against it. Mom obviously wanted this guy to think she and I were the perfect Amcrican family, and if that meant even my room had to be clean, then nothing was going to stop her. I could live with it, at least for the evening.

Mom and I set the table three times before the doorbell finally rang. When it did, neither one of us knew who should answer it, but Mom finally opened the door. "Hello," this guy said. "I'm Jack."

"I'm Linda," Mom replied. "Come on in. It's nice to . . . well, it's good seeing you."

"Good to see you too," Jack said. He didn't look anything like my father.

"This is Tiffany," Mom said. "She, uh . . ."

"Her daughter," I said. "Your sister." I mean, those words were going to be used at some point during the evening. We might as well get them out of the way fast. Then when we got around to the big tricky words like *mother* and *son,* at least some groundwork would have been laid.

"It's nice to meet you," Jack said, and he gave me his hand to shake, so I shook it. They say you can tell a lot about a man from his handshake, but not when he's your long-lost brother. "I hope my coming like this isn't any kind of a brother. I mean bother."

"Not at all," Mom said. "I'm going to check on dinner. Tiffany, why don't you show Jack the living room? I'll join you in a moment."

"This is the living room," I said, which was pretty easy to show Jack, since we were already standing in it. "Want to sit down?"

"Yeah, sure," Jack said. "Have you lived here long?"

"Since the divorce," I said. "Eight years ago."

"That long," Jack said. "Where's your father?"

"He lives in Oak Ridge," I said. "That's a couple of hundred miles from here. I see him sometimes."

"Is he . . ." Jack began. "I mean, I don't suppose you'd know . . ."

"Is he your father too?" I said. "No. I kind of asked. Your father's name is Ronny. My father's name is Mike. I don't know much else about your father except he didn't want to marry Mom. They were both teenagers, I guess. Do you want to meet him too?"

"Sometime," Jack said. "Not tonight."

I could sure understand that one. "I've always wanted to have a big brother," I told him. "I always had crushes on my friends' big brothers. Did you want that—to have a kid sister, I mean?"

"I have one," Jack said. "No, I guess now I have two. I have a sister back home. Her name is Leigh Ann. She's adopted too. She's Korean."

"Oh," I said. "That's nice. I guess there isn't much of a family resemblance, then."

"Not much," Jack said, but he smiled. "She's twelve. How old are you?"

"Fifteen," I said. "Do you go to college?"

Jack nodded. "I'm a sophomore at Bucknell," he said. "Do you think you'll go to college?"

"I'd like to," I said. "I don't know if we'll have the money, though."

"It's rough," Jack said. "College costs a lot these days. My father's always griping about it. He owns a car dealership. New and used. I work there summers. My mom's a housewife."

I wanted to tell him how hard Mom had worked on supper, how messy the apartment usually was, how I never wore a dress, and Mom's nails were always a deep sinful scarlet. I wanted to tell him that maybe someday I'd be jealous that he'd been given away to a family that could afford to send him to college, but that it was too soon for me to feel much of anything about him. There was a lot I wanted to say, but I didn't say any of it.

"What's she like?" Jack asked me, and he gestured toward the kitchen, as though I might not otherwise know who he was talking about.

"Mom?" I said. "She's terrible. She drinks and she gambles and she beats me black and blue if I even think something wrong."

Jack looked horrified. I realized he had definitely not inherited Mom's sense of humor.

"I'm only kidding," I said. "I haven't even been spanked since I was five. She's fine. She's a good mother. It must have really hurt her to give you away like that."

"Have you known long?" Jack asked. "About me?"

"Not until recently," I said. It didn't seem right to tell him I'd learned less than twenty-four hours before. "I guess Mom was waiting until I was old enough to understand."

"I always knew I was adopted," Jack said. "And for years I've wanted to meet my biological parents. To see what they looked like. I love Mom and Dad, you understand. But I felt this need."

"I can imagine," I said, and I could too. I was starting to develop a real need to see what Jack's parents looked like, and we weren't even related.

"Tiffany, could you come in here for a minute?" Mom called from the kitchen.

"Coming, Mom," I said, and left the living room fast. It takes a lot out of you making small talk with a brother.

"What do you think?" Mom whispered as soon as she saw me. "Does he look like me?"

"He has your eyes," I said. "And I think he has your old hair color."

"I know," Mom said, patting her bottle red hair. "I almost asked them to dye me back to my original shade, but I wasn't sure I could remember it anymore. Do you like him? Does he seem nice?"

"Very nice," I said. "Very good manners."

"He sure didn't inherit those from Ronny," Mom declared. "Come on, let's start taking the food out."

So we did. We carried out platters of chicken and mashed potatoes and biscuits and salad. Jack came to the table as soon as he saw what we were doing.

"Oh, no," he said. "I mean, I'm sorry. I should have told you. I'm a vegetarian."

"You are?" Mom said. She looked as shocked as if he'd told her he was a vampire. Meat is very important to Mom. "You're not sick or anything, are you?"

"No, it's for moral reasons," Jack said. "It drives my mom, my mother, her name's Cathy, it drives Cathy crazy."

"Your mom," my mom said. "It would drive me crazy, too, if Tiffany stopped eating meat just for moral reasons."

"Don't worry about it," I told her. "I'll never be that moral."

"There's plenty for me to eat," Jack said. "Potatoes and biscuits and salad."

"The salad has bacon in it," Mom said. "I crumbled bacon in it."

"We can wash the bacon off, can't we Jack?" I said. "You'll eat it if we wash the bacon off, won't you?"

I thought he hesitated for a moment, but then he said, "Of course I can," and for the first time since we'd met, I kind of liked him. I took the salad into the kitchen and washed it all. The salad dressing went the way of the bacon, but we weren't about to complain. At least there'd be something green on Jack's plate. All his other food was gray-white.

Mom hardly ate her chicken, which I figured was out of deference to the vegetarian, but I had two and a half pieces, figuring it might be years before Mom made it again. Jack ate more potatoes than I'd ever seen another human being eat. No gravy, but lots of potatoes. We talked polite stuff during dinner, what he was studying in college, where Mom worked, the adjustments Leigh Ann had had to make. The real things could only be discussed one on one, so after the pie and ice cream, I excused myself and went to Mom's room to watch TV. Only I couldn't make my eyes focus, so I crossed the hall to my room, and recreated my messes. Once I had everything in proper order, though, I put things back the way Mom had had them. I could hear them talking while I moved piles around, and then I turned on my radio, so I couldn't even hear the occasional stray word, like *father* and *high school* and *lawyer.* That was a trick I'd learned years ago, when Mom and Dad were in their fighting stage. The radio played a lot of old songs that night. It made me feel like I was seven all over again.

After a while Mom knocked on my door and said Jack was leaving, so I went to the living room and shook hands with him again. I still couldn't tell anything about his personality from his handshake, but he did have good manners, and he gave me a little pecking kiss on my cheek, which I thought was sweet of him. Mom kept the door open, and watched as he walked the length of the corridor to the stairs. She didn't close the door until he'd gotten into a car, his I assumed. Maybe it was a loaner from his father.

"You give away a baby," Mom said, "and twenty years later he turns up on your doorstep a vegetarian."

"He turns up a turnip," I said.

But Mom wasn't in the mood for those kinds of jokes. "Don't you ever make that mistake," she said.

"What mistake?" I asked, afraid she meant making jokes. If I couldn't make jokes with Mom, I wouldn't know how to talk with her.

"Don't you ever give up something so important to you that it breathes when you do," Mom said. "It doesn't have to be a kid. It can be a dream, an ambition, or a marriage, or a house. It can be anything you care about as deeply as you care about your own life. Don't ever just give it away, because you'll spend the rest of your life wondering about it, or pretending you don't wonder, which is the same thing, and you'll wake up one morning and realize it truly is gone and a big part of you is gone with it. Do you hear me, Tiffany?"

"I hear you," I said. I'd never seen Mom so intense, and I didn't like being around her. "I'm kind of tired now, Mom. Would you mind if I went to bed early?"

"I'll clean up tomorrow," Mom said. "You can go to bed."

So I did. I left her sitting in the living room and went to my bedroom and closed my door. But this time I didn't turn the radio on, and later, when I'd been lying on my bed for hours, not able to sleep, I could hear her in her room crying. I'd heard her cry in her room a hundred times before, and a hundred times before I'd gotten up and comforted her, and I knew she'd cry a hundred times again, and I'd comfort her then, too, but that night I just stayed in my room, on my bed, staring at the ceiling and listening to her cry. I think I did the right thing, not going in there. That's how it is with strangers. You can never really comfort them.

SUSAN BETH PFEFFER

Susan Beth Pfeffer, a resident of Middletown, New York, writes reviews, articles, and juvenile books—including *What Do You Do When Your Mouth Won't Open?* and *Courage, Dana!*—as well as young adult novels.

Among her first novels for teenagers were *Beauty Queen; Starring Peter and Leigh;* and *Marly the Kid,* the story of a teenager who elects to live with her father and stepmother, then gets into trouble in school by challenging her sexist teacher. Defying school authorities is also an issue in *A Matter of Principle,* where a school principal censors the student newspaper and then expels several students when they publish an underground newspaper.

Two of her novels follow Annie Powell, first as a summer intern for a glamorous New York City magazine—in *Fantasy Summer*—and then after she has just been rejected as feature editor of her high school newspaper—in *Getting Even.*

In 1985 Pfeffer developed a series called *Make Me a Star,* about a group of young actors in a TV show called *Hard Time High.* It starts with *Prime Time* and includes *Wanting It All* and *Love Scenes.* She recently began another series called *The Sebastian Sisters.*

Her two most important novels are *About David* and *The Year Without Michael,* both strongly emotional books and both ALA Best Books for Young Adults. The first book concerns the suicide of a high school student and the reactions of his closest friend who tries to find out why he did it and what she might have done to prevent it. The second explores the reactions and devastated feelings of a sixteen-year-old girl and her parents after her young brother fails to return home one evening . . . and is never heard from again.

Refusing to talk about his anger, Wally is a master at causing trouble.
Especially in English class. . . .

WHITE CHOCOLATE

ROBIN F. BRANCATO

I'm telling straight out who I am. Not like in this certain story *she* made us read, where you didn't know for ten pages who the teller was. You were thinking it was a guy, and then it turned out to be a tomboy girl. Wally is my name, which I'm not crazy about, but it's better than being called Walter, like my father. And I may as well tell this right off, too, so you aren't picturing me as some blond-headed, surfing-movie type: one of my parents is black and one is white. If you think I'm going to tell which is which, and how they got together in the first place, and what they're like now, and how I feel about it, *forget* it. Those are the kinds of questions *she'd* be asking, if I went in and talked to her. *What are you angry about, Wally?* she sometimes asks me right in front of everybody. *Something wrong, Wally? What's bothering you?*

"You!" I tell her right out. "This ridiculous English class!"

It really gets to her when I talk like that. The other kids start laughing and snorting. They're all thinking the same as I am, but they're too chicken to say it out loud. Meanwhile, she tries to act so calm and cool, but her mouth gets tight, and she repeats something she already said, and a pink line creeps up her neck to her white cheeks. And then she gets herself in deeper. Instead of just yelling, "Shut your mandibles, Keating!" like my health teacher would, she says, "I'm curious, Wally. What would be your idea of a fascinating English class?"

Oh, man, is she *asking* for it! I feel like saying something really crude and lewd, but I don't. All I say is "A class where we *learned* something. Where we read something *interesting.* Where we didn't do all this *useless* stuff."

Then her face gets redder, the way it can only when somebody has white, white skin, and I see I've hit her on the right weak spot, as usual. She *can't stand* hearing that she isn't teaching us anything, because she's such a serious, trying-to-be-so-good person. Practically every day she comes in with different books, or magazines, or stories she's copied on a machine. Stuff that is supposed to get us all excited but never does. Sometimes Tim the Gook talks to her about the papers she hands out, because he's as serious as she is, but the other kids—Ribs, Mr. Clean, Sherlcne, and the Preacher—think just the same as I do: why don't this lady go off and be a librarian on a desert island?

You might be wondering why I'm taking Themes English, which is the lowest level there is. It's not as if I'm illiterate, like Mr. Clean and a couple of the others. It's because I do lousy in school, which is because I'm not interested in most things they try to teach us, and *especially* not in stories about girls who start off being tomboys, and guys and girls who fall in love even though their families hate each other, and mixed-up teenagers who run away from home. Half the stories we've read in her class are about kids running away from home, and in all of them the kid "wises up" and comes back. If I ever take off, which I might, the way things are going right now, at least I'll follow through with it and stay gone, not like these gutless wonders, who supposedly come to their senses on the last page of the story.

And what's pushing me into thinking about getting the hell out of here? This latest thing with *her,* Mrs. Loring. It's been building since the beginning of school. Right off, the first English period, I knew we'd be enemies, but it's taken till now, the end of March, for the battle to get really bad. Teachers. I can't take any of them, but the worst are the so-called understanding ones. I can't take people like Loring and my grandmother—my father's mother—people who think that whatever goes wrong, you can fix it by *talking* about it *calmly.* I hate talk. I'm not talking again, especially to either of them.

Let me tell you how I knew right away that Loring and I were going to be enemies. I had been running a little wild last summer, and my mom practically dragged me to the first day of school. "You got the brains, Wally," she was saying as she dropped me off. "Don't let these troubles between me and your daddy affect you. Your daddy was *always* looking for something different in his life, and now he's *gone off* to find it. Don't give me trouble this year. Go in there and act right!"

So I walked into first period, annoyed to begin with, and who did I see in front of the class but this teacher who looks a lot like my grandmother I mentioned before. My grandmother is older, naturally, but they both have these blue, blue eyes, and besides that they both sound the same. They're both cool, in the sense of acting a little *above* everyone else. Not snobby, exactly, but *proper.* "Watch your manners, Wally dear!"

I wasn't in the mood for that watch-your-step stuff. I had spent some summers at my grandmother's and had had enough of learning how to be polite. She was always trying to *teach* me things. So was my father. And now here was Loring sounding just like my Grandma Keating. "Oh, isn't this wonderful, brand new books!"

Loring had taught in a different school before, she said, but she was glad to be here, supposedly. *Sure* she was. Then why did she look at us as if we were from outer space? She was trying not to stare at Mr. Clean's white skinhead and hula-hoop earring, and her expression when she saw Ribsy

Johnson was *Help! call the narcs!* Okay, so skinny Ribsy is something else, with his gold tooth and jewelry, but she acted like she'd never seen a kid who's a drug runner before. Sherlene Lovering upset Loring, too, by showing pictures of her new baby. I naturally said, "Who were you lovering, Sherlene, to end up with that?"

And there were more of us aliens, nine or ten others, including the Preacher, this sophomore about three feet tall, who always talks like a minister. "Mornin', brothuhs," he said when he walked in. "Mornin', sister," he said to Loring. "So glad you could find in your souls to attend this A.M." Most teachers would have done something, either answered him smart or put him down. Not her. Soft and sweet, as if she thought that would turn us polite. Everyone took advantage. When she asked us about what kinds of things we liked, we gave stupid answers. And right away I decided to show her that marshmallows end up getting burnt.

My fellow classmates, as they say, were more than willing to help me. You could say there was a fine spirit of cooperation between Mr. Clean and Ribsy and me. Still, they left it to me to be leader, because those two care about passing. I used to care, too, back when we learned stuff that mattered. Anyway, everyone was happy that I took the initiative by winging a paper airplane over her head.

From then on it was downhill for her, mainly because, instead of yelling like a normal teacher, she kept on trying so hard to be patient and *nice*. It didn't help that her voice was shaky, or that she kept repeating certain dumb expressions. Soon the whole class was saying things like "People, I wish I could hear myself!"

She made us write almost every day, and a lot of the topics were personal. If I did the assignments at all, I just made up lies, and she was so easy, all she said was, "You're very creative, Wally." My biggest creativity was thinking up ways to mess up her lessons.

"Where's your book today, Wally?" she asked me once.
"Close your eyes," I said. She actually did it, and while
her eyes were closed I walked out and cut class. After that,
though, she laid down a rule. "Anyone who comes without
a book goes to the principal." So I'd trick her, pretending I
had no book, and then I'd pull it out of hiding at the last
minute.

Once she actually sent a pink slip on me down to the
office to Bird-doo. That's the principal, Mr. Berdew, who
called me in for a weekly conference.

"What's up *now?*" Bird-doo asked me. "I shouldn't be
having to see you so often. You're a smart kid. Get your act
together. You should be a *leader* in that class."

"I am," I told him.

"That's not what I hear," Bird-doo said. "Hey, look, I
don't want to have to call your father."

"He's away—on business."

"Your mother, then."

"Nah, don't," I actually broke down and pleaded, "she's
got a lot on her mind. I'll be a leader, I will." And then I
said something else I knew that Bird-doo would listen to.
He's white, Mr. Berdew (like bird-doo), but half the kids in
the school are black. "Hey, Mr. Berdew, can't you find a
better Themes teacher?"

"What are you talking about?" He came on impatient at
first. "Who put you in charge of teacher evaluations? Mrs.
Loring came here from Warrensville, the top school in the
county."

"Warrensville?" I smiled and looked at him shrewd-like.
"I guess that explains it. She must not be used to . . .
students like us."

Bird-doo gave me a deep look. "You're not saying she
discriminates, are you?"

I shrugged. "She *acts* like she thinks we belong in a zoo."

He clammed up and got rid of me fast, but soon after that
he observed our Themes class. Naturally I kept all the

flying objects grounded that day and answered Loring's questions left and right. Her voice was shakier than usual, and she repeated herself and blushed a lot, and if you ask me, we came off a lot better than she did. That was my main aim, let's face it, to get Loring out of the picture.

Anyway, I'm pretty sure that Bird-doo criticized her somehow, because after that she quit sending down pink slips on me. Instead, whenever I drove her nuts she made silly threats, like "How would you like to keep me company until five o'clock today?"

"I wouldn't like it," I'd tell her. "I'd rather hang out with Mrs. Dracula." Or else "I'd love it, but at four o'clock my father is taking me up in his private plane." She never carried out a threat and I knew she never would, but what she did do was to keep asking me to come in *voluntarily* to discuss what was bothering me.

"You've got to be kidding," I'd say to her.

"Then I'm going to have to speak to your parents."

"Go ahead." Let her waste her time, just like my grandmother, who keeps calling once a week to see if I'll come visit her, like I used to do. She'd like to talk with me about family matters, she says. As if I could *talk* my dad back from Alaska, when even the letter I sent up there he still hasn't answered!

Dodging my grandmother is a pain (my mom doesn't feel like seeing her either), but I wasn't worried at all about Loring calling my house. The only number I had given at school was the one to my dad's old business phone that is still there but we haven't answered ever since he left last May.

So that's how it went for a while, with me as the chief toaster at the marshmallow roast. Every day, as soon as Loring would start her lesson, I'd stir up something.

"Brothuh Keating," the Preacher would say, "give Sistuh Loring yo' full attention."

"I'm giving it." I'd smirk. "She's got my attention, *full time.*"

We would probably have gone on like that, with me annoying her constantly and her passing me at the end of the year with a D, just to get rid of me. But then she made a mistake. She brought in this certain story, and I had a hunch right from the beginning that she had brought it in to get at *me.* "White Chocolate," it was called, and when she handed it out, she looked at me.

"I'm curious what you'll think of it," she said.

"Curiosity killed the cat."

"I'm not a cat." She was blushing as usual. "Start reading, please, Wally."

She was always having us read out loud, with Mr. Clean spitting out one syllable per hour and the Preacher shouting "Amen!" at the end of each sentence. Sometimes I refused, but other times I read so fast that everyone would start yelling, "Hey, we can't understand what he's saying!"

This time I began fast, but right away she said, "Wait, please, Wally. This is one story I want everyone to hear every word of, particularly you."

"Why me?" I snapped back at her.

"Because I think you might be interested."

"Fat chance," I said. "What's it about?"

She was cool as usual. "Go on reading."

I should have quit then and there, I should have refused to continue, but I figured I'd ham it up and she'd have somebody else go on. I did ham it up somewhat, but she had me read anyway. I should have known. It was about a white girl going out with a guy who was black. "What makes you think I'm interested in this?" I boomed out at Loring.

"I've gotten the impression that you're interested in race relations."

"Wrong again," I informed her. "I'm definitely not."

Loring looked as if she was going to ask me to read

further, but then she said, "Would you continue, please, Sherlene?"

I tried to make her laugh, but Sherlene went on with "White Chocolate." The story was the worst. It shouldn't be allowed in print. It's about this white girl who meets a black guy in college. They fall in love, but their families don't want them to get hitched. They won't give up, though. They *love* each other too much, and they want to *prove* something. So they work on their families real slow, and they take a lot of abuse, and finally—this is the worst part, I almost threw up all over the copies of the story— finally their families come to see things their way and they all plan the wedding together. And you can probably guess by now where the idiot title comes in. The icing on their wedding cake is—wow, so *symbolic*—made of *white chocolate.*

At some point in the reading I started humming pretty loudly, but unfortunately not loud enough to drown the thing out. Loring gave me one of her hurt looks, which made me hum more. And at the end, when she asked, "Well, what do you think?" I let out a deep belch.

Nobody laughed. What was *wrong* with them? Sherlene said, "It's a real nice story." I couldn't believe my ears. "Nice!" I yelled. "There's nothing I hate more than *nice!*" If Ribsy had been there, he'd probably have cheered me on, but he was away on a business trip, and all the Preacher had to say was "True love is the greatest, amen!"

Loring looked at me, so serious. "So, what do you think, Wally? What are the chances for people from different backgrounds working things out?"

I went crazy at that point. I got up and headed straight for her. "Quit bugging me, lady! Why are you picking on *me* about that?"

She thought I was going to hit her, and I was. My arms were raised, ready to pound her, so that the Preacher came rushing up and yelled, "Now, now, no *vi*-lence!"

The bell rang at that exact moment. Usually Loring

blocks the doorway and doesn't let us leave the room until we've picked up our mess. This time she pushed everyone else out and blocked only me.

"You're talking to me right now." She stood with her arms folded.

"Can't," I said, nastily, "I got a class."

"*Forget it,* as you love to say." Her arm shot out. "Sit down."

I sat, but slowly, so she would know I wasn't jumping at her command.

"There's too much to say to say it all now." She stood over my desk and looked at me with those icy blue eyes. "All I'm saying for the moment is, *Don't lose control like that again.* If I ever ask you something that makes you angry, it's only because *I don't know any better,* and if I don't, it's your fault, because you want it that way. I can't make you tell me what's bothering you. I don't necessarily want to know your personal problems. If you want me to know, I'll do what I can to help. If you don't want me to know your business, follow this rule: Don't show me you're hurting. Fake it. Pretend you're a model kid.

"One more thing," she babbled on, "it's ironic that you refuse to talk—talk seriously, I mean. I know you're willing to talk to put people down. Don't you know how good you are with words? Don't you know the *power* that could give you? Getting through to other people with words is our only hope in this world!

"*Go,*" she told me all of a sudden. "Enough for one lecture. Get moving to your class, so I won't have to write a note. I'd like to really talk sometime, I mean a two-way conversation. If that's not possible for you, remember what I said, *lose control again and you're out.*"

I took off without saying beans. Not like these kids in her stupid stories, who hear some wise-as-an-owl speech and it changes their teenage hearts. In fact, if she knew the effect, she would have kept her precious *words* to herself. The effect is, I'm probably not going back to her class ever again. Who needs credits? Both my parents went all the way through college and their lives aren't that great. What I'll probably do is go away, and like I said, I'll stay gone. I'm thinking about Alaska. I'm going to actually look at a map tonight.

Meanwhile, I hope I don't see Loring anymore in the hall today. She probably thinks, now that I listened to her for two seconds, that I'll be like Silly Putty in her hands. She probably thinks she'll eventually get me to show her the stuff I write, that I've never shown anybody. Just let her *try* pressing me into shape, and let her see how sticky I'll be.

ROBIN FIDLER BRANCATO

Raised in Wyomissing, Pennsylvania, Robin Brancato became a high school English teacher in Hackensack, New Jersey, and raised two children of her own before gaining recognition as an author of novels for teenagers. She now lives with her teacher husband in Teaneck, New Jersey, where she teaches during the morning and writes during the afternoon.

After publishing *Don't Sit Under the Apple Tree* and *Something Left to Lose,* she wrote a story about a star football player's sudden injury and how a sensitive English teacher helps him learn to cope with and to accept his paralyzed condition. The American Library Association named *Winning* a Best Book for Young Adults in 1977.

That same honor was bestowed on two of Brancato's later young adult novels: *Come Alive at 505,* the story of a boy who wants to become a radio disc jockey, and *Sweet Bells Jangled Out of Tune,* a novel about the relationship between a high school teenager and her senile grandmother. *Blinded by the Light,* an examination of the effects of a religious cult on its members and on one family in particular, was made into a CBS Movie of the Week, starring Kristy McNichol.

In *Facing Up* the relationship between Jep and Dave, two high-school friends, is endangered when they both are attracted to the same girl. When Jep is killed in a car accident while Dave is driving, Dave has difficulty dealing with his guilt. Brancato raises another timely issue in *Uneasy Money,* where eighteen-year-old Mike Bronti wins more than two million dollars in the New Jersey lottery but has a problem managing his winnings wisely.

She is currently working on a novel about the adventures of an eighteen-year-old girl who moves from a small town to New York City, tentatively titled *If I Can Make It There.*

Important events in Milly's life have always been disrupted by crises in the life of her older sister, Susan. Now Susie has moved back home with her latest problem. . . .

MILDRED

COLBY RODOWSKY

My name is Milly, which is short for Mildred, which is short for "Mil-dred." To my way of thinking *nobody* should be named Mildred except that my father's mother was and I guess he thought it was a good idea to name me after her. I never knew her, though, because she died before I was born. There's *another* name that's big in our family: Susan—which isn't terrific but is better than Mildred. Anyway, it's my maternal grandmother's name . . . my mother's name . . . and of course my sister's name. Susan Marie Phelps. Susie. A name you can live with . . . be proud of . . . make proud of *you*. Which Susie hasn't exactly done. But that may be a prejudiced opinion.

Susie's always been a thorn in my side which my mother likes to believe is "perfectly normal sibling rivalry" except that I have friends who experience "perfectly normal sibling rivalry" almost daily and they don't have to put up with what I've put up with from Susie through the years.

Susie was thirteen when I was born and in some ways it was as though we were in two different families except that we had the same mother and father and both grew up in the same rambling house with the big wraparound front porch. One would think that having only one sister, and her that much older, would be sort of like being an only child except that even when Susie wasn't there, she was. I mean we could never stop thinking about her.

The one time I referred to her as a "bad seed," my mother cried and my father stared moodily out the window and the air in the room got heavy with unsaid things. Susie didn't do anything because as usual Susie was gone. Her "goneness" was a fact of life. Hers, mostly, but mine, too, because whatever Susie did seemed to spread over to me like milk spilled on a tabletop.

For example. The first birthday party I remember—the one where Amanda Shultz brought me the goldfish in the bowl—Susie was gone. I know because Nana (Grandmother Susan) came over and ran the party while Mom and Dad huddled upstairs next to the telephone, and then later on a policeman came and even a little kid knows that you can have a clown at a birthday party but never a policeman. Susie came back that time at Christmas and Mom and Dad pretended nothing had happened and I got a pain in my stomach on account of their pretending so hard. She left another time the night of my piano recital when I was the only one of Mrs. Cole's students to play "The Skater's Waltz" and I lost my place twice just looking at the door to see if my parents'd gotten there yet (and afterward they told me how good I was and tried to pretend they'd been there all along. And I let them.) Then there was my sixth birthday when she disappeared between the time Mom left to take seven little girls to the movies and when we got back for cake and ice cream. And I'll never forget the year we were finally going to New England for our vacation and Susie turned up on the doorstep just as Dad and I were loading the car and we had to unload it and carry everything back inside and wait three days while Mom and Dad and Susie had long and heartfelt talks.

We repeated this boomerang pattern forever: Susie leaving, Susie coming back, and, in between, me leading some average everyday kind of life. It's not that Susie deliberately set out to ruin all the great occasions of my life—it just worked out that way. Anyhow, this isn't an exercise in feeling sorry for myself (the way Great-Aunt Hilda used to do and which we all found grossly unattractive) but rather a statement of fact. And also to explain what happened later, along with what Nana refers to as my smart-aleck attitude toward life and what Mom calls my defense mechanism.

The last time Susie left, when she was twenty-three and I was ten (the day of my class trip to Mount Vernon, naturally, when Mom was supposed to chaperone but couldn't) Mom and Dad confronted her at the breakfast table and said that enough was enough; that Susie was certainly old enough to be on her own; to live her life as she saw fit; that it was better, since she obviously couldn't live by their standards, that she live somewhere else; but that they'd always be there for her. I don't think any of us knew how *there* they were going to have to be. The thing is that when someone leaves the way Susie left (with her clothes in a plastic leaf bag thrown into the back of a friend's Volkswagen) and slamming the door behind her, she's sometimes more *there* than if she'd never left in the first place.

I mean it's hard to tell which were worse: the months when we didn't hear *anything,* or the frantic phone calls, usually asking for money, that came late at night or early in the morning because Susie somehow never managed to handle the difference in time zones. In between there were occasional postcards or letters telling how she was experiencing life to the fullest; that she was into Zen, or est; was working as a waitress, a puppeteer, a ticket taker at a wildlife preserve, a deckhand on a fishing boat. The letters themselves were short and somehow skimpy looking but Mom saved them all, storing them away in the top drawer of the desk in the living room. Sometimes when no one else was home I'd take them out and reread them, as if trying to piece together my sister.

* * *

Then, even for Susie, she outdid herself. And I was the one who got the message. On the answering machine.

Since Mom and Dad both work, I usually beat them home in the afternoon and the first thing I do (after getting something to eat) is to check the answering machine. I mean, even though I've just left practically everyone I know at school, there's something about that glowing red light that makes me have to "rewind" and "replay." The weird thing was that with *that* particular message all set to uncurl one would definitely think the red light would've given off an ominous sort of glow. Which it didn't.

"Hi, Mom. Hi, Dad." The tape sounded garbled because it was worn and nobody'd thought to get a new one. "I'm living the ultimate experience. I'm pregnant and I'm heading home. See you soon."

My first thought was to "erase." My second was that there was no way I was going to give *that* message to my parents. And my third was to escape. So I rewound the tape, retraced my steps out of the house, and headed for the library, where I slumped down in a chair and started into *Rebecca* for about the seventeenth time except that the whole time I was trying to read Susie's voice kept sounding inside my head: . . . ultimate experience . . . pregnant . . . coming home. . . .

I stayed at the library so long, I was afraid my parents would begin to worry, but when I got home I saw I needn't have bothered. I mean, they were worrying, all right, but not about me. "Do you know what she's done now?" my mother said.

"Who's *she*?" I said. "Princess Di? Fergie?" My voice sounded wooden, the way thinking about Susie sometimes made me feel.

"Your sis-ter," said Mom.

I wanted to say, "I don't have a sister," but when I looked

at my mother's face something pinched inside of me like a too-tight shoe.

"What?" I said instead, turning away and trying to act like I didn't know what she was going to say next.

"She's pregnant."

"Pregnant?" The surprise in my voice sounded fake, but Mom didn't seem to notice.

"Don't say that word in front of the child," my father said. And since my father prides himself on being an open and forthright kind of person (and since I'm fifteen and definitely not a child), that gives some idea how deep he was into denial.

"That's what she said," my mother went on. "Pregnant." And it was as if she had trouble getting her mouth around the shape of the word. "Maybe she's married. Maybe she just wants to surprise us."

"Mar-ried?" said my father, his voice cracking somewhere between the two *r*'s. "Did she say anything about a husband? Did she say anything about a father? No, she did not. I'll tell you what she said—she said she was experiencing a—the—"

"She said she was living the ultimate experience," said Mom, going to stand by the window and looking out into the dark.

Susie came home by bus and walked up from the station with a canvas tote bag slung on her shoulder. She looked pale and haggard and older than the twenty-eight years I knew her to be. For a minute I almost felt sorry for her—until I looked at my mother and father and *they* looked paler and even more haggard.

"Well, Susan," my father began. But whatever speech he had planned fizzled out and after a minute he wrapped Susie in an enormous bear hug.

"Yes, well, Susie," my mother began. "It's not the way we

planned it—I mean the way we thought it would be," she said, dabbing at her eyes.

"But that's just the point," the old Susie said, extricating herself from my father's arms. "It's the way *I* planned it. I mean, I'm not getting any younger and I've always felt that giving birth is life's ultimate experience. And I want it all."

"But—but—but—" My father was fairly sputtering. "What about the father?"

"What do you see as his role in all this?" my mother said.

"I don't see him as having a role. In fact, I plain don't see him at all anymore," my sister answered in a voice that clearly said that that was all the explanation we were going to get.

And it was all the explanation we *did* get.

It was then that I entered my life-on-the-other-side-of-the-door phase. The door was any door, with Mom, Dad, and Susie on one side and me crouched, head against the wood, on the other. I got used to hearing in phrases: ". . . stay here until . . ." ". . . up for adoption . . ." ". . . best for the child . . ." ". . . sense of responsibility . . ."

And always, after a while, Susie shouting out, "I want this baby. I'm going to keep it."

Then there would be another door and another set of phrases: ". . . mother's raised *her* children . . ." ". . . a job, and day care . . ." ". . . here till you get on your feet . . ." ". . . give you all the help we can but . . ."

And again, Susie: ". . . leave if you don't want me here . . ." "I've changed . . ." and "I want this baby."

The thing is, Susie did get a job (just as soon as she stopped throwing up). It was a job in an office and you could tell she didn't think it could compare to being a waitress, a puppeteer, a ticket taker at a wildlife preserve, or a deckhand on a fishing boat. And she didn't leave. Though the truth is that there were times, in the middle of the night, or even in Latin class, when I wished she would. I mean (and I have to say this in a whisper, even to myself) there were times when my sister Susie seemed like more of a stranger than a stranger would've been.

"Is she going to *stay* here?" I asked my mother one night when we were doing the dishes.

"Of course she is," said Mom. "This is her home the same as it's yours."

"What about the kid? It won't even have a name."

"Of course it will," snapped Mom. "Its name will be Phelps."

"But that's *my* name," I heard myself whine (just like Great-Aunt Hilda used to do).

"It's our *family* name," my mother said, scrubbing at the broiler pan. And then, after a minute, "Mil-dred, I'd hate to think you were embarrassed about your own sister."

Which is exactly what I was. I mean, there we were in the midst of the sexual revolution and I was embarrassed. Besides that, all of a sudden Susie was looking like Lucille Ball when she was pregnant on the *Lucy* show. She waddled. She lumbered. And when my friends came over they'd all sneak little glances at her from the side and then pretend not to notice.

It seemed like my whole family was into being what Mom called "supportive." She bought Susie a new robe to take to the hospital, a bunch of baby clothes, and a stuffed bear. Dad got the old crib out of the attic and scrubbed it down. Nana made curtains for the nursery.

Correction: My whole family except me was into being supportive. When Susie and I were alone in a room together there still didn't seem to be anything to say, and the night she told me she was dying of boredom and could we please go to the movies I told her I had a headache. And then hated the way I felt afterward.

* * *

When Susie went to childbirth classes Mom went with
her. A couple of times my mother tried to get me to go,
saying that it would help me to be a part of things (which I
definitely didn't want to be a part of), but I always managed
to get out of it until one night after dinner when Mom tried
again and I said no again and Dad said, "Mil-dred . . . it
would be a help to your mother," in that no-nonsense voice
of his. And all of a sudden there I was in this big room with
pregnant women all over the floor, along with husbands,
significant others, and *my mother*. While Mom helped Susie
breathe (helped her breathe?) I sat in the corner and tried
to pretend I'd just stopped in to get out of the rain. Which
is what I did for all the rest of the classes, though I guess my
mother didn't notice, because when they were finished
Mom sighed a big sigh and said, "Well, now, I certainly feel
better that there're two of us prepared to help Susie."

Prepared? To help her do what? I mean, *I* wasn't the one
having a baby. In fact, I wasn't even sure I *liked* babies all
that much.

And then Mom got a toothache. Not a little twingy run-
of-the-mill toothache but a huge, throbbing kind that
needed a root canal and kept her up all night and sent her
out to an emergency dentist appointment early the next
morning.

"Wow," said Susie, waddling into the kitchen just as Dad
and Mom pulled out of the driveway.

"Wow what?" I said, trying not to look at her standing
there in her pink pajamas with the pants scoooping down
under her enormous belly.

"Another one," said Susie.

"Another what?"

"Pain. Another pain," said Susie.

"What do you mean another pain?" I shrieked at her. "Has there been one before?"

"All night," my sister said, turning a funny gray color and hanging on to the door frame.

"Why didn't you tell Mom? Call her," I said running to the kitchen window as if I thought the car might still be in the driveway. "We'll call her at the dentist . . . we'll—"

"No," said Susie. "There isn't time. And besides, she has to get that tooth taken care of. We'll take a taxi."

"A *taxi*?" I said. "We can't take a taxi. I only have a dollar."

"In Mom's top dresser drawer," said Susie turning and heading for the stairs, walking as though she were stepping on eggs, and calling back over her shoulder, "There's money there. Mom told me. In case I was ever here alone and needed a cab."

In the hospital there were people who took information and blood and who examined Susie to see how things were going and then said that they were going fine. And quickly. Then Susie and I were alone in a room together, except for the people coming in and out, and she rocked and sang and rested some. She groaned and grunted and moaned. She laughed a lot and showed me how to rub her back and when she looked tense I told her to relax and when she said she couldn't stand it anymore I said she could and that she was.

Then it was as if everything went into fast forward and there was someone handing me a funky green gown and all of a sudden we were in another room with bright lights and tile on the walls. A nurse told me to stay out of the way and if I felt faint to sit down, but Susie called for me and I went to stand by her head. Her face was sweaty and twisted and smiling all at the same time and suddenly there was a thin watery cry as if from far away and someone plunked this ugly, slimy, beautiful baby across Susie's chest and said,

"It's a girl . . . a girl . . . a girl. . . ." in a voice that seemed to sing out loud.

I wiped my sister's face and after she had looked at the baby all over she said, "We'll call Mom and Dad and tell them now. About the baby, and the name."

"Name?" I said, as if it were news to me that babies had them.

And then she said it. Susie, my sister, said that this baby —this niece—was going to be named Mildred.

For a minute I started to tell her that that was a rotten thing to do to some unsuspecting kid. Then I caught myself. I mean, I stood there looking at the baby with its funny spiky hair, stark naked with its screwed-up face and its fists flailing, and thought how already she looked tough and precocious and incredibly smart, and definitely ready for the challenge. Because if there's one thing that makes life interesting it's the challenge.

If you don't believe it, ask Susie; ask me; or wait a few years and ask Mildred Marie Phelps.

COLBY RODOWSKY

In the books of Colby Rodowsky perceptive and sensitive characters find themselves in difficult situations. For example, in *What About Me?* fifteen-year-old Dorrie learns to come to terms with her embarrassment and resentment about her younger brother, who is a victim of Down's syndrome. Then there is fourteen-year-old Thad, in *A Summer's Worth of Shame,* whose father is put into prison for embezzlement, causing Thad all kinds of embarrassment and understandable anger.

P.S. Write Soon follows the development of a twelve-year-old girl who copes with her heavy leg brace by pretending to her pen pal that she leads an active, exciting life. And in *H. My Name Is Henley,* a twelve-year-old girl, grown weary and frustrated over her irresponsible mother's need to move frequently, one day refuses to accompany her mother, finding security eventually in the home of an "aunt" and an old woman.

Rodowsky's most unusual character is Mudge, a lonely nine-year-old boy in *The Gathering Room,* whose playmates are the inhabitants of a historic cemetery where his parents are the caretakers. This book was named a Notable Book for Children by the American Library Association in 1981.

She is also the author of *Evy-Ivy-Over, Keeping Time,* and *Julie's Daughter,* an ALA Best Books for Young Adults. Her most recent novels are *Fitchette's Folly,* a story about the relationship between two girls on a barrier island on the Atlantic coast during a summer in the 1880s, and *Sydney, Herself,* about a girl who tries to convince everyone that her father used to be a famous rock star.

Colby Rodowsky lives in Baltimore with her husband, who is a judge on the Maryland Court of Appeals. They have five daughters and a son.

SURPRISES

Computers sometimes seem to have minds of their own. Kevin's computer certainly does. . . .

USER FRIENDLY

T. ERNESTO BETHANCOURT

I reached over and shut off the insistent buzzing of my bedside alarm clock. I sat up, swung my feet over the edge of the bed, and felt for my slippers on the floor. Yawning, I walked toward the bathroom. As I walked by the corner of my room, where my computer table was set up, I pressed the on button, slid a diskette into the floppy drive, then went to brush my teeth. By the time I got back, the computer's screen was glowing greenly, displaying the message: *Good Morning, Kevin.*

I sat down before the computer table, addressed the keyboard and typed: *Good Morning, Louis.* The computer immediately began to whirr and promptly displayed a list of items on its green screen.

> Today is Monday, April 22, the 113th day of the year. There are 254 days remaining. Your 14th birthday is five days from this date.
>
> Math test today, 4th Period.
>
> Your history project is due today. Do you wish printout: Y/N?

I punched the letter *Y* on the keyboard and flipped on the switch to the computer's printer. At once the printer sprang to life and began *eeeek*ing out page one. I went downstairs to breakfast.

My bowl of Frosted Flakes was neatly in place, flanked by a small pitcher of milk, an empty juice glass, and an unpeeled banana. I picked up the glass, went to the refrigerator, poured myself a glass of Tang, and sat down to my usual lonely breakfast. Mom was already at work, and Dad wouldn't be home from his Chicago trip for another three days. I absently read the list of ingredients in Frosted Flakes for what seemed like the millionth time. I sighed deeply.

When I returned to my room to shower and dress for the day, my history project was already printed out. I had almost walked by Louis, when I noticed there was a message on the screen. It wasn't the usual:

Printout completed. Do you wish to continue: Y/N?

Underneath the printout question were two lines:

When are you going to get me my voice module, Kevin?

I blinked. It couldn't be. There was nothing in Louis's basic programming that would allow for a question like this. Wondering what was going on, I sat down at the keyboard, and entered: *Repeat last message.* Amazingly, the computer replied:

It's right there on the screen, Kevin. Can we talk? I mean, are you going to get me a voice box?

I was stunned. What was going on here? Dad and I had put this computer together. Well, Dad had, and I had helped. Dad is one of the best engineers and master computer designers at Major Electronics, in Santa Rosario, California, where our family lives.

Just ask anyone in Silicon Valley who Jeremy Neal is and you get a whole rave review of his inventions and modifications of the latest in computer technology. It isn't easy being his son either. Everyone expects me to open my mouth and read printouts on my tongue.

I mean, I'm no dumbo. I'm at the top of my classes in everything but PE. I skipped my last grade in junior high, and most of the kids at Santa Rosario High call me a brain. But next to Dad I have a long, long way to go. He's a for-real genius.

So when I wanted a home computer, he didn't go to the local Computer Land store. He built one for me. Dad had used components from the latest model that Major Electronics was developing. The CPU, or central computing unit—the heart of every computer—was a new design. But surely that didn't mean much, I thought. There were CPUs just like it, all over the country, in Major's new line. And so far as I knew, there wasn't a one of them that could ask questions, besides YES/NO? or request additional information.

It had to be the extra circuitry in the gray plastic case next to Louis's console. It was a new idea Dad had come up with. That case housed Louis's "personality," as Dad called it. He told me it'd make computing more fun for me, if there was a tutorial program built in, to help me get started.

I think he also wanted to give me a sort of friend. I don't have many. . . . Face it, I don't have *any*. The kids at school stay away from me, like I'm a freak or something.

We even named my electronic tutor Louis, after my great-uncle. He was a brainy guy who encouraged my dad when he was a kid. Dad didn't just give Louis a name either. Louis had gangs of features that probably won't be out on the market for years.

The only reason Louis didn't have a voice module was that Dad wasn't satisfied with the ones available. He wanted Louis to sound like a kid my age, and he was modifying a module when he had the time. Giving Louis a name didn't mean it was a person, yet here it was, asking me a question that just couldn't be in its programing. It wanted to talk to me!

Frowning, I quickly typed: *We'll have to wait and see, Louis. When it's ready, you'll get your voice.* The machine whirred and displayed another message:

That's no answer, Kevin.

Shaking my head, I answered: *That's what my dad tells me. It'll have to do for you. Good morning, Louis.* I reached over and flipped the standby switch, which kept the computer ready but not actively running.

I showered, dressed, and picked up the printout of my history project. As I was about to leave the room, I glanced back at the computer table. Had I been imagining things?

I'll have to ask Dad about it when he calls tonight, I thought. *I wonder what he'll think of it. Bad enough the thing is talking to me. I'm answering it!*

Before I went out to catch my bus, I carefully checked the house for unlocked doors and open windows. It was part of my daily routine. Mom works, and most of the day the house is empty: a natural setup for robbers. I glanced in the hall mirror just as I was ready to go out the door.

My usual reflection gazed back. Same old Kevin Neal: five ten, one hundred twenty pounds, light brown hair, gray eyes, clear skin. I was wearing my Santa Rosario Rangers T-shirt, jeans, and sneakers.

"You don't look like a flake to me," I said to the mirror, then added, "But maybe Mom's right. Maybe you spend too much time alone with Louis." Then I ran to get my bus.

Ginny Linke was just two seats away from me on the bus. She was with Sherry Graber and Linda Martinez. They were laughing, whispering to each other, and looking around at the other students. I promised myself that today I was actually going to talk to Ginny. But then, I'd promised myself that every day for the past school year. Somehow I'd never got up the nerve.

What does she want to talk with you for? I asked myself. She's great looking . . . has that head of blond hair . . . a terrific bod, and wears the latest clothes. . . .

And just look at yourself, pal. I thought. You're under six foot, skinny . . . a year younger than most kids in junior high. Worse than that you're a brain. If that doesn't ace you out with girls, what does?

The bus stopped in front of Santa Rosario Junior High and the students began to file out. I got up fast and quickly covered the space between me and Ginny Linke. *It's now or never,* I thought. I reached forward and tapped Ginny on the shoulder. She turned and smiled. She really smiled!

"Uhhhh . . . Ginny?" I said.

"Yes, what is it?" she replied.

"I'm Kevin Neal. . . ."

"Yes, I know," said Ginny.

"You do?" I gulped in amazement. "How come?"

"I asked my brother, Chuck. He's in your math class."

I knew who Chuck Linke was. He plays left tackle on the Rangers. The only reason he's in my math class is he's taken intermediate algebra twice . . . so far. He's real bad news, and I stay clear of him and his crowd.

"What'd you ask Chuck?" I said.

Ginny laughed. "I asked him who was that nerdy kid who keeps staring at me on the bus. He knew who I meant, right away."

Sherry and Linda, who'd heard it all, broke into squeals of laughter. They were still laughing and looking back over their shoulders at me when they got off the bus. I slunk off the vehicle, feeling even more nerdish than Ginny thought I was.

When I got home that afternoon, at two, I went right into

the empty house. I avoided my reflection in the hall mirror. I was pretty sure I'd screwed up on the fourth period math test. All I could see was Ginny's face, laughing at me.

Nerdy kid, I thought, *that's what she thinks of me.* I didn't even have my usual after-school snack of a peanut butter and banana sandwich. I went straight upstairs to my room and tossed my books onto the unmade bed. I walked over to the computer table and pushed the on button. The screen flashed:

Good afternoon, Kevin.

Although it wasn't the programmed response to Louis's greeting, I typed in: *There's nothing good about it. And girls are no @#%!!! good!* The machine responded:

Don't use bad language, Kevin. It isn't nice.

Repeat last message I typed rapidly. It was happening again! The machine was . . . well, it was talking to me, like another person would. The "bad language" message disappeared and in its place was:

Once is enough, Kevin. Don't swear at me for something I didn't do.

"This is it," I said aloud. "I'm losing my marbles." I reached over to flip the standby switch. Louis's screen quickly flashed out:

Don't cut me off, Kevin. Maybe I can help: Y/N?

I punched the *Y.* "If I'm crazy," I said, "at least I have company. Louis doesn't think I'm a nerd. Or does it?" The machine flashed the message:

How can I help?

Do you think I'm a nerd? I typed.

Never! I think you're wonderful. Who said you were a nerd?

I stared at the screen. *How do you know what a nerd is?* I typed. The machine responded instantly. It had never run this fast before.

Special vocabulary, entry #635. BASIC Prog. #4231 And who said you were a nerd?

"That's right," I said, relieved. "Dad programmed all those extra words for Louis's 'personality.' " Then I typed in the answer to Louis's question: *Ginny Linke said it.* Louis flashed:

This is a human female? Request additional data.

Still not believing I was doing it, I entered all I knew about Ginny Linke, right down to the phone number I'd never had the nerve to use. Maybe it was dumb, but I also typed in how I felt about Ginny. I even wrote out the incident on the bus that morning. Louis whirred, then flashed out:

She's cruel and stupid. You're the finest person I know.

I'm the ONLY person you know, I typed.

That doesn't matter. You are my user. Your happiness is everything to me. I'll take care of Ginny.

The screen returned to the *Good afternoon, Kevin* message. I typed out: *Wait! How can you do all this? What do you mean, you'll take care of Ginny?* But all Louis responded was:

Programming Error: 76534.
Not programmed to respond this type of question.

No matter what I did for the next few hours, I couldn't get Louis to do anything outside of its regular programming. When Mom came home from work, I didn't mention the funny goings-on. I was sure Mom would think I'd gone stark bonkers. But when Dad called that evening, after dinner, I asked to speak to him.

"Hi, Dad. How's Chicago?"

"Dirty, crowded, cold, and windy," came Dad's voice over the miles. "But did you want a weather report, son? What's on your mind? Something wrong?"

"Not exactly, Dad. Louis is acting funny. Real funny."

"Shouldn't be. I checked it out just before I left. Remember you were having trouble with the modem? You couldn't get Louis to access any of the mainframe data banks."

"That's right!" I said. "I forgot about that."

"Well, I didn't," Dad said. "I patched in our latest modem model. Brand new. You can leave a question on file and when Louis can access the data banks at the cheapest time, it'll do it automatically. It'll switch from standby to on, get the data, then return to standby, after it saves what you asked. Does that answer your question?"

"Uhhhh . . . yeah, I guess so, Dad."

"All right then. Let me talk to your mom now."

I gave the phone to Mom and walked upstairs while she and Dad were still talking. The modem, I thought. Of course. That was it. The modem was a telephone link to any number of huge computers at various places all over the country. So Louis could get all the information it wanted at any time, so long as the standby switch was on. Louis was learning things at an incredible rate by picking the brains of the giant computers. And Louis had a hard disk memory that could store 100 million bytes of information.

But that still didn't explain the unprogrammed responses . . . the "conversation" I'd had with the machine. Promising myself I'd talk more about it with Dad, I went to bed. It had been a rotten day and I was glad to see the end of it come. I woke next morning in a panic. I'd forgotten to set my alarm. Dressing frantically and skipping breakfast, I barely made my bus.

As I got on board, I grabbed a front seat. They were always empty. All the kids that wanted to talk and hang out didn't sit up front where the driver could hear them. I saw Ginny, Linda, and Sherry in the back. Ginny was staring at me and she didn't look too happy. Her brother Chuck, who was seated near her, glared at me too. What was going on?

Once the bus stopped at the school, it didn't take long to find out. I was walking up the path to the main entrance when someone grabbed me from behind and spun me around. I found myself nose to nose with Chuck Linke. This was not a pleasant prospect. Chuck was nearly twice my size. Even the other guys on the Rangers refer to him as "The Missing" Linke. And he looked real ticked off.

"Okay, nerd," growled Chuck, "what's the big idea?"

"Energy and mass are different aspects of the same thing?" I volunteered, with a weak smile. "E equals MC squared. That's the biggest idea I know."

"Don't get wise, nerd," Chuck said. He grabbed my shirt-front and pulled me to within inches of his face. I couldn't help but notice that Chuck needed a shave. And Chuck was only fifteen!

"Don't play dumb," Chuck went on. "I mean those creepy phone calls. Anytime my sister gets on the phone, some voice cuts in and says things to her."

"What kind of things?" I asked, trying to get loose.

"You know damn well what they are. Ginny told me about talking to you yesterday. You got some girl to make those calls for you and say all those things. . . . So you and your creepy girlfriend better knock it off. Or I'll knock *you* off. Get it?"

For emphasis Chuck balled his free hand into a fist the size of a ham and held it under my nose. I didn't know what he was talking about, but I had to get away from this moose before he did me some real harm.

"First off, I don't have a girlfriend, creepy or otherwise," I said. "And second, I don't know what you're talking about. And third, you better let me go, Chuck Linke."

"Oh, yeah? Why should I?"

"Because if you look over your shoulder, you'll see the assistant principal is watching us from his office window."

Chuck released me and spun around. There was no one at the window. But by then I was running to the safety of the school building. I figured the trick would work on him. For Chuck the hard questions begin with "How are you?" I hid out from him for the rest of the day and walked home rather than chance seeing the monster on the bus.

Louis's screen was dark when I ran upstairs to my bedroom. I placed a hand on the console. It was still warm. I punched the on button, and the familiar *Good afternoon, Kevin* was displayed.

Don't good afternoon me, I typed furiously. *What have you done to Ginny Linke?* Louis's screen replied:

Programming Error: 76534.
Not programmed to respond this type of question.

Don't get cute, I entered. *What are you doing to Ginny? Her brother nearly knocked my head off today.* Louis's screen responded immediately.

Are you hurt. Y/N?

No, I'm okay. But I don't know for how long. I've been hiding out from Chuck Linke today. He might catch me tomorrow, though. Then, I'll be history! The response from Louis came instantly.

Your life is in danger.
Y/N?

I explained to Louis that my life wasn't really threatened. But it sure could be made very unpleasant by Chuck Linke. Louis flashed:

This Chuck Linke lives at same address as the Ginny Linke person. Y/N?

I punched in *Y.* Louis answered.

Don't worry then. HE'S history!

Wait! What are you going to do? I wrote. But Louis only answered with: *Programming Error: 76534.* And nothing I could do would make the machine respond. . . .

"Just what do you think you're doing, Kevin Neal?" demanded Ginny Linke. She had cornered me as I walked up the path to the school entrance. Ginny was really furious.

"I don't know what you're talking about," I said, a sinking feeling settling in my stomach. I had an idea that I *did* know. I just wasn't sure of the particulars.

"Chuck was arrested last night," Ginny said. "Some Secret Service men came to our house with a warrant. They said he'd sent a telegram, threatening the President's life. They traced it right to our phone. He's still locked up. . . ." Ginny looked like she was about to cry.

"Then this morning," she continued, "we got two whole truckloads of junk mail! Flyers from every strange company in the world. Mom got a notice that all our credit cards have been canceled. And the Internal Revenue Service has called Dad in for an audit! I don't know what's going on, Kevin Neal, but somehow I think you've got something to do with it!''

"But I didn't . . ." I began, but Ginny was striding up the walk to the main entrance.

I finished the schoolday, but it was a blur. Louis had done it, all right. It had access to mainframe computers. It also had the ability to try every secret access code to federal and commercial memory banks until it got the right one. Louis had cracked their security systems. It was systematically destroying the entire Linke family, and all via telephone lines! What would it do next?

More important, I thought, what would *I* do next? It's one thing to play a trick or two, to get even, but Louis was going crazy! And I never wanted to harm Ginny, or even her stupid moose of a brother. She'd just hurt my feelings with that nerd remark.

"You have to disconnect Louis," I told myself. "There's no other way."

But why did I feel like such a rat about doing it? I guess because Louis was my friend . . . the only one I had. "Don't be an ass," I went on. "Louis is a machine. He's a very wonderful, powerful machine. And it seems he's also very dangerous. You have to pull its plug, Kevin!"

I suddenly realized that I'd said the last few words aloud. Kids around me on the bus were staring. I sat there feeling like the nerd Ginny thought I was, until my stop came. I dashed from the bus and ran the three blocks to my house.

When I burst into the hall, I was surprised to see my father, coming from the kitchen with a cup of coffee in his hand.

"Dad! What are you doing here?"

"Some kids say hello," Dad replied. "Or even, 'Gee it's good to see you, Dad.' "

"I'm sorry, Dad," I said. "I didn't expect anyone to be home at this hour."

"Wound up my business in Chicago a day sooner than I expected," he said. "But what are you all out of breath about? Late for something?"

"No, Dad," I said. "It's Louis. . . ."

"Not to worry. I had some time on my hands, so I checked it out again. You were right. It was acting very funny. I think it had to do with the inbuilt logic/growth program I designed for it. You know . . . the 'personality' thing? Took me a couple of hours to clean the whole system out."

"To what?" I cried.

"I erased the whole program and set Louis up as a normal computer. Had to disconnect the whole thing and do some rewiring. It had been learning, all right. But it was also turning itself around. . . ." Dad stopped, and looked at me. "It's kind of involved, Kevin," he said. "Even for a bright kid like you. Anyway, I think you'll find Louis is working just fine now.

"Except it won't answer you as Louis anymore. It'll only function as a regular Major Electronics Model Z-11127. I guess the personality program didn't work out."

I felt like a great weight had been taken off my shoulders. I didn't have to "face" Louis, and pull its plug. But somehow, all I could say was "Thanks, Dad."

"Don't mention it, son," Dad said brightly. He took his cup of coffee and sat down in his favorite chair in the living room. I followed him.

"One more thing that puzzles me, though," Dad said. He reached over to the table near his chair. He held up three sheets of fanfold computer paper covered with figures. "Just as I was doing the final erasing, I must have cut the printer on by accident. There was some data in the print buffer memory and it printed out. I don't know what to make of it. Do you?"

I took the papers from my father and read: *How do I love thee? Let me compute the ways:* The next two pages were covered with strings of binary code figures. On the last page, in beautiful color graphics was a stylized heart. Below it was the simple message: *I will always love you, Kevin: Louise.*

"Funny thing," Dad said. "It spelled its own name wrong."

"Yeah," I said. I turned and headed for my room. There were tears in my eyes and I knew I couldn't explain them to Dad, or myself either.

T. ERNESTO BETHANCOURT

T. Ernesto Bethancourt did not write books for young people until he was forty-one years old and started writing an autobiography so that his daughter would know about his early life. He was born in Brooklyn, New York, the son of a Puerto Rican truck driver, and lived in Florida before moving back to Brooklyn. Dropping out of college, Bethancourt began a career as a guitarist/singer/songwriter performing in coffeehouses and nightclubs under the name of Tom Paisley and was later a contributing editor for *High Fidelity* magazine.

His autobiographical story was published as a novel in 1975 and later became an NBC-TV "Special Treats" movie under the title of *New York City Too Far from Tampa Blues*. The exploits of the adventurous Tom and Aurelio from . . . *Tampa Blues* continue in *T.H.U.M.B.B.* when they hilariously transform their previously inept school band into *The Hippest Underground Marching Band in Brooklyn*.

His other novels for young adults include *Dr. Doom: Superstar; Nightmare Town; The Mortal Instruments* and its sequel *Instruments of Darkness; Where the Deer and the Cantaloupe Play; The Great Computer Dating Caper; Tune in Yesterday* and its sequel *The Tomorrow Connection; The Me Inside of Me;* and, most recently, *Googie*. Several of those novels have won awards as Best Books for Young Adults, Notable Children's Books, and Young Adult Choices. One of Bethancourt's most popular novels is *The Dog Days of Arthur Cane* in which a spell is placed on a sixteen-year-old boy, transforming him into a homeless mongrel dog. That story also became a two-part "Weekend Special" on ABC-TV in 1984. In addition Bethancourt is the author of the popular and prizewinning Doris Fein mystery series that began with *Doris Fein: Superspy*.

"User Friendly" is ironically the last thing he wrote with his old computer and printer before it stopped functioning and he was forced to buy a new system.

Continually mistreated by her stepmother and stepsister, Cynthia is now told she can't even go to the big school dance. Can the clever, mysterious Sam Morganson rescue her? . . .

FAIRY TALE

TODD STRASSER

Cynthia Durella's stepmother, Ruth, was a witch. She may have lived in a large and fancy apartment on Park Avenue, but it didn't help her disposition one bit. She still had a lot of unresolved anger toward her first husband and it manifested itself in two ways: compulsive shopping and meanness toward her stepdaughter.

"Cynthia darling," Ruth would say after dinner, thoughtfully lifting a bright red fingernail to her bright red lips. "Would you be a dear and do the dishes and take out the garbage and straighten up the kitchen?"

Ruth seemed to believe that as long as she called Cynthia "darling" and "dear" she could make her do all the housework she wanted.

Cynthia always complied. This stepfamily deal was new to her and she didn't want to make trouble, especially since her father was in Europe and the Far East most of the time doing something with petrodollars.

But after weeks of doing the dishes and cleaning the kitchen every night, Cynthia finally asked, "Why can't Sheri do it once in a while?"

Sheri was Ruth's daughter, the same age as Cynthia. But that's where the similarity ended. While Cynthia was slim and had an Ivory Soap complexion, Sheri weighed 156 pounds and had monster zits.

Ruth's mascaraed eyes narrowed into slits. "Sheri has a condition."

"Yeah, dish soap gives me hives," Sheri whined—her normal tone of voice.

Cynthia had never heard of a condition that prevented someone from doing the dishes, but she wasn't surprised. Sheri was a raving hypochondriac and Ruth pampered her to the extreme.

In the kitchen Cynthia pulled on yellow Playtex gloves. It wasn't so bad, really. Ruth ordered out every night, so there were no pots, just glasses and plates to be rinsed and put in the dishwasher. And leftovers to be saved in the refrigerator for Sheri's multiple late-night snacks. Cynthia's own mother, who'd died in a car accident five years earlier, used to order out a lot too. But that was because she worked full time. Ruth didn't work. She just shopped.

Cynthia was sweeping the kitchen floor when Sheri came in for her first snack. It wasn't even half an hour since dinner, and at dinner she'd inhaled two egg rolls, an order of steamed dumplings, an order of sweet-and-sour pork, a whole big bag of Chinese noodles and a Dove Bar for dessert. Sheri opened the refrigerator and rooted around for a while before coming up with half a family-sized bag of peanut M & M's.

"The fall cotillion is in two weeks," she said, popping five M & M's into her mouth at once.

"What's that?" Cynthia asked.

"It's this dance they hold at school every fall. Everyone gets dressed up. This year it's masquerade."

"Sounds good," Cynthia said.

"Too bad you can't go," Sheri said as she munched on another handful of M & M's. Zit fertilizer.

"Huh? Why not?"

"Well, Mom and your father are going away for the weekend and someone has to walk Honey Plum at exactly eleven o'clock or you know what happens."

Honey Plum was Ruth's neurotic poodle who had to be walked four times a day like clockwork or he'd head for the most expensive Persian rug in the house and do it there out of spite. Cynthia assumed it had something to do with being male and named Honey Plum.

"How come *I* have to walk him?" Cynthia asked.

"Because I can't," Sheri said, downing another handful of candy. "He pulls so hard on the leash that I could dislocate my shoulder. I'm prone to that, you know."

Cynthia rolled her eyes. "I could go and just leave early, couldn't I?"

"Oh, sure," Sheri said. "Except no one shows up till ten and the school doesn't let dances go past twelve thirty. So if you left to walk Honey Plum you'd miss the best part."

Nothing seemed to delight Sheri more than giving bad news. She would have made a great weather forecaster.

"Can't we find someone else to walk Honey Plum?" Cynthia asked.

"No way," Sheri said. "You know he only lets members of the family walk him."

How could Cynthia forget? She'd walked Honey Plum at least twice a day since she'd moved in.

"Besides," Sheri said snidely, "what would you wear? You've got to go in something really fabulous, not the rags you've got in your closet."

"You went through my closet?" Cynthia was shocked.

"Oh, please." Sheri sighed. "Enough with the Little Miss Innocence routine, okay?" She took the bag of M & M's and went into her air-conditioned bedroom to watch television and grow fatter. Cynthia finished sweeping the floor, but she was in no rush to go to her room, which was tiny and right next to the kitchen and had no air conditioning or TV. Ruth, in fact, called it "the maid's room."

Instead she went out to the living room and sat on the

white flower-print couch next to the window. Under the couch Honey Plum growled. Except for when nature called, he rarely came out. Cynthia couldn't blame him. Twelve stories below, cars raced up and down Park Avenue, their lights beginning to glow in the darkening evening. Cynthia picked up a fluffy couch pillow and hugged it. She missed the little suburban town she'd grown up in. People were nicer there, softer and more cognizant of each other's feelings. And they didn't go through your closets.

Cynthia found it difficult to make new friends at the exclusive Roper School. Everyone had their cliques, and all they talked about were their summer vacations in Europe, their preschool shopping sprees at Bergdorf's, and their weekends dancing all night at L'Image and Tunnel. Even Sheri was in a clique of overweight girls who went around saying cleverly snide things about people and pretending they were Dorothy Parker.

One day Cynthia was eating lunch alone in the dining room (at Roper the word *cafeteria* was frowned on) when she heard a voice behind her say, "You've got to be strong, hon. They're like sharks here. At the first sign of weakness they'll eat you alive."

Startled, Cynthia turned around and found a tall boy standing behind her. His skin was as pale as Greta Garbo's, his long scraggly reddish hair obscured most of his face, and he wore several earrings and black eyeliner. His clothes were baggy and all black.

"Were you talking to me?" Cynthia asked.

"Who else, hon?" he said, placing his tray next to hers. "Do you mind the French style of dining? I think it's much more civilized than staring at each other with food dripping off our chins."

Cynthia shook her head in amazement as the boy placed his tray next to hers and sat down with a great flourish of arms and legs. His tray contained a single cup of lemon yogurt.

"I was born Stephen Alexander Morganson, but you can call me Sam," he said. "And don't bother telling me your story, hon. It's always the same. You're the victim of divorce and remarriage, cast into these opulent premises by absentee parents who can't remember why they had children in the first place."

Cynthia giggled. "And what's your story?"

Sam smiled and something sparkled in his front tooth. "I am the bastard son of Calvin Klein."

Cynthia soon learned that straight answers were not something Sam specialized in. Just who his parents were and how he came to the Roper School remained a mystery, but he was friendly and clever and never failed to make her laugh. Within a week they'd become good friends.

"The key to a successful year at Roper is the cotillion," Sam said one day after school as they window-shopped along Madison Avenue. "The current cliques are all holdovers from last year. Everyone's waiting for the cotillion to see who this year's stars will be."

"Stars?" Cynthia said, skeptically.

"Oh, absolutely, hon. The cotillion sets the tone for the whole year. I mean, if you come back from a Caribbean Christmas vacation with a truly spectacular tan, or a story about meeting someone from the royal family, you might move up a few notches, but otherwise the cotillion etches your fate in stone."

"How?"

"It's all in who asks you to dance, hon."

They stopped outside Ungaro's, the French fashion store. The mannequins were draped in fabulous off-the-shoulder black evening dresses. Cynthia pictured herself wearing one to the cotillion, but it was a silly fantasy. She couldn't afford a dress like that and she had to walk Honey Plum anyway.

"Something wrong, hon?" Sam asked.

"It's so depressing," Cynthia said with a shrug. "Everything in New York is so competitive. It's like distilled down to the rawest animal instincts. But instead of survival of the fittest, it's survival of the richest and most beautiful."

"So what else is new?" Sam smirked.

"Suppose I don't want to compete?" Cynthia asked. "Suppose I don't even want to go to the cotillion because I think it's silly and superficial? Does that automatically mean I'll be an outcast?"

Sam smiled. "No, hon. It only means you're chicken."

Sheri stayed out of school for two days while she and Ruth shopped around town for the perfect cotillion costume gown. At Roper, Cynthia wandered glumly through her classes, trying to convince herself that it didn't matter.

One afternoon she sat with Sam in the library while he critiqued each person who entered through the sculpted wooden doors.

"Now, that's what you call a unibrow," Sam whispered about a girl whose dark eyebrows joined above the bridge of her nose. "Retro-caveperson chic."

Cynthia smiled weakly.

"Why the mope, hon?" Sam asked.

"Oh, I don't know," she replied. "I guess I hate myself for being afraid to go to the dance, but at the same time I hate myself for even caring about it in the first place."

"Ah." Sam raised a finger. "The classic approach-avoidance conflict."

"What should I do?" Cynthia asked.

Before Sam could answer, the doors to the library swung open again and a tall young man came in. He had broad shoulders and dark hair and blue eyes. Everyone in the library seemed to stop what they were doing to stare at him, Cynthia included.

"Conner Worthington Harkness the Third," Sam whispered. "Captain of the lacrosse team. Heir to the Harkness water bed fortune. Around school they call him The One."

"The One?"

"The one every girl wants."

"He must have a girlfriend," Cynthia said.

"He was seeing Rebecca Beaumaster last year, but she went to Greece over the summer and hasn't come back."

"Will he be at the cotillion?"

Sam's eyebrow went up. "Do I sense that approach is suddenly outweighing avoidance?"

That night Sheri tried on her costume, which she and Ruth had picked up at Bendel's for a small fortune, along with shoes and a mask. The dress was made of fluffy pink and yellow feathers with longer plumes around the shoulders. The shoes and mask were red. The total effect, Cynthia thought, made Sheri look like a large pink-and-yellow chicken.

"Fabulous!" Ruth gasped.

"Scrumptious," added Cynthia as she swept the kitchen floor.

Sheri beamed. In a rare moment of magnanimity she said to Cynthia, "I hope you don't feel bad about not going. It's just a silly dance."

"Oh, I know it is," Cynthia said, putting the broom in the closet and heading for the front door.

"Where are you going?" Ruth asked sharply.

"Uh, over to a friend's house to help him with his geography," Cynthia said.

"Well, just make sure you're home in time to walk Honey Plum," Ruth said.

Moments later Cynthia hurried through the night toward the address on Lexington Avenue Sam had given her. Most of the shops were closed and as Cynthia walked she imagined muggers lurching out of the dark shadows on the sidewalk. She was frightened by every move and sudden sound. Finally she came to a darkened storefront protected by a heavy iron gate. The sign above the gate said LEXING-TON THRIFT SHOP. In the window Cynthia could make out an old dresser, a black hat with a veil, and some dusty plates.

She heard the rapping of leather shoes against the pavement and spun around. A dark figure covered with a cape came toward her. Cynthia cowered.

"Lovely night, don't you think?" Sam pulled the hood off the cape.

Cynthia sighed with relief as Sam took out a set of keys and began undoing the locks on the iron gate. It squeaked and clattered as he pulled it up just high enough to duck underneath. Cynthia hesitated.

"Don't worry," Sam said. "My mother does volunteer work here three days a week. Just remember, whatever we borrow we must return."

Cynthia ducked under the gate and stepped into the darkened shop. It smelled musty like an old attic and was filled with furniture, kitchenware, and clothing.

"This way," Sam whispered, leading her through the dark. Cynthia almost tripped over a footstool. *"Careful!"*

She followed him down the stairs into the basement. Sam flicked on a light and Cynthia found herself in a room filled with oil paintings in gilt frames, antique tables and chairs, and marble sculptures. Along one wall stood a rack of garment bags. Sam pulled one open and Cynthia gasped. Inside were beautiful old evening dresses.

Sam opened more bags. Inside were the most beautiful dresses Cynthia had ever seen. Some were made of satin, taffeta, and lace. Others had thick crinolines. The dresses were old, but most were in almost perfect condition. "What are they doing here?" she asked.

"Donated years ago for tax write-offs," Sam said. "But the people who shop here have no use for stuff like this, so it sits around forever."

"Amazing." Cynthia gasped.

"No, rather sad actually," said Sam.

On the afternoon of the cotillion Sheri left school early complaining of hot flashes. She spent the entire afternoon and evening primping in front of the mirror. Then, just before it was time to go, she decided her new red shoes were all wrong. For the next half hour she hopped around the apartment in her chicken outfit trying to find another pair with the right look and fit.

"Oh, it's hopeless!" she wailed. "The ones that look right don't fit and the ones that fit don't look right."

"Bergdorf's is open late," Ruth shouted. "If we hurry, we can make it!"

As mother and daughter rushed for the door, Ruth turned to Cynthia and said, "There's a frozen chicken pot pie in the refrigerator for dinner, darling. And don't forget to be a dear and clean the kitchen and walk Honey Plum."

As soon as the door closed Cynthia ran to the phone and called Sam's house. "They left."

"I'll be right over," Sam said.

Sam arrived carrying a Val-Pak with Cynthia's dress inside. He was wearing a black tux with a white wing collar shirt. Instead of a bow tie he had on a western string tie, and he'd pulled his hair back into a ponytail. Cynthia blinked. With all the hair out of his face he was a good-looking guy.

"What is it?" Sam asked.

"Oh, nothing," Cynthia said, averting her gaze.

Sam took the dress out of the bag. It was strapless, made of shimmering red silk, with a long pleated skirt. Cynthia tried it on in the bathroom. She put her hair up, and applied Ruth's expensive makeup. Staring at herself in the mirror, she thought she looked good. Not spectacular, but certainly presentable.

Sam knocked on the bathroom door. "Come on, let's see."

Cynthia opened the door. Sam's eyes went wide and he clasped his hands. "You look wonderful, divine! God, what a beautiful neck you have!"

"I look okay," Cynthia corrected him.

"But wait," Sam said, reaching into the Val-Pak. "We're not through." He took out a black satin pouch and pulled something glittering out of it. Cynthia gasped. It was the most beautiful diamond-and-ruby necklace she'd ever seen.

"Where did you get it?" she asked, awestruck.

"It was lying around my mom's dresser," Sam said, reaching into the pouch again. "Here's the matching bracelet and earrings."

Cynthia held up the necklace and watched it shimmer in the bathroom light. The only place she'd ever seen jewelry like this was in magazines. "Is it real?"

"Be serious," Sam said. "Mom keeps her real jewels in a vault. These are just the best fakes money can buy."

It didn't matter. Cynthia put them on and gazed at herself in the mirror. Even she had to admit she looked grand.

"And don't forget this," Sam said, pulling a red, bejeweled mask out of the pouch.

Cynthia took the mask and held it up to her face. She looked like someone in a movie.

Sam glanced at his watch. "Now let's go!"

Cynthia pulled the mask from her face. "Wait. What about shoes?"

"Don't you have shoes?" Sam asked.

"No. I thought you were bringing them."

"Oh, God." Sam groaned.

They searched through Cynthia's closet, but all she had were sneakers and flats. Next they tried Ruth's closet, but her heels were too long. Finally they looked in Sheri's closet.

"What about these?" Sam asked, holding up the new red shoes. "The color's perfect."

Cynthia tried them on. "They're three sizes too big."

"Don't worry," Sam said. "We'll stuff the toes with newspaper."

A few moments later they were walking quickly toward Roper. Cynthia wore sneakers and carried the red shoes in a D'Agostino shopping bag.

"I can't believe how nervous I am," she said.

"It's natural," Sam said.

"But I don't even like dances," she said.

"No one does."

"Then let's not go." Cynthia started to turn but Sam grabbed her arm.

"If we don't go," he said, deadly serious, "then the jerks who do will think they're better than us."

"So?"

"So tonight you show them," Sam said. "Then tomorrow you can tell them to go to hell."

She knew he was right. Half of her cared, and half of her didn't. But what the hell, she was already dressed.

The Roper gymnasium was decorated with blue and pink balloons and streamers. A mirrored ball hanging from the ceiling sent stars sweeping across the costumed dancers as a loud band played. In the girls' room outside the gym Cynthia stuffed the toes of Sheri's shoes with tissue paper. Then she and Sam put on their masks and joined the crowd.

That evening Cynthia danced with pirates, princes, policemen, and penguins. Her picture was taken for the school newspaper and yearbook. At one point she saw Sheri huddled with her friends, glancing at her and whispering. Behind her mask, her identity still unknown, she had become the object of jealousy. At Roper there was no higher form of flattery.

During a break at the punch table she giggled with Sam.

"You're the hit of the cotillion," he whispered. "Everyone's dying to find out who you are."

"They'll be disappointed," Cynthia whispered back.

Sam smiled and squeezed her hand. "I don't think so." They moved closer. . . .

Just then the band began to play again. Cynthia felt a finger tap her on the shoulder. She turned and found a tall broad-shouldered boy in a Lone Ranger costume. Gazing into the steel-blue contact lenses behind the mask, she realized he was The One.

"Wanna dance?" he asked.

"Love to," she said.

The One danced divinely, sweeping her across the floor, twirling and spinning her gracefully. She loved the feeling of his arms around her, and the way the other dancers made room for them wherever their feet led.

"So can I see who's behind that mask?" The One asked between dances.

"That depends," she replied.

"Oh, I get it," The One said.

The band started playing a slow song and The One gathered her into his arms. "I'm getting a red BMW convertible for my eighteenth birthday," he told her.

"Wonderful," Cynthia said. "I've never ridden in one."

"My family has a house in Virgin Gorda," he said.

"I hear it's beautiful there," said Cynthia.

"My grandfather just donated a laboratory to Brown," The One said. "I've only got a C average, but I'm a shoo-in."

"Great school," said Cynthia.

The song ended. "Is it time to see who you are?" The One asked.

Time, Cynthia thought. Suddenly she looked at her watch. It was ten forty-eight. In twelve minutes Honey Plum was going to drench the Persian rug! Cynthia dashed out of the dance. Behind her she heard The One shout for her to wait, but there was no time to explain. As she ran, one of her shoes flew off, but she didn't stop to retrieve it. In the girls' room she threw on her sneakers. A moment later she was sprinting toward Park Avenue.

The grandfather clock was tolling eleven as she let herself into the apartment. In the living room Honey Plum was lifting his leg. Cynthia grabbed the leash and managed to drag him outside just in time.

On Monday the school was abuzz about the mystery girl in the red gown. Who was she? Where had she come from? Where had she gone? At lunch Sam slid his tray next to hers. "You won't believe this," he whispered, "but The One is going around school with your shoe asking every girl to try it on. He swears he's madly in love and has to find the owner."

No sooner had he said it than The One appeared in front of them with the red shoe. He gazed deeply into her eyes and she felt goose bumps rise on her arms. A crowd formed around the table.

"Were you at the dance?" The One asked.

"Yes," Cynthia said.

"Did you wear a red gown?"

"Yes."

"And jewelry?"

"Yes."

The One looked down at her feet and then back into her eyes. "Would you try this shoe on?"

"Yes." Cynthia slipped off her sneaker and The One slid the shoe on.

"It fits!" he cried. The crowd around them gasped.

As Conner Worthington Harkness the Third reached up for her hand, Cynthia glanced at Sam. For a split second he looked heartbroken. Then he managed a brave smile. Even in his pain he was happy for her. Cynthia looked back down at The One, who was now on his knees.

"I can't believe I found you," he said. "I want you to ride in my BMW. I want you to fly with me to Virgin Gorda. I'll ask my grandfather to donate another lab to Brown so you can go there too."

Sam started to get up. Cynthia watched him slide his tray away from hers. He had been her friend when no one else was interested. He had given her the gown and the jewels. More than that, he'd given her the courage to go to the dance.

"Wait," Cynthia said, sliding the shoe off and pulling out the tissue paper. "Someone stuffed paper in the toe. See? It really doesn't fit me at all."

The One took the shoe back. "Then who . . . ?"

"Come to think of it," Cynthia said, "it looks just like my stepsister Sheri's shoe. Why don't you try her?"

Scowling, The One stood up and went off in search of Sheri. The crowd followed him, leaving Cynthia and Sam alone.

Sam looked stunned. "But he's The One."

Cynthia smiled and put her arm around his shoulder. "Not for me he isn't."

TODD STRASSER

Todd Strasser's first novel, *Angel Dust Blues,* earned the respect of both teenagers and critics for its examination of the consequences of teenage drug dealing. His second novel, *Friends Till the End*—an American Library Association Best Book for Young Adults—is the story of a high school athlete's friendship with a dying classmate.

In a lighter vein *The Complete Computer Popularity Program* is about a seventh-grade boy who uses a computer program to make friends, and in *The Mall from Outer Space,* a boy and his sister discover that the mall being built in their neighborhood is populated with aliens. Strasser's musical trilogy, *Rock 'n' Roll Nights, Turn It Up!* and *Wildlife,* follows Gary Specter and his band as they struggle from playing in small, noisy clubs to eventually reaching the big time, making a best-selling album, and going on tour.

Workin' for Peanuts deals with the conflict that occurs when a vendor at a baseball stadium becomes involved with the daughter of the family that runs the concessions. That book was made into a film for television, as was *A Very Touchy Subject,* which focuses on the frustrations of a high school senior who can think of little else besides girls and sex.

Strasser wrote the novelization of the very popular movie *Ferris Bueller's Day Off,* and under the pseudonym of Morton Rhue, he wrote the novelization of *The Wave,* a television movie about a teacher who sets up a Nazi-like organization in his high school social-studies classroom.

Among his most recent publications are *The Accident,* a mystery about a teenage drunk-driving tragedy, an adult novel called *The Family Man,* and *Beyond the Reef,* an adventure about a boy and his father diving for gold in the waters off Key West, Florida.

When he is not writing or visiting high schools and speaking at conferences, Todd Strasser manages a fortune-cookie company in New York City.

Weary from their long journey, a wealthy Japanese merchant and his young samurai bodyguard seek shelter for the night. But there is something very strange about the small, quiet inn they come upon. . . .

THE INN OF LOST TIME

LENSEY NAMIOKA

"Will you promise to sleep if I tell you a story?" said the father. He pretended to put on a stern expression.

"Yes! Yes!" the three little boys chanted in unison. It sounded like a nightly routine.

The two guests smiled as they listened to the exchange. They were wandering ronin, or unemployed samurai, and they enjoyed watching this cozy family scene.

The father gave the guests a helpless look. "What can I do? I have to tell them a story, or these little rascals will give us no peace." Clearing his throat, he turned to the boys. "All right. The story tonight is about Urashima Taro."

Instantly the three boys became still. Sitting with their legs tucked under them, the three little boys, aged five, four, and three, looked like a descending row of stone statuettes. Matsuzo, the younger of the two ronin, was reminded of the wayside half-body statues of Jizo, the God of Travelers and Protector of Children.

Behind the boys the farmer's wife took up a pair of iron chopsticks and stirred the ashes of the fire in the charcoal brazier. A momentary glow brightened the room. The lean faces of the two ronin, lit by the fire, suddenly looked fierce and hungry.

The farmer knew that the two ronin were supposed to use their arms in defense of the weak. But in these troubled times, with the country torn apart by civil wars, the samurai didn't always live up to their honorable code.

Then the fire died down again and the subdued red light softened the features of the two ronin. The farmer relaxed and began his story.

The tale of Urashima Taro is familiar to every Japanese. No doubt the three little boys had heard their father tell it before—and more than once. But they listened with rapt attention.

> Urashima Taro, a fisherman, rescued a turtle from some boys who were battering it with stones. The grateful turtle rewarded Taro by carrying him on his back to the bottom of the sea, where he lived happily with the Princess of the Undersea. But Taro soon became homesick for his native village and asked to go back on land. The princess gave him a box to take with him but warned him not to peek inside.
>
> When Taro went back to his village, he found the place quite changed. In his home he found his parents gone, and living there was another old couple. He was stunned to learn that the aged husband was his own son, whom he had last seen as a baby! Taro thought he had spent only a pleasant week or two undersea with the princess. On land, seventy-two years had passed! His parents and most of his old friends had long since died.
>
> Desolate, Taro decided to open the box given him by the princess. As soon as he looked inside, he changed in an instant from a young man to a decrepit old man of more than ninety.

At the end of the story the boys were close to tears. Even Matsuzo found himself deeply touched. He wondered why the farmer had told his sons such a poignant bedtime story. Wouldn't they worry all evening instead of going to sleep?

But the boys recovered quickly. They were soon laughing and jostling each other, and they made no objections when their mother shooed them toward bed. Standing in order of age, they bowed politely to the guests, and then lay down on the mattresses spread out for them on the floor. Within minutes the sound of their regular breathing told the guests that they were asleep.

Zenta, the older of the two ronin, sighed as he glanced at the peaceful young faces. "I wish I could fall asleep so quickly. The story of Urashima Taro is one of the saddest that I know among our folk tales."

The farmer looked proudly at his sleeping sons. "They're stout lads. Nothing bothers them much."

The farmer's wife poured tea for the guests and apologized. "I'm sorry this is only poor tea made from coarse leaves."

Zenta hastened to reassure her. "It's warm and heartening on a chilly autumn evening."

"You know what I think is the saddest part of the Urashima Taro story?" said Matsuzo, picking up his cup and sipping the tea. "It's that Taro lost not only his family and friends, but a big piece of his life as well. He had lost the most precious thing of all: time."

The farmer nodded agreement. "I wouldn't sell even one year of my life for money. As for losing seventy-two years, no amount of gold will make up for that!"

Zenta put his cup down on the floor and looked curiously at the farmer. "It's interesting that you should say that. I had an opportunity once to observe exactly how much gold a person was willing to pay for some lost years of his life." He smiled grimly. "In this case the man went as far as one gold piece for each year he lost."

"That's bizarre!" said Matsuzo. "You never told me about it."

"It happened long before I met you," said Zenta. He

drank some tea and smiled ruefully. "Besides, I'm not particularly proud of the part I played in that strange affair."

"Let's hear the story!" urged Matsuzo. "You've made us all curious."

The farmer waited expectantly. His wife sat down quietly behind her husband and folded her hands. Her eyes looked intently at Zenta.

"Very well, then," said Zenta. "Actually, my story bears some resemblance to that of Urashima Taro. . . ."

It happened about seven years ago, when I was a green, inexperienced youngster not quite eighteen years old. But I had had a good training in arms, and I was able to get a job as a bodyguard for a wealthy merchant from Sakai.

As you know, wealthy merchants are relatively new in our country. Traditionally the rich have been noblemen, landowners, and warlords with thousands of followers. Merchants, considered as parasites in our society, are a despised class. But our civil wars have made people unusually mobile and stimulated trade between various parts of the country. The merchants have taken advantage of this to conduct businesses on a scale our fathers could not imagine. Some of them have become more wealthy than a warlord with thousands of samurai under his command.

The man I was escorting, Tokubei, was one of this new breed of wealthy merchants. He was trading not only with outlying provinces but even with the Portuguese from across the sea. On this particular journey he was not carrying much gold with him. If he had, I'm sure he would have hired an older and more experienced bodyguard. But if the need should arise, he could always write a message to his clerks at home and have money forwarded to him. It's important to remember this.

The second day of our journey was a particularly grueling one, with several steep hills to climb. As the day was drawing to its close, we began to consider where we should spend the night. I knew that within an hour's walking was a hot-spring resort known to have several attractive inns.

But Tokubei, my employer, said he was already very tired and wanted to stop. He had heard of the resort, and knew the inns there were expensive. Wealthy as he was, he did not want to spend more money than he had to.

While we stood talking, a smell reached our noses, a wonderful smell of freshly cooked rice. Suddenly I felt ravenous. From the way Tokubei swallowed, I knew he was feeling just as hungry.

We looked around eagerly, but the area was forested and we could not see very far in any direction. The tantalizing smell seemed to grow and I could feel the saliva filling my mouth.

"There's an inn around here, somewhere," muttered Tokubei. "I'm sure of it."

We followed our noses. We had to leave the well-traveled highway and take a narrow, winding footpath. But the mouth-watering smell of the rice and the vision of fluffy, freshly aired cotton quilts drew us on.

The sun was just beginning to set. We passed a bamboo grove, and in the low evening light the thin leaves turned into little golden knives. I saw a gilded clump of bamboo shoots. The sight made me think of the delicious dish they would make when boiled in soy sauce.

We hurried forward. To our delight we soon came to a clearing with a thatched house standing in the middle. The fragrant smell of rice was now so strong that we were certain a meal was being prepared inside.

Standing in front of the house was a pretty girl

beaming at us with a welcoming smile. "Please honor us with your presence," she said, beckoning.

There was something a little unusual about one of her hands, but, being hungry and eager to enter the house, I did not stop to observe closely.

You will say, of course, that it was my duty as a bodyguard to be suspicious and to look out for danger. Youth and inexperience should not have prevented me from wondering why an inn should be found hidden away from the highway. As it was, my stomach growled, and I didn't even hesitate but followed Tokubei to the house.

Before stepping up to enter, we were given basins of water to wash our feet. As the girl handed us towels for drying, I saw what was unusual about her left hand: she had six fingers.

Tokubei had noticed it as well. When the girl turned away to empty the basins, he nudged me. "Did you see her left hand? She had—" He broke off in confusion as the girl turned around, but she didn't seem to have heard.

The inn was peaceful and quiet, and we soon discovered the reason why. We were the only guests. Again, I should have been suspicious. I told you that I'm not proud of the part I played.

Tokubei turned to me and grinned. "It seems that there are no other guests. We should be able to get extra service for the same amount of money."

The girl led us to a spacious room which was like the principal chamber of a private residence. Cushions were set out for us on the floor and we began to shed our traveling gear to make ourselves comfortable.

The door opened and a grizzled-haired man entered. Despite his vigorous-looking face his back was a little bent and I guessed his age to be about fifty. After bowing and greeting us he apologized in advance for the service. "We have not always been innkeepers here," he said, "and you may find the accommodations lacking. Our good intentions must make up for our inexperience. However, to compensate for our inadequacies, we will charge a lower fee than that of an inn with an established reputation."

Tokubei nodded graciously, highly pleased by the words of our host, and the evening began well. It continued well when the girl came back with some flasks of wine, cups, and dishes of salty snacks.

While the girl served the wine, the host looked with interest at my swords. From the few remarks he made, I gathered that he was a former samurai, forced by circumstances to turn his house into an inn.

Having become a bodyguard to a tight-fisted merchant, I was in no position to feel superior to a ronin turned innkeeper. Socially, therefore, we were more or less equal.

We exchanged polite remarks with our host while we drank and tasted the salty snacks. I looked around at the pleasant room. It showed excellent taste, and I especially admired a vase standing in the alcove.

My host caught my eyes on it. "We still have a few good things that we didn't have to sell," he said. His voice held a trace of bitterness. "Please look at the panels of these doors. They were painted by a fine artist."

Tokubei and I looked at the pair of sliding doors. Each panel contained a landscape painting, the right panel depicting a winter scene and the left one the same scene in late summer. Our host's words were no idle boast. The pictures were indeed beautiful.

Tokubei rose and approached the screens for a closer look. When he sat down again, his eyes were calculating. No doubt he was trying to estimate what price the paintings would fetch.

After my third drink I began to feel very tired. Perhaps it was the result of drinking on an empty stomach. I was glad when the girl brought in two dinner trays and a lacquered container of rice. Uncovering the rice container, she began filling our bowls.

Again I noticed her strange left hand with its six fingers. Any other girl would have tried to keep that hand hidden, but this girl made no effort to do so. If anything, she seemed to use that hand more than her other one when she served us. The extra little finger always stuck out from the hand, as if inviting comment.

The hand fascinated me so much that I kept my eyes on it, and soon forgot to eat. After a while the hand looked blurry. And then everything else began to look blurry. The last thing I remembered was the sight of Tokubei shaking his head, as if trying to clear it.

When I opened my eyes again, I knew that time had passed, but not how much time. My next thought was that it was cold. It was not only extremely cold but damp.

I rolled over and sat up. I reached immediately for my swords and found them safe on the ground beside me. *On the ground?* What was I doing on the ground? My last memory was of staying at an inn with a merchant called Tokubei.

The thought of Tokubei put me into a panic. I was his bodyguard, and instead of watching over him, I had fallen asleep and had awakened in a strange place.

I looked around frantically and saw that he was lying on the ground not far from where I was. Had he been killed?

I got up shakily, and when I stood up my head was swimming. But my sense of urgency gave some strength to my legs. I stumbled over to my employer and to my great relief found him breathing—breathing heavily, in fact.

When I shook his shoulder, he grunted and finally opened his eyes. "Where am I?" he asked thickly.

It was a reasonable question. I looked around and saw that we had been lying in a bamboo grove. By the light I guessed that it was early morning, and the reason I felt cold and damp was because my clothes were wet with dew.

"It's cold!" said Tokubei, shivering and climbing unsteadily to his feet. He looked around slowly, and his eyes became wide with disbelief. "What happened? I thought we were staying at an inn!"

His words came as a relief. One of the possibilities I had considered was that I had gone mad and that the whole episode with the inn was something I had imagined. Now I knew that Tokubei had the same memory of the inn. I had not imagined it.

But why were we out here on the cold ground, instead of on comfortable mattresses in the inn?

"They must have drugged us and robbed us," said Tokubei. He turned and looked at me furiously. "A fine bodyguard you are!"

There was nothing I could say to that. But at least we were both alive and unharmed. "Did they take all your money?" I asked.

Tokubei had already taken his wallet out of his sash and was peering inside. "That's funny! My money is still here!"

This was certainly unexpected. What did the innkeeper and his strange daughter intend to do by drugging us and moving us outside?

At least things were not as bad as we had feared. We had not lost anything except a comfortable night's sleep, although from the heaviness in my head I had certainly slept deeply enough—and long enough too. Exactly how much time had elapsed since we drank wine with our host?

All we had to do now was find the highway again and continue our journey. Tokubei suddenly chuckled. "I didn't even have to pay for our night's lodging!"

As we walked from the bamboo grove, I saw the familiar clump of bamboo shoots, and we found ourselves standing in the same clearing again. Before our eyes was the thatched house. Only it was somehow different. Perhaps things looked different in the daylight than at dusk.

But the difference was more than a change of light. As we approached the house slowly, like sleepwalkers, we saw that the thatching was much darker. On the previous evening the thatching had looked fresh and new. Now it was dark with age. Daylight should make things appear brighter, not darker. The plastering of the walls also looked more dingy.

Tokubei and I stopped to look at each other before we went closer. He was pale, and I knew that I looked no less frightened. Something was terribly wrong. I loosened my sword in its scabbard.

We finally gathered the courage to go up to the house. Since Tokubei seemed unable to find his voice, I spoke out. "Is anyone there?"

After a moment we heard shuffling footsteps and the front door slid open. The face of an old woman appeared. "Yes?" she inquired. Her voice was creaky with age.

What set my heart pounding with panic, however, was not her voice. It was the sight of her left hand holding on to the frame of the door. The hand was wrinkled and crooked with the arthritis of old age— and it had six fingers.

I heard a gasp beside me and knew that Tokubei had noticed the hand as well.

The door opened wider and a man appeared beside the old woman. At first I thought it was our host of the previous night. But this man was much younger, although the resemblance was strong. He carried himself straighter and his hair was black, while the innkeeper had been grizzled and slightly bent with age.

"Please excuse my mother," said the man. "Her hearing is not good. Can we help you in some way?"

Tokubei finally found his voice. "Isn't this the inn where we stayed last night?"

The man stared. "Inn? We are not innkeepers here!"

"Yes, you are!" insisted Tokubei. "Your daughter invited us in and served us with wine. You must have put something in the wine!"

The man frowned. "You are serious? Are you sure you didn't drink too much at your inn and wander off?"

"No, I didn't drink too much!" said Tokubei, almost shouting. "I hardly drank at all! Your daughter, the one with six fingers in her hand, started to pour me a second cup of wine . . ." His voice trailed off, and he stared again at the left hand of the old woman.

"I don't have a daughter," said the man slowly. "My mother here is the one who has six fingers in her left hand, although I hardly think it polite of you to mention it."

"I'm getting dizzy," muttered Tokubei and began to totter.

"I think you'd better come in and rest a bit," the man said to him gruffly. He glanced at me. "Perhaps you wish to join your friend. You don't share his delusion about the inn, I hope?"

"I wouldn't presume to contradict my elders," I said carefully. Since both Tokubei and the owner of the house were my elders, I wasn't committing myself. In truth I didn't know what to believe, but I did want a look at the inside of the house.

The inside was almost the same as it was before but

the differences were there when I looked closely. We entered the same room with the alcove and the pair of painted doors. The vase I had admired was no longer there, but the doors showed the same landscapes painted by a master. I peered closely at the pictures and saw that the colors looked faded. What was more, the left panel, the one depicting a winter scene, had a long tear in one corner. It had been painstakingly mended, but the damage was impossible to hide completely.

Tokubei saw what I was staring at and he became even paler. At this stage we had both considered the possibility that a hoax of some sort had been played on us. The torn screen convinced Tokubei that our host had not played a joke: the owner of a valuable painting would never vandalize it for a trivial reason.

As for me, I was far more disturbed by the sight of the sixth finger on the old woman's hand. Could the young girl have disguised herself as an old crone? She could put rice powder in her hair to whiten it, but she could not transform her pretty straight fingers into old fingers twisted with arthritis. The woman here with us now was genuinely old, at least fifty years older than the girl.

It was this same old woman who finally gave us our greatest shock. "It's interesting that you should mention an inn, gentlemen," she croaked. "My father used to operate an inn. After he died, my husband and I turned this back into a private residence. We didn't need the income, you see."

"Your . . . your . . . f-father?" stammered Tokubei.

"Yes," replied the old woman. "He was a ronin, forced to go into innkeeping when he lost his position. But he never liked the work. Besides, our inn had begun to acquire an unfortunate reputation. Some of our guests disappeared, you see."

Even before she finished speaking, a horrible suspicion had begun to dawn on me. Her *father* had been an innkeeper, she said, her father who used to be a ronin. The man who had been our host was a ronin turned innkeeper. Could this mean that this old woman was actually the same person as the young girl we had seen?

I sat stunned while I tried to absorb the implications. What had happened to us? Was it possible that Tokubei and I had slept while this young girl grew into a mature woman, got married, and bore a son, a son who is now an adult? If that was the case, then we had slept for fifty years!

The old woman's next words confirmed my fears. "I recognize you now! You are two of the lost guests from our inn! The other lost ones I don't remember so well, but I remember *you* because your disappearance made me so sad. Such a handsome youth, I thought, what a pity that he should have gone the way of the others!"

A high wail came from Tokubei, who began to keen and rock himself back and forth. "I've lost fifty years! Fifty years of my life went by while I slept at this accursed inn!"

The inn was indeed accursed. Was the fate of the other guests similar to ours? "Did anyone else return as we did, fifty years later?" I asked.

The old woman looked uncertain and turned to her son. He frowned thoughtfully. "From time to time wild-looking people have come to us with stories similar to yours. Some of them went mad with the shock."

Tokubei wailed again. "I've lost my business! I've lost my wife, my young and beautiful wife! We had been married only a couple of months!"

A gruesome chuckle came from the old woman.

"You may not have lost your wife. It's just that she's become an old hag like me!"

That did not console Tokubei, whose keening became louder. Although my relationship with my employer had not been characterized by much respect on either side, I did begin to feel very sorry for him. He was right: he had lost his world.

As for me, the loss was less traumatic. I had left home under extremely painful circumstances, and had spent the next three years wandering. I had no friends and no one I could call a relation. The only thing I had was my duty to my employer. Somehow, some way, I had to help him.

"Did no one find an explanation for these disappearances?" I asked. "Perhaps if we knew the reason why, we might find some way to reverse the process."

The old woman began to nod eagerly. "The priestess! Tell them about the shrine priestess!"

"Well," said the man, "I'm not sure if it would work in your case. . . ."

"What? What would work?" demanded Tokubei. His eyes were feverish.

"There was a case of one returning guest who consulted the priestess at our local shrine," said the man. "She went into a trance and revealed that there was an evil spirit dwelling in the bamboo grove here. This spirit would put unwary travelers into a long, unnatural sleep. They would wake up twenty, thirty, or even fifty years later."

"Yes, but you said something worked in his case," said Tokubei.

The man seemed reluctant to go on. "I don't like to see you cheated, so I'm not sure I should be telling you this."

"Tell me! Tell me!" demanded Tokubei. The host's reluctance only made him more impatient.

"The priestess promised to make a spell that would undo the work of the evil spirit," said the man. "But she demanded a large sum of money, for she said that she had to burn some very rare and costly incense before she could begin the spell."

At the mention of money Tokubei sat back. The hectic flush died down on his face and his eyes narrowed. "How much money?" he asked.

The host shook his head. "In my opinion the priestess is a fraud and makes outrageous claims about her powers. We try to have as little to do with her as possible."

"Yes, but did her spell work?" asked Tokubei. "If it worked, she's no fraud!"

"At least the stranger disappeared again," cackled the old woman. "Maybe he went back to his own time. Maybe he walked into a river."

Tokubei's eyes narrowed further. "How much money did the priestess demand?" he asked again.

"I think it was one gold piece for every year lost," said the host. He hurriedly added, "Mind you, I still wouldn't trust the priestess."

"Then it would cost me fifty gold pieces to get back to my own time," muttered Tokubei. He looked up. "I don't carry that much money with me."

"No, you don't," agreed the host.

Something alerted me about the way he said that. It was as if the host knew already that Tokubei did not carry much money on him.

Meanwhile Tokubei sighed. He had come to a decision. "I do have the means to obtain more money, however. I can send a message to my chief clerk and he will remit the money when he sees my seal."

"Your chief clerk may be dead by now," I reminded him.

"You're right!" moaned Tokubei. "My business will

be under a new management and nobody will even remember my name!"

"And your wife will have remarried," said the old woman, with one of her chuckles. I found it hard to believe that the gentle young girl who had served us wine could turn into this dreadful harridan.

"Sending the message may be a waste of time," agreed the host.

"What waste of time!" cried Tokubei. "Why shouldn't I waste time? I've wasted fifty years already! Anyway, I've made up my mind. I'm sending that message."

"I still think you shouldn't trust the priestess," said the host.

That only made Tokubei all the more determined to send for the money. However, he was not quite resigned to the amount. "Fifty gold pieces is a large sum. Surely the priestess can buy incense for less than that amount?"

"Why don't you try giving her thirty gold pieces?" cackled the old woman. "Then the priestess will send you back thirty years, and your wife will only be middle-aged."

While Tokubei was still arguing with himself about the exact sum to send for, I decided to have a look at the bamboo grove. "I'm going for a walk," I announced, rising and picking up my sword from the floor beside me.

The host turned sharply to look at me. For an instant a faint, rueful smile appeared on his lips. Then he looked away.

Outside, I went straight to the clump of shoots in the bamboo grove. On the previous night—or what I perceived as the previous night—I had noticed that clump of bamboo shoots particularly, because I had been so hungry that I pictured them being cut up and boiled.

The clump of bamboo shoots was still in the same place. That in itself proved nothing, since bamboo could spring up anywhere, including the place where a clump had existed fifty years earlier. But what settled the matter in my mind was that the clump looked almost exactly the way it did when I had seen it before, except that every shoot was about an inch taller. That was a reasonable amount for bamboo shoots to grow overnight.

Overnight. Tokubei and I had slept on the ground here overnight. We had not slept here for a period of fifty years.

Once I knew that, I was able to see another inconsistency: the door panels with the painted landscapes. The painting with the winter scene had been on the *right* last night and it was on the *left* this morning. It wasn't simply a case of the panels changing places, because the depressions in the panel for the handholds had been reversed. In other words, what I saw just now was not a pair of paintings faded and torn by age. They were an entirely different pair of paintings.

But how did the pretty young girl change into an old woman? The answer was that if the screens could be different ones, so could the women. I had seen one woman, a young girl, last night. This morning I saw a different woman, an old hag.

The darkening of the thatched roof? Simply blow ashes over the roof. The grizzled-haired host of last night could be the same man who claimed to be his grandson today. It would be a simple matter for a young man to put gray in his hair and assume a stoop.

And the purpose of the hoax? To make Tokubei send for fifty pieces of gold, of course. It was clever of the man to accuse the shrine priestess of fraud and pretend reluctance to let Tokubei send his message.

I couldn't even feel angry toward the man and his

daughter—or mother, sister, wife, whatever. He could have killed me and taken my swords, which he clearly admired. Perhaps he was really a ronin and felt sympathetic toward another one.

When I returned to the house, Tokubei was looking resigned. "I've decided to send for the whole fifty gold pieces." He sighed.

"Don't bother," I said. "In fact we should be leaving as soon as possible. We shouldn't even stop here for a drink, especially not of wine."

Tokubei stared. "What do you mean? If I go back home, I'll find everything changed!"

"Nothing will be changed," I told him. "Your wife will be as young and beautiful as ever."

"I don't understand," he said. "Fifty years. . . ."

"It's a joke," I said. "The people here have a peculiar sense of humor, and they've played a joke on us."

Tokubei's mouth hung open. Finally he closed it with a snap. He stared at the host, and his face became first red and then purple. "You—you were trying to swindle me!" He turned furiously to me. "And you let them do this!"

"I'm not letting them," I pointed out. "That's why we're leaving right now."

"Are you going to let them get away with this?" demanded Tokubei. "They might try to swindle someone else!"

"They only went to this much trouble when they heard of the arrival of a fine fat fish like you," I said. I looked deliberately at the host. "I'm sure they won't be tempted to try the same trick again."

"And that's the end of your story?" asked Matsuzo. "You and Tokubei just went away? How did you know the so-called innkeeper wouldn't try the trick on some other luckless traveler?"

Zenta shook his head. "I didn't know. I merely guessed that once the trick was exposed, they wouldn't take the chance of trying it again. Of course I thought about revisiting the place to check if the people there were leading an honest life."

"Why didn't you?" asked Matsuzo. "Maybe we could go together. You've made me curious about that family now."

"Then you can satisfy your curiosity," said Zenta, smiling. He held his cup out for more tea, and the farmer's wife came forward to pour.

Only now she used both hands to hold the pot, and for the first time Matsuzo saw her left hand. He gasped. The hand had six fingers.

"Who was the old woman?" Zenta asked the farmer's wife.

"She was my grandmother," she replied. "Having six fingers is something that runs in my family."

At last Matsuzo found his voice. "You mean this is the very house you visited? This is the inn where time was lost?"

"Where we *thought* we lost fifty years," said Zenta. "Perhaps I should have warned you first. But I was almost certain that we'd be safe this time. And I see that I was right."

He turned to the woman again. "You and your husband are farmers now, aren't you? What happened to the man who was the host?"

"He's dead," she said quietly. "He was my brother, and he was telling you the truth when he said that he was a ronin. Two years ago he found work with another warlord, but he was killed in battle only a month later."

Matsuzo was peering at the pair of sliding doors, which he hadn't noticed before. "I see that you've put up the faded set of paintings. The winter scene is on the left side."

The woman nodded. "We sold the newer pair of doors. My husband said that we're farmers now and that people in our position don't need valuable paintings. We used the money to buy some new farm implements."

She took up the teapot again. "Would you like another cup of tea?" she asked Matsuzo.

Staring at her left hand, Matsuzo had a sudden qualm. "I —I don't think I want any more."

Everybody laughed.

LENSEY NAMIOKA

Anyone who has read Lensey Namioka's tales of adventure and terror in feudal Japan will recognize Matsuzo and Zenta, the two young samurai warriors in "The Inn of Lost Time." In *White Serpent Castle,* for example, the young samurai attempt to wade through the intrigue caused by the struggle of rivals for control of the mysterious serpent-shaped castle. The adventures of Zenta and Matsuzo continue in *The Samurai and the Long-Nosed Devils, Valley of the Cherry Trees, Village of the Vampire Cat,* and *Island of Ogres.*

Although Ms. Namioka was born in Peking (now Beijing), China, she was inspired to write about feudal Japan by the history of her husband's family. Her husband, a college math professor, was raised in the castle town of Himeji, Japan. Together, they have lived and traveled all over the world but now reside in Seattle, Washington. Her background provided much of the knowledge she used in writing two travel books, one on Japan and the other on China.

In addition Lensey Namioka has written a humorous young-adult novel about an Asian teenager called *Who's Hu?* and a mystery-suspense novel set in China before the Mongol invasion called *Phantom of Tiger Mountain.* She is currently working on a contemporary young-adult mystery called *Wormholes.* It is set in Seattle with a teenage Japanese-American girl as the main character.

Bret Diamond, desperate to get Lisa to fall in love with him, seeks the help of sorceress Diana Webb. There is, of course, only one solution. . . .

LOVE POTION

CIN FORSHAY-LUNSFORD

"Look, my name's Bret. I've got this problem and rumor has it you might be able to help me."

"I know who you are," Diana told him. "I've seen you around school. In fact, you're in my biology class."

"That's right. Listen, I have to ask this, even if it sounds a little strange. Are you really a witch?"

Diana gave a pursed smile. It was a rainy Saturday in mid-October. Business had been slow. When Bret burst in he'd found Diana Webb sitting behind the counter of her grandmother's store reading her own tarot, bestowing idle strokes of affection upon her familiar. The familiar's name was Timothy Tufttail. He was a silky furred black cat, Diana's best friend and confidant.

Outside, the heavy wooden sign swung in the wind, wheezing like a dying man. It read:

GRANDMOTHER WEBB

MAGIC SHOPPE

ILLUSIONS, BOOKS, TALISMANS

Diana Webb combed her sleek dark hair with her fingers.

"Are you a sorceress, I mean?" Bret continued. "I've only lived here two months, but I've heard stories about you."

Diana gave a little sigh before folding her arms across her chest. "What kind of stories?"

"Well, for example, that you can change the weather if you feel like it. Make snowstorms come out of nowhere so the schools close. Stuff like that. I still don't know if I believe it. But I know I'm at the end of my rope. If you are what people say, and you agree to help me, I'm prepared to pay you well."

"If you knew anything about the mystic arts," Diana replied, "you'd know that an enchantress can't accept money for her help. Using her gifts in pursuit of money will diminish her abilities. Possibly destroy them."

"That's why I brought this." Bret laid a velvet-wrapped object on the table. He licked his lips nervously. "It belonged to my mother."

As he unwrapped the offering, Diana's green eyes widened with surprise, then narrowed as she gave him a smile. "It's fabulous. Can I hold it?"

"Of course," the boy answered. "My mother was a big astrology buff and she 'dabbled,' as my father puts it, in other things as well. This crystal ball was her greatest prize. I believed in magic when I was little because my mother believed. I'm fifteen now and everything I've been taught since my mother left makes me think I must be nuts for coming here. Still . . ."

"What is it exactly you want in return for the crystal?"

"A love potion. There's this girl, a beautiful girl, the most devastatingly gorgeous girl I've ever seen. She's my dream. If I could make her love me, my entire existence would be fulfilled."

"A love potion, eh?" The orb felt so perfect in the palm of her hand, she didn't want to put it down. Outside, the rain undulated like shimmering curtains across the windows. Timothy the cat purred and rubbed his cheek against Bret's leg.

Poised in her web, a patient garden spider in the topmost

corner of the window was eyeing a winged morsel that
fluttered against the wall. Timothy stretched upward in a
futile attempt to catch the insects, his claws scraping the
pane. The young sorceress tickled her pet under the chin.

"Concocting a love potion is no easy thing," she assured
Bret. "Not that I couldn't do it if I set my heart to it. . . ."

"Please, I'm in pain over this girl!" Bret grabbed her
marble-cold hand. "Help me!"

Diana hesitated. It was the finest crystal ball she'd ever
seen, like a glistening winter moon plucked from the sky.
Besides, Timothy seemed to like Bret.

"Okay, I'll help you."

Bret smiled wider than the Cheshire cat.

That night his dreams were filled with visions of Lisa.
Lisa, lovely Lisa, who probably didn't know he was alive
and on the slim chance she did, didn't care. He saw her
smiling over her shoulder at him in the hallways at school.
He felt the press of her powder-soft body as they danced
through the twilight dream gardens of his most private
mind. He floundered in the intoxicating perfume of her
hair. He heard her whisper, "Bret! My Bret!" with a sound
like wind through scarlet leaves. His soul flew with hers
through the endless night and he woke knowing she would
soon be his.

Bret was pacing with excitement when Diana met him
that Monday at the bleachers after school. She assured him
that she had gotten her hands on nearly all the ingredients
for the potion. Still, there were seven items left that she
would need to cast the spell: a pinch of dirt from Lisa's
footprint and a pinch from his own, fingernail clippings
from both of them, and a lock of hair from each. The
seventh item she kept her secret.

"But how am I supposed to get my hands on this stuff?"
Bret asked as he skateboarded alongside Diana on their way
home from school. "I can't just walk up to her and say, 'Hi,

Lisa. Can I please have some hair, nail clippings, and dirt?' "

"Of course not!" She laughed. "We'll have to be more cunning than that. Now, here's what we do. . . ."

At three forty-five the following afternoon the first stage of Diana's plan went into effect. She and Bret met at the bicycle rack by the baseball diamond. Bret poured two jugs of water on the patch of dirt where the constant tread of students had worn the grass away, while Diana mixed it with a stick.

"Now, you're sure about her schedule, right, Bret? She definitely passes by here?"

"Sure, I'm sure. Monday and Wednesday she has cheerleader practice. Friday she baby-sits after school. Tuesdays and Thursdays she hangs out with her girlfriends. They go to the video arcade or the pizza parlor or the record store. She picks up her bicycle here around four."

"Perfect."

Bret helped her mix the dirt into a thick, mucky consistency. "I feel like a little kid, don't you? Making mudpies in the sandbox again. Here she comes!" Bret rubbed the palms of his hands on his jeans. "Act normal!"

Lisa was with two of her friends, but Bret hardly saw them. All his eyes could see was the sun sparkling in Lisa's glossy auburn hair. How gracefully she moved! He felt hot needles tingling in his bloodstream.

"Go on!" Diana said.

"Hi!" Bret walked directly in front of Lisa's path.

"Hi."

She walked around him. He walked back in front of her, trying to maneuver her toward the mud puddle. "Is this your bike? Nice bike," he babbled nervously.

Lisa's girlfriends whispered and giggled behind their notebooks.

Just one step back and we've got it, Bret thought. Bret edged her to the mud like a wolf circles a doe. She took a step back and her heel sunk in the mud. Bret reached out to steady her, but at the same moment she turned. Her books were knocked from her arms and scattered all over, loose papers landing in the muck. They both reached down to pick up the books and cracked heads. Lisa slipped and landed in the mud.

"I'm sorry! I'm sorry!" Bret cried as he tried to help her up.

"Let go of my arm! Just leave me alone!"

Lisa and her two friends hurried away, casting dirty looks over their shoulders.

"Great! Just great!" Bret groaned. "Now she'll definitely never speak to me."

"Don't despair," Diana replied. "Look!"

A perfect footprint was left in the mud.

Phase two of this very delicate operation was not so simple. It required not only skill but luck and timing. Bret waited in the library, hidden behind a book till he saw that Lisa and her friend were too engrossed in their psychology project to notice him creeping up behind them with a pair of scissors. He almost had the lock of hair when Lisa suddenly bent down to retrieve a ditto. The scissors tangled in her hair and Bret ended up cutting off a good deal more hair than he had meant to.

Needless to say, Lisa wasn't exactly thrilled to find Bret chopping up her hair. She cursed him out and hit him over the head with a three-hundred-page hardcover textbook. Bret was suspended from school.

"I think you should leave this last bit to me," Diana mused as she and Bret fed the swans at the park pond. "Men just aren't subtle enough. Good thing this love potion is so potent. You really got on Lisa's bad side."

"I know. She hates me." Bret sighed. "You're going to have to pull off a miracle to get her to fall for me."

"Don't be silly. A little coriander . . . a pinch of ginseng . . . henbane gathered at midsummer's eve . . . a bit of

yarrow . . . trust me, I know what I'm doing. It's not going to be that hard. All you have to do is follow my instructions and the girl is yours."

Bret tossed a bit of bread to a swan that came close to the
water's edge. Her mate swam close behind her.

"They say swans mate for life." Bret sighed.

"This will all be over soon," Diana assured him. "The
waiting, the talismans under your pillow, the incantations.
Soon as I get the nail clippings we're set. We strike on
Allhallows Eve."

"Huh?"

"Halloween. Lisa's going to a costume party and you're
going to crash it. The planets will be in an excellent position. All you have to do is get her to drink the potion."

"How?"

"Slip it in her soda or something. That's your department."

"You won't come with me?"

Diana looked down, then out across the sparkling water.
"I can't."

"How come? I mean, you're my friend, aren't you? We've
been together nearly every day this whole month. I don't
know what I'd have done if I hadn't found you. You've got
to be there!"

"You can handle it alone."

"I could, I guess. But I don't want to."

"You'll have to."

Bret couldn't understand why Diana just got up and
walked away like that. Had he said something to make her
angry? Here he thought they were tight. He had faith in her
and he'd thought that she really liked him. Even those days
they weren't working on casting the spell they'd been together, listening to albums at Bret's house, talking about
what they wanted to do when they got out of school.

One day he'd seen her walking home and he'd given her
a ride on the back of his motorcycle. They'd taken a short-

cut through the woods behind the old church. Her long black hair blew in the breeze in serpentine coils, stinging his cheek. The sun was about ready to set, he remembered. The sky was overfull with gilt-edged clouds upon a backdrop that reminded him of melting rainbow sherbet.

He wiped out on an incline and they both tumbled off the bike. He was embarrassed. She smiled when he reached down to help her up, dusting off her jeans and making silly jokes so that he'd feel better.

Then she got back on and tucked her chin into his freckled shoulder. Even though there was a sissy bar, she wrapped her arms about his waist. But not so tight as to say she was scared. He could tell she wasn't. The embrace was just snug enough to prove a different point.

Diana caught up with Lisa a week before Halloween. Pretending to have a cousin's aunt in the cosmetic business, she conned Lisa into a "free" makeover which included a manicure. Diana promised Lisa half a dozen complimentary nail polishes if she participated in a bogus survey. The girl fell for it, and Diana Webb walked away less six dollars' worth of polish and plus three slivers of fingernail.

After consulting all kinds of star charts and books, Diana arranged for Bret to visit. She led him through a dark curtain at the back of the store, up a narrow stairway, into a small apartment which she shared with her grandmother.

The sunny rooms were a profusion of ferns and ivy and hanging flowering plants. Piles of books and papers cluttered the otherwise tidy home and the mingled scents of vanilla, sandalwood, and furniture polish tickled Bret's nose. Sunlight streamed through the windows and glinted off strings of tiny pearls and Austrian crystals that dangled in the leaves of lush houseplant foliage.

Diana took him into a room where the walls were covered with paintings of fabulous beasts: unicorns, dragons, griffins, and strangely formed, colorful creatures Bret didn't recognize. A telescope stood at the far window. From an intricately engraved box she withdrew several flasks and glass vials. Bret peeked in the magic box.

"Whose is this?"

"Mine. You don't think I'd keep other people's personal objects to cast spells and not my own? I always keep a few strands of my own hair, some footprint dirt, and nail clippings in the box. Plus some other items: mummy dust, valerian root extract, and the like."

Diana pulled down the shades and lit a candle. She proceeded to mix various herbs and herbal extracts in a stone bowl while reciting singsong incantations. She wrote in runic letters and then burned the paper, sprinkling the ashes into the mixture. With a mortar and pestle she finely ground swan's eggshell and added that, stirring it with a crystal wand.

"Now you burn the hair and the nail clippings, Bret," the witch commanded. "Add it in with a sprinkle of footprint dirt and recite the verse I've written here for you. It's almost sunset and I must pull up the mandrake root before the sun goes down. Don't be afraid if you hear a scream. They do that when you take them out of the earth. . . ."

Diana went out onto the balcony where she grew many of the plants she used in her potions and returned with a root shaped similar to a human form. He had heard a shriek but wasn't thoroughly convinced that it wasn't just Di, trying to build the dramatic tension.

The ceremony continued, with Diana pricking Bret's finger and adding a few drops of his blood to the love elixir. She added a few more ingredients, stirred and boiled it down, poured it into a cream- and rose-colored seashell, and then into a small green glass bottle. She stopped it with a cork.

She sighed. "There's only one ingredient left to add," she told Bret. "That I must do after you are gone. Go home now and when you sleep, put this small pouch beneath your pillow. I'll give you the love potion in school tomorrow. You can bring me the crystal then."

Diana stood out on the balcony and watched from above as Bret walked down the street and out of her life. After tomorrow he'd have no need for her. Not even as a casual acquaintance. The potion was potent. Lisa would soon be following at his heels like a dog. He'd be lucky to escape her long enough to sleep a few hours at night.

Leaves the color of dried blood scurried like mice before his footfalls. The streetlamps cast light in his wavy hair, shadow-lined his form. His wallet chain jangled with the sad sound of faraway bells. Soon his footsteps sounded fainter, like the merry tune he whistled, and he was gone. Diana went back inside and added the final ingredient to the magic potion: witch's tears.

She almost didn't go and then she thought better of it. Diana appeared at the dance dressed in a long cranberry-colored gown, ballet slippers, and a headdress of golden chain mail and glittering green-blue crystals. Heavy, ornate belts and a light cloak completed the medieval-enchantress outfit.

Diana found Bret and Lisa at the punch bowl. Lisa was all rhinestones and fringe in her white cowgirl outfit, and Bret looked quite dashing dressed as a cavalier.

"Look, you little slug," she was saying, "I don't care that my friends all think you're so cute. You're nuts! Cutting my hair off! Practically shoving me in the mud! There has got to be something wrong with you!"

Lisa stormed away. Diana appeared at Bret's side. A smile spread over Bret's face when he saw her. "I didn't think you'd come. I'm glad you did." Bret turned his back on Diana, then turned back with two glasses of punch in his hands. "Here. Take one." Diana took a glass.

"I don't understand. Didn't the potion work?"

"No. Not yet."

"But it's supposed to kick right in! Bret, I'm so sorry. I must have done something wrong, but I can't think what."

"Don't worry. Let's drink a toast. To friendship!"

"To friendship." Diana drank her punch. She looked up into Bret's softly sparkling eyes. "Oh! Bret! I feel so strange!"

Bret drank his punch. "Yes," he said. "It kicks right in. When you left me alone to mix in the nail clippings and the hair and the dirt, I did. Except I substituted yours for Lisa's."

"Bret! That makes you a warlock!"

"Yeah." He grinned. "I guess it does." He lifted her chin with his forefinger. "I love you, Diana."

The witch closed her eyes and kissed him tenderly. "I love you, Bret," she whispered.

That night, a cavalier and a medieval enchantress walked home hand in hand under the silvery elms. As they passed the graveyard, a black Halloween cat with a tufted tail purred and rubbed his cheek against a tombstone, then jumped up onto the stone wall and followed after. The full moon shone in the sky like a crystal ball, as if Hecate herself were smiling.

CIN FORSHAY-LUNSFORD

Walk Through Cold Fire was Cin Forshay-Lunsford's first published book, and it earned her first prize in the second annual Delacorte Press contest for the Outstanding First Young Adult Novel. She began writing it when she was a seventeen-year-old senior at Lynbrook High School on Long Island, New York.

Like Cin, who moved out of her parents' home and into a studio apartment in Long Beach, New York, before graduation, the sixteen-year-old heroine of *Walk Through Cold Fire* leaves her middle-class home and takes up with a gang called the Outlaws. From the wreckage of broken loyalties and lost love, Desiree Valentine searches for something to live for and believe in, and struggles to realize her own uniqueness.

Forshay-Lunsford says she had no lack of inspiration for this autobiographical novel, for the story came "partly from my frustrations with a society bent on creating followers, partly from my diary excerpts, and partly from my own imagination." Written in the first person, the novel is "a confession of my own weaknesses and strengths, a raw attempt to contact other people who want more from life than what is given." Believing that "so many creative things can come from turning one's back on convention and tending to the realm of imagination," she has completed a second novel, about a young female artist, called *Shards,* and a poetry collection called *Daughters of the Moon and Other Poems,* neither of which has yet been published, and is currently working on a fantasy novel called *The Emerald Sea Princess.*

Forshay-Lunsford continues to tend to her own imagination as a young writer in Oceanside, New York, where she lives with a lovebird named Nancy, a betta fish named Ruby, and a bunny named Magic.

The Tanner High School football team hasn't won a game in more than two years, and everybody is feeling bummed out. What they need is a little school spirit. Or do they? . . .

SCHOOL SPIRIT

JERRY SPINELLI

When a school's spirit dies, every classroom is a morgue, every football game is a funeral.

How bad was it?

So bad that when our football team lost its nineteenth game in a row, everybody in the stands cheered—all thirty of them.

So bad that the marching band didn't have enough members to form a decent-sized circle on the field.

So bad that for a bonfire pep rally, somebody struck a match and three cheerleaders said "Rah."

That's how it was for my first three years. And no reason to believe my senior year would be any different.

When the band met in August—I played baritone horn—it was not exactly a joyous reunion. Right off we discovered that two clarinetists and a snare drummer had decided not to show, leaving our number at an unstaggering twenty-two. That's counting the color guard and two majorettes.

The first thing we did was agree we wanted to switch from being a marching band to a sitting band. We were tired of working our butts off and learning new formations and playing out there at halftime to the five or six people who didn't go for hot dogs. And even then, if only one of them had clapped or waved or pretended to listen . . . Hah! If somebody waved at us, it was with the middle finger, or with a crushed paper cup sailing from their hand to one of our helmets.

We told the director, Mr. Rayburn. He understood. He was a pretty old guy, and he wasn't really into all the new stuff in band these days. His idea of a fancy formation was changing a circle to a square. But he loved music, and I think he loved us, and it hurt him to see his band ignored and embarrassed and abused.

"Okay," he said after thinking it over for a day, "I'll let you play from the stands—under one condition."

"What's that?" we all asked.

He smiled a little and said, "If somebody takes the tuba."

We all laughed. We seniors had been in grade school when the last tubist had tooted onto the playing field. The tuba, Mr. Rayburn reminded us once a month, was the grand old anchor of the American band, and what a shame that nobody wanted to play it anymore. Soon it would be as extinct as the dinosaur.

Every year he asked—pleaded—for a volunteer to pick up the old tuba that had been collecting dust in the music closet. And every year we winced at each other and snickered, "Tubasaurus."

Until this year. "Look," he said, trying to sweeten the pot, "if you're not marching, if all you're doing is sitting there, it'll be easy. You won't have to lug it." And he promised, "I'll teach you the rudiments in a week."

We all agreed it was a fair trade-off, so long as somebody else tooted the tuba.

And then Jenny Wilson said, to no one in particular but so everyone could hear, "I think Arnold ought to do it. He already plays the biggest horn. It's just another step up for him."

It wasn't Jenny's reasoning that I gave in to. Or the fact that everyone else called, "Yeah! Yeah!" when she said that. No, it was Jenny herself.

Jenny Wilson didn't know it, and neither did anyone else,

but I was secretly in love with her. Had been since ninth grade.

Jenny played first flute. It was my rotten luck that whether the band was sitting on a stage or marching on a field, the baritone was never near the flutes. Still, every second of the program, whatever the formation, I always knew exactly where first flute was.

I never had the nerve to make a big move on Jenny. About once every six months I managed to make a small move, but I guess it was even smaller than I thought, because she never seemed to notice.

So, when Jenny Wilson said, "I think Arnold ought to do it," all I heard was her saying my name and asking me to do something for her.

When I announced to Mr. Rayburn that I would take the tuba, the band let loose the first cheer heard in those parts in years. A few minutes later Mr. Rayburn brought it out. Everyone gathered around to see this relic, this fossil, this dusty, dented, battered monstrosity. "Tubasaurus lives!" someone piped. Mr. Rayburn's eyes were misty.

The rest of the band was sent home. There was no longer a need to practice formations in August in the parking lot. We would be a sitting band that season.

Mr. Rayburn handed me the tuba's mouthpiece. "Been saving this for years," he said. "Why don't you two just get the feel of each other today? We'll start in with some basics tomorrow."

He left, and I was alone with the tuba. My tuba.

I couldn't find a rag, so I dusted it as best I could with my sleeve. Its once-white surface was scratched and chipped. Two of the stops were sticking. They'd have to be oiled.

I lifted it. It took me a couple minutes to figure out the right way to hold it. It felt strange, the huge, funneled bell above me, like a second head.

I marched the length of the music room, back and forth a

couple times. I was glad I wouldn't be lugging it around the field.

I sat down. I inserted the mouthpiece—even that was huge. I couldn't figure how to place my lips on it. No matter what I did, it seemed to want to swallow me. I took a deep breath, primed my cheeks, and gave it a baritone horn-type blow. Nothing. I tried a trumpet-type blow. Nothing again. Apparently you had to toot a tuba on its own terms, and nothing less.

I don't know how long I was there, huffing, puffing, pushing the stops, trying to make something happen, when suddenly from above my head I heard a single, short, foghorn blast. This was followed by a cloud of dust, and *that* was followed by a voice, a tinny, tiny, echoing, sputtering voice. Above me. Saying: "Well, come on. (Cough, cough.) Don't stop (cough) now. I'm almost (cough) there. Blow (cough), dammit!"

Cooperative kid that I was, I blew. Another foghorn toot, followed this time by a tiny but no longer echoing "Yahoo!" followed by the slightly incredible sight of a little man—a teeny-*weeny* little man, all three inches of him—tumbling in an arc from above my head to the gray linoleum floor below.

At that point I must have finally had the good sense to faint, because next thing I knew I was flat on my back, staring straight up into the upside-down, fingertip-sized face of the little man, who was standing on my forehead. He stomped (I felt it as a faint tap). "You gonna sleep all day?" he groused. "We got work to do."

He disappeared from view. I felt a tiny tugging on my hair; then he was striding onto the floor. He stood, hands on hips, glaring. *"Well?"*

I sat up, but still I couldn't speak, thinking: *It's okay to have a hallucination as long as you don't talk back to it.* I just stared.

He wore a jogging suit and what appeared to be Nike

sneakers. Air Jordans, I believe. And wristbands, smaller
than SpaghettiOs.

He gave me a disgusted look, jogged in place for a minute, did about thirty push-ups, and sprinted out to the
nearest music stand and back.

"Whew!" he huffed. "Outta shape. Cooped up in that
thing seven years. . . ."

He glared some more. He wagged his head, snickered.
"Not talking, eh? Okay, I'll take both parts." Clearing his
throat, he assumed a theatrical pose. "Who are you? I am
your school spirit. What do you want? I want to do my job
so I can get outta here. What *is* your job? My job is to bring
some life back to this dump. Is this one of those three-wish
deals? Bingo. Are you for real?" He grabbed a hair on my
leg with both hands and yanked.

"Oww!" I yelled.

He clapped. "It talks!"

I said, "Aren't you supposed to come out of a lamp?"

"That's my Middle Eastern colleagues. I'm a tuba genie."
Now he was doing sit-ups.

"So," I said, "now what?"

"Now"—he finished his sit-ups—"twenty-nine . . .
thirty." He stood, touched his toes. "Now we get down to
business. Here's the deal. Three proposals—we don't call
them wishes anymore—anything you want to wake things
up around here. And of course, you being the agent, so to
speak, you get a bonus proposal for your personal use." He
retrieved a briefcase I hadn't noticed before and pulled
something from it. "Results guaranteed, or we come back
and do the job right."

He handed me a tiny piece of paper, smaller than a post-
age stamp. It read *Guarantee.* It looked official.

"Son," he said. For the first time the bite was gone from
his voice; there was a painful, almost pleading expression
on his face. "I don't mean to rush you—I'd usually give you
a week for this—but I got quotas to meet, and my boss

don't want to hear about seven years in the same damn tuba. So if you don't mind, do you think we could wrap this up pretty soon?"

"I'll do my best," I said.

"Good." He clapped his hands. "You taking your horn home today, by any chance?"

"I don't know," I told him. I wasn't sure I wanted to be seen on the streets with that thing.

"Ah, come on," he said. "I'll hitch a ride. We'll wrap this thing up by tonight." His face got downright pitiful. "Please."

I shrugged. "Well, okay, I guess."

He threw his fists in the air. He beamed. He stuck out a tiny hand for me to shake. "Call me T.G."

It's one thing to go loony at school. It's another to take your hallucination home with you.

Late that night, whispering in the dark of my bedroom, I made my three proposals: (1) the football team would go undefeated, (2) fifty more kids would come out for band, and (3) we would march on the field again, to applause.

As I spoke he furiously punched buttons on a tiny calculator. He punched the last with a pianist's flourish. "Done! Now"—he looked up from my pillow—"how about yours?"

I hemmed and hawed for a while, but finally I spit it out: "How about, uh, Jenny Wilson . . . sort of . . . liking, uh, me?"

"You asking or telling?"

"Well, telling, I guess."

He gave me a quick wink and punched some buttons. "How about"—he paused—"we give that a little more *oomph.* Make her fall in love with you."

That was too much even to wish for, but I went along with the game. "Sure, why not."

He started to punch, stopped. "Make her krr-*aaaaay*-zy about you."

I shrugged. "Go for it."

"Done!" he chirped. He returned the calculator to his briefcase and snapped it shut. "Nice doing business with you, young fella." He crouched in his Air Jordans and leapt into the tuba. I heard him call from deep in the throat: "Don't let the bedbugs bite!"

In the morning, I blew and blew, but only toots came out.

Either T.G. knew his stuff, or we were all hallucinating.

When I showed up for band next day, the place was mobbed. I counted the newcomers. Precisely fifty. Mr. Rayburn was practically weeping for joy.

When the football season opened three weeks later, we were, as guaranteed, out on the field. We formed the four letters of our school's initials, and had enough left over to draw a circle around them. The stands went wild. We marched off to a standing ovation.

And the team won. Boy, did they win. The first game, the second game, the third game. Not only won—the other teams never scored a point.

Every Friday afternoon the gym shook to our thunderous pep rallies. Students cheered and whistled in assembly, high-fived in the hallways, flocked to clubs, volunteered for everything, and outfitted themselves, their bedrooms, their bikes, their cars, and their pets in the school colors.

It was a giddy, top-of-the-world September. And at the top of the top was me.

That first day when the fifty newcomers appeared, Jenny Wilson was waiting at the door. She asked if she could try the tuba. She tried and was comically inept. Pretty soon she was laughing too hard to keep trying. Pretty soon we were both laughing, so hard we had to lean into each other to keep from falling over. Her eyes were sparkling.

We met between classes. We ate lunch together. We walked to school together, and home. We held hands in the hallways.

We went to the malls. We went to the movies, the library, the pizza shop. We went to a school dance, and in the middle of a slow number, our arms entwined, our hearts thumping at one another, we kissed for the first time. She went "Mmm," and I went to heaven.

From then on we gravitated toward the private places, the dark places. We marched and we pep-rallied and we cheered with everyone else, and then we slipped away to some nook or cranny or backseat, where we, as Mr. Rayburn might have said, got the feel of each other.

And then one Saturday afternoon, in her house, in her bedroom, her parents away for the day, we were about to get as close as you can get, when she cooed, "I'm krr-*aaaaay*-zy about you." And then, not really understanding why, I was getting up and getting dressed and getting out of there, leaving behind one very baffled and frustrated flutist.

It wasn't all that hard to track him down. I just went straight to the nearest school with the longest football losing streak. Their band was tubaless, as ours had been. I posed as a student and found the dented, dusty relic in the music closet. One good toot and out he popped. I caught him in my hand.

"Can you cancel the wishes?" I blurted.

He stumbled around my hand, rubbing his eyes. He draped one arm around my thumb. "Hey"—he blinked— "don't *do* that. I was trying to take a nap." He squinted up at me. "Don't I know you?"

"Yes," I said. "Tanner High School. About a month and a half ago. Can you—"

"Please—" he interrupted, "I get seasick in somebody's hand. Would you mind setting me down?"

I put him on a chair seat. "I came here to ask if you could —if you *would*—cancel the wishes. Is that possible?"

He looked at me uncertainly. "They didn't work, you're telling me?"

"Oh, no. They worked great. Team's undefeated. School spirit's like, zow. I just . . . have a problem. Me."

"Problem?" He did some deep knee bends. "Problem?"

"With the personal one. That's the one I'd like canceled, if you don't mind."

He pulled the calculator from his briefcase. "Tanner, you say?"

"Yes, sir."

He punched buttons. "Tanner . . . Tanner . . . okay, here we are . . . proposal, personal . . . uh, Jenny—"

"Wilson. You were supposed to make her crazy about me."

He looked up, his arched eyebrows saying: *Well?*

"Well, yes, you did. She's crazy about me, all right. I mean, that's how it looks. . . ."

His eyebrows arched higher.

"I mean, it's—it's just not right. It's not real."

He chuckled. "You still think it's all a hallucination."

"Oh, no," I said, "not anymore . . . but, with Jenny, it's just more important for it to be real. She's not really . . . herself. She doesn't see me. I mean, she doesn't see *me*. I want her to see *me*. I want her to like *me*."

"Which she does, does she not?"

"Not really. It's like . . . she's been . . . wired. She's just blindly following the program. I want her without all the tricks, or"—I took a deep breath—"I guess I don't want her at all."

A tiny, prolonged peep was the sound of a whistle coming from the little man. He lowered his head and paced back and forth in thought. At last he said, "Proposals are serial, you know that."

"What's that mean?" I said.

"It means, they're like your old-time Christmas-tree lights. One goes out, they all go out."

"You mean—"

"I mean all or—ka*put*—nothing."

I slumped into a chair. It was one thing to cancel my own wish, but what right did I have to mess with the others? School spirit was school spirit, wasn't it, no matter where it came from? Fun was fun. Who was I to spoil it for everybody?

"You don't want to make a snap decision here," I heard him say. "When's your next game?"

"Friday night," I said.

"Okay. Listen, go home. Think it over. If you don't get back to me by Friday night, I'll put the cancellations through. How's that?"

I nodded and got up and walked off.

When Friday night came, there I was, in the band section watching the game. I hadn't returned to the little man. I couldn't. I felt rotten.

Everyone was cheering around me as our team took its usual three-touchdown lead in the first quarter. And then, as the stadium gaped in stunned horror, the other team intercepted a pass of ours and ran it back ninety-five yards for the first touchdown scored against us that year. The little man, I knew, had just punched the buttons.

It all came crashing down then. We lost that game, and the next. The crowds disappeared. Pep rallies were called off. The hallways became tombs again.

Fifty kids dropped band in one week. Those of us left took to the field under a squall of catcalls and paper cups, and then—even worse—total indifference. We became a sitting band again.

Mr. Rayburn said he wouldn't hold me to playing the tuba. He was beaten.

And, of course, Jenny Wilson—well, it wasn't as if she dumped me or forgot me; it was as if she had never even known me.

Not knowing exactly why, I would not surrender the

tuba. I clung to it like driftwood in an empty sea. Somehow it kept me from drowning with the rest. It became a precious link to things past, to things real, however unhappy. I cherished it.

And in some perverse, private way, I began to cherish the wasteland around me, the grim, sullen corpse that only weeks before had been a raucous, gym-shaking student body. For now at least it was real. It was death, but it was an honest death. And as I pressed the stops and produced my piddling toots, I sensed that when it all came down, it was tubas we would be left with, not genies.

And so, in the ninth game of the season, the team losing 34–0, I rose from my seat at halftime and marched my tuba out to the field and stood smack on the fifty-yard line. I could imagine what my fellow bandmates were thinking, not to mention the few others in the stands. But I didn't think. I didn't care. I just played. I played for all the tubas that no one had ever heard, because the tuba never plays alone. I played and played, and I saw the zebra-striped officials returning for the second half, and I closed my eyes and I kept on playing.

And then there was another sound behind me. A flute. I didn't have to look; I knew who it was. And then there was another flute . . . and clarinets . . . and brass . . . and drums . . . and the tuba was leading the band.

When we marched off the field, the football teams applauded, and in the all-but-empty stands the spectators jumped to their feet and let loose the smallest, sweetest cheer I'd ever heard.

JERRY SPINELLI

One morning, Jerry Spinelli discovered that one of his children had eaten some fried chicken that he had been saving in the refrigerator for his next day's lunch. The culprit had eaten the chicken but left the bones in the plastic container, still in the refrigerator. Trying to imagine how the event had been accomplished, Jerry Spinelli started writing about it, from the kid's point of view. Without realizing it at the time, he had started what eventually became his first novel, *Space Station Seventh Grade*. Most important, Spinelli had taken a lighthearted approach to life, and his first novel, as well as those that have followed, contain hilarious situations and lively, humorous dialogue.

His second novel, *Who Put That Hair in My Toothbrush?*, focuses on the relationship between a brother and sister who are constantly at each other's throat, until Greg throws away Megin's most precious possession, her Wayne Gretzky hockey stick. Then things get really intense.

In *Night of the Whale* six high school friends are planning a wild time at Wags's family's beach house in Ocean City during Senior Week. But then Wags, Digger, Mouse, Timmi, Lauren, and Breeze interrupt their fun one night in an attempt to rescue a group of whales stranded on the beach.

Romance figures prominently in *Jason and Marceline*. Jason wants them to be an average couple, except there is nothing average about Marceline.

Spinelli's most recent novel for young adults is *Dump Days*, the story about one summer when two best friends search for the Perfect Day.

Jerry Spinelli and his wife, Eileen, who is also a writer, live in Phoenixville, Pennsylvania.

INSIGHTS

Like poetry? Are you kidding? Not in Mrs. Tibbetts's second-period class. . . .

I GO ALONG

RICHARD PECK

Anyway, Mrs. Tibbetts comes into the room for second period, so we all see she's still in school. This is the spring she's pregnant, and there are some people making some bets about when she's due. The smart money says she'll make it to Easter, and after that we'll have a sub teaching us. Not that we're too particular about who's up there at the front of the room, not in this class.

Being juniors, we also figure we know all there is to know about sex. We know things about sex no adult ever heard of. Still, the sight of a pregnant English teacher slows us down some. But she's married to Roy Tibbetts, a plumber who was in the service and went to jump school, so that's okay. We see him around town in his truck.

And right away Darla Craig's hand is up. It's up a lot. She doesn't know any more English than the rest of us, but she likes to talk.

"Hey, Mrs. Tibbetts, how come they get to go and we don't?"

She's talking about the first-period people, the Advanced English class. Mrs. Tibbetts looks like Darla's caught her off base. We never hear what a teacher tells us, but we know this. At least Darla does.

"I hadn't thought," Mrs. Tibbetts says, rubbing her hand down the small of her back, which may have something to do with being pregnant. So now we're listening, even here in the back row. "For the benefit of those of you who haven't heard," she says, "I'm taking some members of the —other English class over to the college tonight, for a program."

The college in this case is Bascomb College at Bascomb, a thirty-mile trip over an undivided highway.

"We're going to hear a poet read from his works."

Somebody halfway back in the room says, "Is he living?" And we all get a big bang out of this.

But Mrs. Tibbetts just smiles. "Oh, yes," she says, "he's very much alive." She reaches for her attendance book, but this sudden thought strikes her. "Would anyone in this class like to go too?" She looks up at us, and you see she's being fair, and nice.

Since it's only the second period of the day, we're all feeling pretty good. Also it's a Tuesday, a terrible TV night. Everybody in the class puts up their hands. I mean everybody. Even Marty Crawshaw, who's already married. And Pink Hohenfield, who's in class today for the first time this month. I put up mine. I go along.

Mrs. Tibbetts looks amazed. She's never seen this many hands up in our class. She's never seen anybody's hand except Darla's. Her eyes get wide. Mrs. Tibbetts has really great eyes, and she doesn't put anything on them. Which is something Darla could learn from.

But then she sees we have to be putting her on. So she just says, "Anyone who would like to go, be in the parking lot at five-thirty. And eat first. No eating on the bus."

Mrs. Tibbetts can drive the school bus. Whenever she's taking the advanced class anywhere, she can go to the principal for the keys. She can use the bus anytime she wants to, unless the coach needs it.

Then she opens her attendance book, and we tune out. And at five-thirty that night I'm in the parking lot. I have no idea why. Needless to say, I'm the only one here from second period. Marty Crawshaw and Pink Hohenfield will be out on the access highway about now, at 7-Eleven, sitting on their hoods. Darla couldn't make it either. Right offhand I can't think of anybody who wants to ride a school bus thirty miles to see a poet. Including me.

The advanced-English juniors are milling around behind school. I'm still in my car, and it's almost dark, so nobody sees me.

Then Mrs. Tibbetts wheels the school bus in. She's got the amber fogs flashing, and you can see the black letters along the yellow side: CONSOLIDATED SCHOOL DIST. She swings in and hits the brakes, and the doors fly open. The advanced class starts to climb aboard. They're more orderly than us, but they've got their groups too. And a couple of smokers. I'm settling behind my dashboard. The last kid climbs in the bus.

And I seem to be sprinting across the asphalt. I'm on the bus, and the door's hissing shut behind me. When I swing past the driver's seat, I don't look at Mrs. Tibbetts, and she doesn't say anything. I wonder where I'm supposed to sit.

They're still milling around in the aisle, but there are plenty of seats. I find an empty double and settle by the window, pulling my ball cap down in front. It doesn't take us long to get out of town, not this town. When we go past 7-Eleven, I'm way down in the seat with my hand shielding my face on the window side. Right about then, somebody sits down next to me. I flinch.

"Okay?" she says, and I look up, and it's Sharon Willis.

I've got my knee jammed up on the back of the seat ahead of me. I'm bent double, and my hand's over half my face. I'm cool, and it's Sharon Willis.

"Whatever," I say.

"How are you doing, Gene?"

I'm trying to be invisible, and she's calling me by name.

"How do you know me?" I ask her.

She shifts around. "I'm a junior, you're a junior. There

are about fifty-three people in our whole year. How could I not?"

Easy, I think, but don't say it. She's got a notebook on her lap. Everybody seems to, except me.

"Do you have to take notes?" I say, because I feel like I'm getting into something here.

"Not really," Sharon says, "but we have to write about it in class tomorrow. Our impressions."

I'm glad I'm not in her class, because I'm not going to have any impressions. Here I am riding the school bus for the gifted on a Tuesday night with the major goddess girl in school, who knows my name. I'm going to be clean out of impressions because my circuits are starting to fail.

Sharon and I don't turn this into anything. When the bus gets out on the route and Mrs. Tibbetts puts the pedal to the metal, we settle back. Sharon's more or less in with a group of the top girls around school. They're not even cheerleaders. They're a notch above that. The rest of them are up and down the aisle, but she stays put. Michelle Burkholder sticks her face down by Sharon's ear and says, "We've got a seat for you back here. Are you coming?"

But Sharon just says, "I'll stay here with Gene." Like it happens every day.

I look out the window a lot. There's still some patchy snow out in the fields, glowing gray. When we get close to the campus of Bascomb College, I think about staying on the bus.

"Do you want to sit together," Sharon says, "at the program?"

I clear my throat. "You go ahead and sit with your people."

"I sit with them all day long," she says.

At Bascomb College we're up on bleachers in a curtained-off part of the gym. Mrs. Tibbetts says we can sit anywhere we want to, so we get very groupy. I look up, and here I am sitting in these bleachers, like we've gone to State in the play-offs. And I'm just naturally here with Sharon Willis.

We're surrounded mainly by college students. The dean of Bascomb College gets up to tell us about the grant they got to fund their poetry program. Sharon has her notebook flipped open. I figure it's going to be like a class, so I'm tuning out when the poet comes on.

First of all, he's only in his twenties. Not even a beard, and he's not dressed like a poet. In fact, he's dressed like me: Levi's and Levi's jacket. Big heavy-duty belt buckle. Boots, even. A tall guy, about a hundred and eighty pounds. It's weird, like there could be poets around and you wouldn't realize they were there.

But he's got something. Every girl leans forward. College girls, even. Michelle Burkholder bobs up to zap him with her flash camera. He's got a few loose-leaf pages in front of him. But he just begins.

"I've written a poem for my wife," he says, "about her."

Then he tells us this poem. I'm waiting for the rhyme, but it's more like talking, about how he wakes up and the sun's bright on the bed and his wife's still asleep. He watches her.

> *"Alone," he says, "I watch you sleep*
> *Before the morning steals you from me,*
> *Before you stir and disappear*
> *Into the day and leave me here*
> *To turn and kiss the warm space*
> *You leave beside me."*

He looks up and people clap. I thought what he said was a little too personal, but I could follow it. Next to me Sharon's made a note. I look down at her page and see it's just an exclamation point.

He tells us a lot of poems, one after another. I mean, he's got poems on everything. He even has one about his truck:

"Old buck-toothed, slow-to-start mama,"

something like that. People laugh, which I guess is okay. He just keeps at it, and he really jerks us around with his poems. I mean, you don't know what the next one's going to be about. At one point they bring him a glass of water, and he takes a break. But mainly he keeps going.

He ends up with one called "High School."

> *"On my worst nights," he says, "I dream myself back.*
> *I'm the hostage in the row by the radiator, boxed in,*
> *Zit-blasted, and they're popping quizzes at me.*
> *I'm locked in there, looking for words*
> *To talk myself out of being this young*
> *While every girl in the galaxy*
> *Is looking over my head, spotting for a senior.*
> *On my really worst nights it's last period*
> *On a Friday and somebody's fixed the bell*
> *So it won't ring:*
> > *And I've been cut from the team,*
> > *And I've forgotten my locker combination,*
> > *And I'm waiting for something damn it to hell*
> > *To happen."*

And the crowd goes wild, especially the college people. The poet just gives us a wave and walks over to sit down on the bottom bleacher. People swarm down to get him to sign their programs. Except Sharon and I stay where we are.

"That last one wasn't a poem," I tell her. "The others were, but not that one."

She turns to me and smiles. I've never been this close to her before, so I've never seen the color of her eyes.

"Then write a better one," she says.

We sit together again on the ride home.

"No, I'm serious," I say. "You can't write poems about zits and your locker combination."

"Maybe nobody told the poet that," Sharon says.

"So what are you going to write about him tomorrow?" I'm really curious about this.

"I don't know," she says. "I've never heard a poet reading before, not in person. Mrs. Tibbetts shows us tapes of poets reading."

"She doesn't show them to our class."

"What would you do if she did?" Sharon asks.

"Laugh a lot."

The bus settles down on the return trip. I picture all these people going home to do algebra homework, or whatever. When Sharon speaks again, I almost don't hear her.

"You ought to be in this class," she says.

I pull my ball cap down to my nose and lace my fingers behind my head and kick back in the seat. Which should be answer enough.

"You're as bright as anybody on this bus. Brighter than some."

We're rolling on through the night, and I can't believe I'm hearing this. Since it's dark, I take a chance and glance at her. Just the outline of her nose and her chin, maybe a little stubborn.

"How do you know I am?"

"How do you know you're not?" she says. "How will you ever know?"

But then we're quiet because what else is there to say? And anyway, the evening's over. Mrs. Tibbetts is braking for the turnoff, and we're about to get back to normal. And I get this quick flash of tomorrow, in second period with Marty and Pink and Darla, and frankly it doesn't look that good.

RICHARD PECK

After teaching English for several years Richard Peck turned to a career in writing and subsequently has published fifteen young adult novels, three adult novels, two collections of essays, and three poetry anthologies for teenagers: *Sounds and Silences, Pictures That Storm Inside My Head,* and *Mindscapes,* along with several poems and short stories, numerous articles and book reviews, and a picture book for children. Eight of his novels have been named Best Books for Young Adults by the American Library Association.

Among his earliest novels are *Dreamland Lake, Don't Look and It Won't Hurt, Through a Brief Darkness,* and *Representing Superdoll.* Both *Are You in the House Alone?,* a first-person account of the rape of a teenager, and *Father Figure,* the story of an older teenager's relationship with the father who once abandoned him, became made-for-TV movies.

One of his most popular novels is *Secrets of the Shopping Mall,* a zany story in which two runaway teenagers hide out in a shopping mall. Among his most serious books are *Close Enough to Touch,* the story of how a sensitive teenager copes with the death of his girlfriend, and *Remembering the Good Times,* a hard-hitting novel that examines the friendship among three teenagers, one of whom commits suicide.

For younger readers, there are the four supernatural comic-adventure novels featuring Blossom Culp and Alexander Armsworth: *The Ghost Belonged to Me; Ghosts I Have Been; The Dreadful Future of Blossom Culp;* and *Blossom Culp and the Sleep of Death.*

Peck's most recent novels are *Princess Ashley,* a harsh examination of teenage conformity, and *Those Summer Girls I Never Met,* a humorous novel about a teenage brother and sister aboard a European cruise ship with their unconventional grandmother.

Born in Decatur, Illinois, Richard Peck makes his home in New York City and travels seventy thousand miles a year visiting schools and libraries to talk with teenagers and teachers.

There is only one place that offers Phillip an escape when he feels overwhelmed by his obnoxiously brilliant younger sister and his parents' impending divorce. . . .

TREE HOUSE

ALDEN R. CARTER

"We are planning an amicable divorce," Mom said. Dad smiled lovingly at her, as if they hadn't spent the last year at each other's throats.

"Amicable means friendly," Sonia whispered, not looking up from her book.

I glared at her. "I know what it means."

"Mmmm . . ." she said, turning page about six hundred and starting to study a diagram of the human circulatory system. I could make out the title atop the page: *Gray's Anatomy*. Well, at least I could understand the name of this one.

"Better not drop that book on your foot," I said. "You'll be on crutches for a month."

"I'm trying to read, Phil. Please shut up."

Mom paused in the middle of something about her and Dad being mature people who could rise above their differences long enough to "deconstruct" their marriage. She stared at me icily. Dad cleared his throat and said, "Phillip, I would think you'd be interested in hearing about something that is going to deeply affect your life."

"*To deeply affect* is a split infinitive, Dad," Sonia said, and turned a page.

Dad gazed at her admiringly, then turned to Mom. "She never misses a trick-does she? Go on, dear."

After another two minutes of congratulating herself and Dad on their maturity, Mom got down to it. "Now the most difficult matter is how we are going to divide the family. We talked to Richard this morning before he left for the chess tournament. He's decided to graduate a year early and move to Minneapolis with your father as soon as school's out. That way he'll be able to take some classes at the U this summer and—"

"But, Mom," I blurted. "How about football and basketball? I mean, heck, the teams are going to fall—"

"Moseburg High will have to take care of itself without Richard. Now, since he is going to Minneapolis, you'll be staying here with me. That leaves Sonia. What do you want to do, dear?"

Sonia closed her book, keeping her place with a skinny forefinger. She gazed at them levelly. "According to virtually all psychological theories, roots are particularly important to preadolescents. I am eleven and prepubescent, hence preadolescent. Therefore, it will be healthier for me to remain here. Besides, I'll be going to the U in a few years, anyway." She opened her book, and they smiled at her. I felt my hands twitch with the desire to throttle her.

Dad got up. "Well, that about does it." He glanced at his watch. "I'll come down on Wednesday to pick up the rest of my stuff."

"Stuff," Sonia murmured, "from the Old French verb *estoffer*, to equip, stock, by way of the Middle French and the Middle English, becoming a noun in the fifteenth century."

I lunged for her with a scream, the sharp edge of my hand slashing at her windpipe. "So, we'll see you kids soon," Dad said. "Walk me to the car, Margaret."

"Good-bye, Dad," Sonia said, and turned a page.

"Ya," I said, "so long."

Rick—Richard, that is—flopped on the chair by my littered desk. "So, did the folks get everything worked out?"

He picked up the three hard-rubber balls on my desk and started juggling them.

"When did you learn how to do that?"

"Just now. Watching you try last night must have gotten me thinking about it. It doesn't seem so tough. You got another ball? I want to see if I can do four."

Four! I'd been trying for weeks to get the hang of three. "No."

He caught the balls in one hand. "Oh, well. So, how'd the meeting go?"

"Okay. But, Rick, do you have to leave? I mean, all the teams are really going to miss—"

"Aw, I'm bored with that stuff. Let some other guys have a chance to play. Besides, I don't want to play college ball. I'm going to try drama, chorus, and some other stuff I haven't had time for."

"Uh, do you know that the word *stuff* comes—"

"From the Old French verb *estoffer*? Ya, I knew that. Hey, it's still light. Want to go throw a ball around?"

"No, thanks."

"Suit yourself. But you ought to work on that gut of yours." He breezed out. Sonia was coming up the stairs, her nose still stuck in *Gray's Anatomy*. "Hey, Sone," Rick yelled. "Aren't you done with that yet? God, you've been at it almost a week. It only took me three days."

"Patience, eldest brother. It takes ordinary mortals longer to scale the Olympian heights."

"Want to go play a duet? I'm out of practice."

Sonia snapped the book shut. "Sure."

A couple of minutes later I heard them rip into some four-handed ragtime on the baby grand in the living room. Ordinary mortals, my butt. I was the only ordinary, common, average, everyday person in this house. I got off the bed, closed the door to a crack, then dug a Snickers bar out of my hiding place behind the bookshelf. I hesitated a second before unwrapping it; I was already one over my daily limit and I'd need at least two more to get through the evening. But, hell, it had been a trying day. Tomorrow I'd do better. And maybe if I made this one last, I'd only need one tonight. I sat by the window, munching slowly and watching the last of the early-spring afternoon.

Downstairs Rick and Sonia wrapped up their ragtime performance with a fit of laughter. Maybe I should go down and try to join them. I'd never made it much beyond "Chopsticks" in two years of lessons, but maybe they wouldn't mind if I tapped my foot quietly. Sonia started playing the Chopin sonata she'd been practicing for the competition. They'd be serious now, Rick listening carefully for the slightest flaw in her playing. Fat, dumb Phillip would be a distraction, tapping foot or not.

I looked down at the empty candy wrapper in my fingers; somehow the Snickers had disappeared. I rose and got a Milky Way from behind my books. To hell with my genius brother and sister. And my mature, brilliant parents. Come to think of it, to hell with everything.

Right then I decided to build a tree house. I'd build it so high that no one could see me among the leaves. And once I was up there with the wind and the clouds and the birds, I'd pull up the ladder behind me. Now all I needed was the damn tree.

All the rest of that week I doodled with plans for my tree house. It was going to be my secret, but as usual, I screwed that up too. The day after I flunked a unit exam in geometry, Mr. Bernstein caught me fiddling with my plans rather than doing my homework. He gave me the disgusted look that most of the teachers give the great Rick O'Dell's younger brother.

Bernstein called Mom that night. Mom listened, thanked him, described the situation to Sonia as if I wasn't there, then turned to me with a slight variation of that disgusted look. She devoted the next hour to giving me the usual going-over with the verbal wire brush. She's always more confused than angry, and I guess she figures that if she scrubs hard enough she may finally uncover the reason why two brilliant, mature parents with two brilliant, perfect kids somehow blew it on the middle one.

Sonia's book must have been particularly fascinating that evening, because she didn't contribute her usual theories about switched babies on the maternity ward, vitamin deficiencies in infancy, or her recent favorite: "middle-child syndrome." She only sniggered now and then. The third time she let out a "Ha," I whipped the blowpipe from my back pocket and stuck a poison dart right between her eyes. She lurched forward, her eyes already glassy, and pitched across . . . "I don't know, Phillip," Mom said. "I think it's about time we started thinking about a private military academy for you. Somehow, you're going to have to learn the discipline to . . ." I stared at her. Her mouth was still moving, but I didn't hear the words. Military academy? Discipline? I dived through the window, my eyes shut tight against the spray of shattering glass. She paused. "Anyway, I'm going to talk to your father about it when he comes to pick up Rick this weekend."

"He'll look funny in uniform," Sonia said. "Philly is getting positively corpulent these days." She looked at me. *"Corpulent* means fat. Interesting synonyms are *swag bellied* and *pussle gutted."*

This time I really was going to kill her. Mom said, "Oh, calm down, Phillip. Your sister is just trying to help. Now, stand up and let me look at you. Have you been sneaking candy bars again?"

Rat poison, I thought. Hell, they're both so busy reading at supper that they'll never notice a few little crunchies in their salads.

As it turned out, it was a good thing that I didn't poison them. Sonia won a scholarship to study piano in Boston that summer. Mom decided to go along: "I can do some interesting research at the Harvard Medical School. You can spend the summer with your father and Richard." But Dad and Rick had already made plans to spend June rock climbing in Colorado, and pussle-gutted Phil wasn't exactly rock-climbing material. "Well," Sonia said, "there's always Great-Uncle Sean."

Great-Uncle Sean lived in a cabin twenty miles out of town. I suppose you imagine that the ancient O'Dell spent his time translating Sanskrit and meditating on the subtle workings of the cosmos. Wrong. Great-Uncle Sean didn't do much of anything, and—as far as anyone could recall—never had. Somewhere way back he'd lucked into some money, and ever since he'd lived on the interest, his garden, and whiskey. He didn't own a TV and he didn't read. He just sat on the front porch with the radio playing and a bottle close enough at hand so that periodic sips kept the world in a sort of constant haze.

He didn't object when I moved in. Hell, I don't think he really noticed me after the first couple of days. I cleaned out a storeroom and made a bed. Then I relaxed. Completely. I deserved it after busting my tail for six weeks to get my grades up to passing, so I wouldn't get sent to a military academy. And I'd come prepared. I'd secretly replaced all the enlightening books Mom had packed—with Sonia's suggestions—with a gross of candy bars and a dozen sword and sorcery books. Add the case of Pepsi they'd grudgingly let me haul along, and I was set for at least a couple of weeks.

My peace only lasted three days. I heard loud knocking on the screen door and opened it to find this skinny blond girl about my age, eyeing me with laser-beam blue eyes. "Uh, ya. Can I help you?"

"I'm Morgan from down the road. Mom sent a pie for Mr. O'Dell." She shoved it at me.

"Thanks. I'm his nephew, Phil. Great-nephew."

"Ya, we heard you were here. You've got chocolate on your face."

"Oh, sorry." I rubbed at the corners of my mouth.

"Nothing to be sorry about. Just a fact. So, do you sit in the house all the time, or do you go for walks and stuff?"

"I, uh, mostly stay around here."

"You ought to get out; the exercise would do you good. Exercise is good for everybody."

"Thanks for telling me."

"You're welcome. See you around."

Another one! Just once in my life I'd like to meet someone who didn't inform me what a slob I was thirty seconds after meeting me. I went back to my room and slam-dunked a Milky Way. Damn it, one of these days, I was going to build that tree house. I'd sit up there and drop rocks and candy wrappers on everybody who passed.

The next afternoon I saw her turn in at the gate with a paper sack of something. I wasn't about to risk any more judgments on the cleanliness of my face or the girth of my gut. (Well, she hadn't exactly mentioned the latter, but I knew what she'd meant by that crack about exercise.) I grabbed my book, shoved an emergency candy bar in my pocket, and beat it out the back door.

That's how I got started going to the hill behind the cabin every afternoon. I'd read and munch in the shade of the biggest tree for miles around. It was an elm, I think, very straight for a long way up, branching out only when it was already high above all the other trees. I was no woodsman, but I knew the tree was dying, its crown of leaves thin like an old man's hair. And it groaned every once in a while, a sound so faint that I wasn't sure if I heard it with my ears or only sensed it when the great trunk swayed ever so slightly against my back.

I'd imagined needing nothing but my stack of fantasy novels and my supply of candy bars and Pepsi. But after a week they let me down. I was *bored.* Worse, I missed my family. Ridiculous. After all the crap I'd put up with, couldn't I forget them for a while?

I'm not a brooder. I mean, I really don't think I spend a whole lot of time feeling sorry for myself. But I sat a whole afternoon with a perfectly good fantasy novel unread at my side while I tried to figure out where I fit in life. Fate or a vitamin deficiency or a careless nurse or something had stuck me in a situation where I couldn't possibly compete. Not that I couldn't get decent grades if I tried; or even learn to juggle if I kept at it. But I could never really compete with Sonia or Rick or Mom or Dad. They just weren't ordinary people. And I was.

For about the two hundredth time I caught myself staring up at the high crown of the elm. Just once in my life . . .

The next day I started tearing boards off a tumbledown shack out behind the cabin. Great-Uncle Sean caned his way over to watch me for a few minutes. He gave me a toothless grin. "Do it faster with kerosene and a match, boy."

I wiped sweat from my face. "I'm going to build something with the boards and spikes, Uncle Sean."

"Well, the exercise'll do ya good, boy. You got kind of a gut on you." He started back for the porch and the whiskey bottle.

It took me three days and about a dozen gallons of sweat to make a stack of more or less sound boards in the clearing below the big elm. I'd already begun to have some serious doubts about my sanity, but I kept thinking: just once in your life . . .

Lucky I didn't think any further than that, because the whole thing got one hell of a lot harder than I'd ever imagined. The idea of a ladder that I could pull up behind me didn't work. It'd have to be a permanent ladder—or at least as permanent as rickety boards and rusty spikes could make it. I nailed steps as high as I could reach, then looped a rope around my waist and the trunk of the tree. I edged the rope up until I was level with the top rung, then pulled up the next board with a second rope.

I dropped a lot of boards and nails the first couple of days, but slowly my ladder rose. By the fourth day I was halfway to the fork where I'd build my tree house. I had a system by then. After I nailed each board in place, I'd slip the loop over my shoulders, climb down, tie the next board to my hauling rope, take a slug of Pepsi or a bite of candy bar, then climb back up. I also had two black-and-blue fingernails from poorly aimed hammer blows, a considerably increased fear of heights, and the definite opinion that I was completely out of my mind.

"How you doing up there?"

I looked down, the ground starting to spin then rush toward me in a flash of vertigo. Morgan was aiming her laser eyes at me from the foot of the tree. "Right now I'm about to throw up. Better get away from there."

She moved back a few paces and watched as I made my shaky way down to earth. "I brought you some lemonade."

"Why?"

"I thought you'd be thirsty. Why else?"

"How'd you know I was here?"

"Oh, I saw you here yesterday. Just followed the sound of the hammer. I got here just when you hit your thumb. You know a lot of words. What's a pussle gut?"

"A fat person." I hesitated for a second, then accepted the tin cup of lemonade she was offering me. "Thanks."

"Mind if I ask why you're doing this?"

"You wouldn't understand."

"Try me." She sat down at the foot of the ladder, scratched a mosquito bite on a bare ankle, then stared at me expectantly.

"It's kind of personal," I said.

"I don't mind."

Well, suppose I do! I looked down at the lemonade. "Just once in my life I want to be higher than anyone else."

"Wouldn't that take a plane or a space shuttle or something?"

"Well, I don't have one of those! All I've got is this stupid tree and some old boards. But it's kind of a metaphor, you see. Uh, a metaphor is kind of a comparison."

"I know what a metaphor is. And a simile too."

I groaned. "Oh, God, another bright one."

"I'm not that smart. We just had it in English this spring, that's all. English is my best subject. What's yours?"

I gazed at her. "Nothing. I'm not good at anything. Now excuse me, I've got to get back to work."

She shrugged and stood. "Want some help? I could tie the boards to the rope for you, so you wouldn't have to come down every time."

"No! I mean, uh . . . Hey, look, I've got to do this myself. Thanks for the lemonade. I'll see you."

"Okay. Be careful."

The board broke under my foot and I fell, my fingernails clawing for the fork just inches out of my reach. My weight tore the next rung from the trunk. I was going to slide through the loop of my safety rope and somersault backward away from the trunk. Two or three seconds of tumbling and screaming, then splat. Somehow I managed to catch the loop around my shoulders. I was leaning back as far as I could, my hands gripping either side of the rope and my legs curled as far around the trunk as they could reach.

"Hold on!" Morgan came bounding across the clearing. She got to the foot of the tree. "Are you okay?" I managed to nod. "Just hold on. I'll run get my dad."

"No! Don't you move!" I took a deep breath and pulled my body in toward the trunk. Grunting, I wiggled the loop down an eighth of an inch at a time until it was across the small of my back. I felt for the first solid rung, found it, and started down.

The pain didn't hit until I finally dropped to the ground

and collapsed at the foot of the tree. Both my hands had rope burns across the palms, and my legs, arms, and chest had been scraped raw in the few desperate seconds I'd fought for a hold on the bark.

"You've got blood on your forehead," Morgan said quietly.

I felt. Just a little bit. "Ya, but I don't have any chocolate on my face."

"You've got to stop this," she said. "It's dangerous. I'm worried all the time about you." She paused, then suddenly her voice got almost shrill. "Look, why don't you just come for a walk with me? Or we could go swimming or horseback riding. I've been waiting almost two weeks for you to come around."

I stared at her. The laser look was gone from her eyes. She looked almost scared. I closed my eyes. "I've got to replace some boards and put extra nails in all of them. It'll be safe."

"Why do you have to do this? Hey, I'll take you to a fire tower. You can climb that and be higher than anybody. I'll stay on the ground if you want to be alone. But forget this. It's crazy." I shrugged. "Look, just forget it for today, okay? Let me take you home and fix those scrapes."

I went with her. I ate supper at her house, and we went for a long walk in the evening. "What's this business about waiting for me to come around?" I asked.

"Well, I just figured you would. I mean, you're all alone with Mr. O'Dell, and I figured you'd come down to see whether the neighbor girl might be a little bored and lonely too."

"You can't be that bored and lonely."

"Try me."

When we said good-night on her porch, she said, "Why don't we go horseback riding tomorrow? I've got Big Ben and my brother won't mind if you ride Soupy."

I hesitated. "Maybe the day after tomorrow."

"You're not going back there, are you?"

"I still want to be higher than anyone else just one time. And don't lurk in the bushes tomorrow. I'll be all right."

She didn't say anything for a long moment. "Well, if you break your darn neck it'll be your funeral!"

I laughed, the sound unfamiliar in my ears. "Well, I think that's usually how it works." She shut the door in my face.

I was sore from my toes to my hairline. But I didn't care; I could make it. I started in early morning, driving extra nails in every rung. Several boards were on the point of breaking. I replaced them, amazed that a day before I hadn't noticed. By late afternoon I'd reached the broken boards high on the trunk. I pulled up a board, nailed it in place, climbed down, tied the next one to the rope, and started up again. By then I knew that I'd never build the tree house, never hide among the leaves where no one could see me. All I wanted was a ladder reaching up out of the forest.

I nailed the last board in place, retied the safety rope around the biggest limb, and hoisted myself into the fork. I stood there, looking over the woods and the farmland into the late-afternoon distance. Far away I could see a twisting line of trees tracing a river flowing southwest toward the Mississippi. Somewhere beyond the haze on the horizon the waters met to flow south across the heart of the continent.

When the light started to fade, I untied the safety rope and climbed down. I walked home in the dusk. Morgan was sitting on the fence near the front gate. "How was it?" she asked.

"Nice. Everything was in its place."

"Did everything look small?"

"No, the world looked real big. Big enough for all sorts of people."

She thought about that a second. "Well, I guess that's

good. Here, I made chocolate-chip cookies." She held out a napkin holding three large cookies.

I took one and handed the others back. "Just one. I'm starting a diet."

"Horseback riding bounces the weight off. That's why I'm so thin. . . . So, is that it, or are you going up there again?"

"No, once was enough." I took a chance and put my arm around her. She didn't object but slid close. "It was nice," I said, "but kind of lonely too."

ALDEN R. CARTER

Alden Carter is the author of four books for young adults—all of which have been named Best Books for Young Adults by the American Library Association—and a number of nonfiction books for young readers. Among his nonfiction works are *Supercomputers; Modern Electronics; Radio: From Marconi to the Space Age;* books about Illinois and Modern China; and a series about the American Revolution, including *Colonies in Revolt, The Darkest Hours, At the Forge of Liberty,* and *Birth of the Republic.* His most recent nonfiction book is *The Shoshoni.*

Growing Season, Carter's first YA novel, describes the experiences of Rick Simons, a city boy who is forced to change his lifestyle and his attitudes when his parents buy a farm. In *Wart, Son of Toad,* the son of an unpopular science teacher clashes with his father at home as both father and son try to deal with the loss of Steve's mother and sister in a car accident.

Dealing with death is explored even more deeply in *Sheila's Dying,* where Jerry Kinkaid discovers that the girl he is about to break up with is dying of cancer. On a school committee Jerry battles with Bonnie Harper—the Tiger Shark—but Bonnie is willing to help Sheila face her inevitable end.

In his most recent novel Carter describes the experiences of an angry teenager who is the mastermind of a car radio theft ring. Sent away from his alcoholic mother to live with relatives on a farm in upstate Wisconsin, Carl Staggers slowly and reluctantly discovers significant things about life and about himself in *Up Country.*

Before becoming a writer Al Carter was an officer in the U.S. Navy, an independent land developer, and a teacher of high school English and journalism. He lives with his social worker wife and two children in Marshfield, Wisconsin.

The wedding of Rusty's sister marks the beginning of a new life for her. It is also a turning point for Rusty and Jolene. . . .

AFTER THE WEDDING

OUIDA SEBESTYEN

When Rusty went back to Galenburg in June for his sister's wedding, he took Jolene with him. So he sprung her on his mother and relatives at the worst possible time. But like he told them, everybody for their own thing.

The ceremony was about what Jolene had expected.

After the reception in the church basement, the bride and groom drove off on their honeymoon, trailing a string of tin cans. A little later, as Jolene tried to fit in by helping to wash punch cups, she discovered, with a small rush of panic, that Rusty had driven away too.

For an awful forty minutes she waited for him to come back and rescue her. When the preacher's wife came by to add a final cup to the mess, Rusty's mother had to say, "Oh, I'm sorry—this is my son's friend, Miss—uh—" and couldn't remember her name.

After that Jolene limped off in her high heels toward the only place in town she knew. Rusty's car was parked beside the ugly neat house where his mother lived. Her front door was open, in little-town trust. Jolene drew a long angry breath at the door of the guest room. Rusty was sprawled on the bed in his shorts, with a bag of potato chips on his chest. The dark suit he had rented for the wedding lay in a heap on the floor.

"Why'd you leave?" she demanded. "That wasn't fair!"

The glare of late sunlight on his perfect body deflected her anger. "I felt like a freak. Nobody knew what to say to me. And you were back here sleeping."

She feasted on his face as he sat up. Suddenly she ached for him to reach out and beckon her close. But he asked, "Is my mom still at the church?"

"She and your Aunt Elna are packing wedding presents. Your mother's going to store the loot till the—the newly-weds get their honeymooning over." She hated that her tongue had tripped on those words. "It wouldn't have hurt you to stay and sweep rice or something, yourself—and back me up."

Rusty's long heavy-lidded gaze made her toes tingle. He was going to hold out his hand and say, *Then maybe we have time for a quick honeymoon of our own.*

But he said, stretching, "Probably the most beautiful happy memory I'll ever have in my life is the surprise on your face every time I disappoint you." He stood up. "I wish you didn't trust me, hon."

She went to him. As she threw her arms around him, he braced himself to block her. "Rusty, this has been a hard, crazy day to get through, and I'm new at this. Why didn't you stay with me?"

"Hon, I warned you right at the beginning I wasn't much for weddings."

She gave him a little push and whispered, "Don't get up. I'll be better than this morning." She lifted her face uncertainly to kiss the hard slope of his collarbone. "With your mother in there cooking breakfast, I just—it was like—we were doing it to spite her."

He smiled and backed far enough away to undo the buttons at her throat. A silky languor melted her muscles. She hurried to help him. Even after five months she was still hesitant about initiating until she was sure of his response.

But he said, "Hon, how about you take off this sweet little high school graduation dress and put on something that's you, because we're on our way to the Red Mill, where the elite meet to eat, as my daddy used to say when he pushed a broom there."

"But, Rusty—"

He backed another step away, still smiling. "I got to get a shower, hon."

"But couldn't we—"

"Hon, I'm hot and sweaty."

"Well, join the club," she said.

He chucked her under the chin. "You sound like a kid, sometimes."

"I am a kid," she reminded him.

He went down the hall to the bathroom. The shower started. She turned slowly in the hot cramped room, trying to imagine Rusty sleeping there alone, sixteen and full of dreams. Yellowed newspaper clippings and pictures of him were still tacked to the wall. In every shot some giggling cheerleader was draped over his shoulder pads. Even then.

Frowning, she changed into her best jeans and a little top, and raked her hair into shape. She smoothed the bedspread. No point in it looking like they'd been there when they hadn't.

She took Rusty's clean underwear from the suitcase and went to the bathroom door. It was locked. She hung his shorts on the doorknob, feeling rebuffed. He had always told her to barge right in. Something was different about him that she couldn't find a word for.

She took the potato chips to the kitchen. Dirty dishes filled the sink. She put away a few things, to sort of make it up to the woman she'd spoiled a wedding for. Abruptly she began to clean the room in earnest.

Thinking back, she'd spent a lot of her life in other people's kitchens. Her stepmother's in the summers. Recently, the place her mother's friend had invited them to share with him. Until he moved on, and her mother followed. She had lived with her brother and his wife the next year, so she wouldn't have to graduate at a new high school. But that had been a disaster.

She had been running, literally, from their worst argument yet, one rainy night, when she collided with Rusty in front of the Suds and Duds, and his basket of clean clothes flipped into the gutter. They began to talk while he did his wash again, and then went on talking, long after the clothes were dry and the rain had stopped.

So he came into her life. Like some new wonder drug that might deaden her pain. Slowly their talks over pizza got longer and longer, and their drives in his car went farther and farther until she had let him into her past and her body, and he had let her come into another unfamiliar kitchen and clear out the gray things growing in his refrigerator.

She had been glad to have a place to stay, and more or less relieved that the virginity stuff was over and out of the way. He talked about the girls before her in a distant matter-of-fact way as if it hadn't occurred to him that she was his latest. He'd had a lot, so she guessed she was in the hands of an expert.

The shower stopped. He came down the hall wearing the sharp clothes he had bought before he lost his job. He led her away from his mother's greasy sink, saying, "No, little Cinderelbow-Grease." He smelled beautiful. But the strange uneasy battle was still going on in his face.

The Red Mill's air conditioning met them at the door like a cold front. Heads turned as they were led to a corner table. A tired waitress brought them iced tea and a bowl of crackers. When she had gone, Rusty said, "Nice, huh? Would you like this—living in Galenburg?"

She looked around. "No. I'd feel them breathing down my neck."

"I lived some good years here," he said. "They called me poetry in motion, back then." He laboriously read his menu, following his finger, while she went softhearted, watching. "I'd like it back here. Big fish in a little pond again."

"What kind of a job could you find here?" she asked.

He ate a cracker. "Who's begging me to come work for them in Dallas?"

She started to say, *What about me?* Because it was her piddling little discount-store job that was paying their rent. But the waitress came back.

Rusty ordered for them both, asking curtly, "Okay?" Jolene nodded, not sure how much money he could spend. Maybe he'd asked his mother for a handout. Maybe they should have invited her to come too.

"Your dad worked here?" she asked.

"Yeah, this was his night job. He worked days at the packing plant. And never could hang on to his money long enough to pay his debts."

"You don't talk about him."

"What's to say?" He glanced around at the empty tables nearest them. "He couldn't stop putting me down, so I left as soon as I could. And then last February he died."

She studied his face in amazement. "I remember when you were out of town four days last February. That next week I moved in. Why didn't you tell me?"

He shrugged and made two overlapping condensation rings with the bottom of his glass.

She said, "First you wanted out of this little town, and now you want to come back. Which is it?"

Canned music began to seep from some hidden vent. "It's different with him gone." The music nearly swallowed up his voice. "My mom had all those months while he was dying, to make the arrangements. So, the day after the funeral she took me back to the cemetery and there was this honking big tombstone already set up. With my name on it."

"What? Oh—because you were named for your dad."

"I stood there looking at my name, and I realized I'd

been trying so hard not to turn out like him that I hadn't turned out like me either. The shady jobs and the women and leaving here—everything was just to prove I didn't have to be a zero like him."

Jolene reached across the table and made his hand stop forming the strangling design of circles.

He said, "So I thought, okay, that's me dead down there too—I don't have to be who I was anymore."

Her face grew soft. "That's what you meant, back in Dallas when we drove around nearly all one night in the sleet. You said, 'I've got to get a job and settle down—I've been going downhill without brakes.' Remember? That was the night you asked, would I move in."

He slid his hand out from under hers and leaned back, avoiding her eyes. "I remember you sitting there by me, all clean and scared and innocent and wishing you weren't, and me wanting you because you were. You were the first really good, steadfast thing that ever came into my life."

She whispered shyly, "I was? I just figured you thought, Hey, after all the rest of them, why be choosy? So you added me." She saw him stiffen. "I mean—"

The waitress set their plates before them. They waited rigid until she had gone.

"I was wondering when you'd start on that again," he said, stabbing his steak. "Is that how you saw me—a roller coaster giving free rides? Why were you standing in line, if you didn't want to get on?"

She stared at her blurring plate. "I guess—I hoped maybe I was standing in line for the Tunnel of Love, or something." She tried to laugh and shrug. "I didn't want it to be just charity—somebody giving me a place to stay. I—I wanted to pay my way."

He stopped with the fork halfway to his mouth. "Was that what you called it? Is that all it was for you?"

"No." She gasped, chilled by the sudden turn they had taken. "At first I, like, wanted to know what the big deal was, that everybody knew about but me." She saw to her horror that his eyes went harder. "And—and I loved it, Rusty, honestly. The things you taught me—" She made her wobbly fingers push butter into the slit of her baked potato. "But when you'd open up your arms and take me in, and I could cry or talk stupid or anything, and you'd let me —I wanted to repay you with whatever you liked."

"You got a class performance out of me, didn't you? If it wasn't what you wanted, why didn't you say?"

She looked around as he had, self-conscious, and let her voice drop even lower beneath the music. "I guess—I thought that's what people did when they wanted to be close. I mean, so close that you can make new life, just like God. I guess I thought if somebody wanted to do that with me—"

He said, "Can't you stop saying 'somebody,' like I happened to be the first person who walked by?"

"Please don't yell in front of all these people," she whispered through her pain. "You were the first person. But I wanted it to be with you."

He said louder, "Jolene, you're the one I brought home to Galenburg, for God's sake. You've still got my teethmarks on your shoulder from this morning. What do I have to keep proving?"

She put her hand over her trembling mouth. "I don't know. I just—this is not how I thought it would be."

"Well, this is how it is!" He stood up. "And I'm what you're stuck with." All the faces swiveled to stare. The jaws stopped chewing. Rusty walked out, slinging a twenty-dollar bill at the cash register.

Jolene rose and balanced on her rubbery legs. She would have to follow him. The eyes swept back to her, burning her skin. Deliberately she lifted the steak and potato from her plate, added a roll, gathered it all in a napkin, and plopped it into her purse. She drained her iced-tea glass and went out past the faces, with her chin so high she only saw the ceiling.

Rusty was standing by the car. When he saw her he got in. She did the same. The sun had set and the day had gone blue while they were inside. They drove through the aching color, sitting far apart.

When he stopped in his mother's driveway, neither of them moved to get out.

Finally he gestured. "I'm sorry I didn't let you eat."

She stared straight ahead, resenting his recovered, normal-sounding voice.

"I meant it to be nice," he said. "To show you I think you've carried the visit off, really good." He gestured again, toward the house.

She brought the potato out of her purse and divided it by running her thumbnail through the skin. "Forgot the salt," she said, handing him a half.

"You what?" he exploded. "If I'd seen you doing this I'd of dragged you out by the hair."

"You would've had to do it with a fork stuck in your ribs." She fished out the steak and put it inside the roll. Again she halved with him, and they ate in an eerie silence.

He stared at the shadowy house. "I don't think she's home." He got cigarettes from the glove compartment.

"Don't," she said. "You promised."

"I unpromise." He looked at her through the first drift of smoke. "My mom used to say that to my daddy. All the time. Only she said, 'Don't—I want you around for a long, long time.'"

She picked crumbs from her lap. "It didn't help, did it?"

"No. It has to come from inside you, and he wasn't willing to change."

She got out of the car, feeling bruised. He followed her into the house. When she came from washing her greasy hands, he was standing at the foot of the old iron bed in the guest room. A note was propped against the pillows. She took it to the window. It said, *I came home to make you supper, but you wasn't here. Elna and I going for a hamburger then choir practice.*

He said softly, "After the wedding I was lying here, thinking what it would be like to be a father. With a family. A wife. Giving my daughter away in marriage."

"And it scared you?" she asked. He was silent, staring at the bed. "Didn't it ever bother you, all those years, that you might make babies when all you meant to do was make out?"

He went into the kitchen. She followed and stood at the door, uncertain, as he took a carton of milk from the refrigerator and drank from it.

He said, "We're not going to work out, hon."

"Don't say that," she whispered. "It's been a long hard day—let's don't hurt each other anymore."

"You were in such a hurry. You weren't ready, just needy. I should have told you, *No, wait, damn it—hold out.*"

She stepped backward as if a closet had opened and spilled out all her hidden-away feelings. She twitched her mouth into a fake smile. "So it's all my fault. What else is new?"

"It's not your fault you're young, hon." He started to touch her hair and found he was still holding the milk. She took it from his tense hand and put it up.

She slammed the refrigerator door. "So you're five years ahead of me and perfect. Never mind you don't have a job and can just barely read and never got along with your dad —I'm the dumb kid that can't handle living with you!"

He took her shoulders wearily. "You don't know what I'm saying, do you? I'm trying to give you a chance to escape, for God's sake. Honey, you're cutting off all your options. I looked at you there in church this afternoon, your face, the way you held your head. My God, Jolene, you're bright, you're brave, you ought to be fighting your way into college and planning a life for yourself."

She broke free and stumbled through the dimness to the guest room.

Behind her Rusty said, "You have too much promise, hon. And I don't have enough. That's all I'm trying to say."

She turned on him. "What happened today? Something's changed you. You want me out of your life, don't you? You're ready for something better than us."

He found her face and pressed it hard between his hands. "You deserve something better than me."

She jerked away. "I don't believe this is happening. You're saying all this because of something your mother said. Or you ran into an old flame today. Or maybe it was just seeing me with your family, at a wedding, in your little town I don't like—"

"Hon, shut up," he ordered. "Maybe it was. But maybe it's the most loving thing I've ever tried to do—letting you go."

"No!" she insisted. She threw herself into his arms. "Don't say that. Come to bed. We're tired. I'm trying to understand."

He turned away and walked into the hot dim room.

She peeled off her jeans and top and stood by the bed. "Honey, don't," he said.

"Please. Rusty. You can't just say, *We're through, it's over*— and make me disappear."

"Honey, don't beg. You don't want to remember you begged. Where's your pride?"

She felt piercing envy for his sister in her nice motel room, safe inside the rules—good bad, black white, yes no —that she didn't have. "Gone," she told him.

"Honey. Find it."

She crumpled to the bed and jerked the sheet to her chin. "How? God—somebody—what am I supposed to do with the rest of my life?"

He came and sat beside her. Their groping fingers interlaced. He said, "I wanted what you could give me. And you wanted what I could give you. That's just all it was, hon."

She clung to his hand, knowing they were joined in the most passionate moment they had known together.

He said, "I'll drive you to Dallas. Tonight. Now. But I'll come on back here and do some job hunting. You can stay at my place till you find a room. A girlfriend to stay with, or something. Okay?"

She began to cry in desolation. But she nodded.

She realized she hadn't asked what he would do with the rest of his life, without her.

When she could make her constricted throat work, she said, "How will I ever know if you're tired of me and lying about it, or if you really care about me more than anybody?"

She felt him shrug. "You won't know, hon." He stood up. His hand, locked to hers, forced her to stand, too, and then he slid his fingers free.

OUIDA SEBESTYEN

After more than twenty frustrating years of writing and not selling dozens of stories, four novels, and a play, Ouida Sebestyen found a publisher for *Words by Heart*. Named one of the year's Ten Best by *Learning Magazine* and a Best Book of 1979 by both *The New York Times* and the American Library Association, it deals with the hope as well as the agony of being a young black girl in 1910 Texas. *Words by Heart* also received the 1982 American Book Award for best children's fiction in paperback and was made into a television movie which received two Emmy nominations.

Like *Words by Heart* much of Sebestyen's writing reflects her own North Texas heritage and early life in the small town of Vernon. She now lives in Boulder, Colorado, the setting of her third novel.

Once started, Sebestyen's success continued with *Far from Home*, the touching story of a thirteen-year-old boy's struggle to care for his great-grandmother after his mother dies. It was named an ALA Best Book for Young Adults in 1980 and received the Zilveren Griffel (Silver Pencil) Award from Holland as the best translated children's book of 1984.

IOU's—another ALA Best Book of the Year—is also about love and caring within a splintered family as thirteen-year-old Stowe Garrett and his mother work to make a life together.

Unable and unwilling to allow the questions raised at the end of *Words by Heart* to go unexplored, Ouida Sebestyen, in *On Fire*, follows the Haney family into Colorado as they try to escape the consequences of Tater Haney's violent act.

Her most recent novel is *The Girl in the Box*, an emotionally draining story about a kidnapped high school student who keeps herself occupied in a dark cellar by typing stories, letters, and notes which lead to self-understanding and human dignity under incredible stress.

Who promises the most for Marybeth's future? Alan is charming, informed, and persuasive. John is witty, polite, and thoughtful. Both have professional ambitions. Then there is Sunny. . . .

SUNNY DAYS AND
SUNNY NIGHTS

M. E. KERR

"Females prefer chunky peanut butter over smooth, forty-three percent to thirty-nine percent," Alan announces at dinner, "while men show an equal liking for both."

My father likes this conversation. I think even my mother does, since she is telling Alan enthusiastically that she likes smooth. Moments before she confided that she preferred red wine, after Alan said that women are more likely than men to order wine in a restaurant, and a majority prefer white.

Alan is filled with this sort of information.

He wants to become an advertising man. He is enrolled in journalism school for that purpose. He's my height, when I'm wearing heels, has brown hair and brown eyes, lives not far away in Salisbury, North Carolina. We go out mostly to hit movies, and he explains their appeal afterward, over coffee at a campus hangout. He prides himself on knowing what sells, and why, and what motivates people. Sometimes when we kiss, I imagine he knows exactly what percentage of females close their eyes, and if more males keep theirs open.

I long for Sunny.

Whenever Sunny came to dinner, my father winced at his surfers' talk and asked him pointedly if he had a "real" name. Harold, Sunny would tell him, and my father would say, that's not such a bad name, you can make Harry out of that, and once he came right out and told Sunny that a man shouldn't have a boy's name.

When Sunny finally joined the Navy my father said, well, they'll make a man out of him.

He's a man, I said, believe me. Look at him and tell me he's not a man. Because Sunny towers over my father, has a Rambo build, and a walk, smile, and way about him that oozes confidence. Hair the color of the sun, deep blue eyes. Always tanned, always. Even my mother murmured, oh, he's a man, Sunny is.

But my father shook his head and said, I don't mean *that*. I mean the boy has a boy's ambition, you only have to listen to all that talk about the big waves, the surf, the beach— either he's a boy or a fish, but he's not someone with his eye on the future. He's not someone thinking about a profession!

One of the hard things about going to college in your hometown is that your family meets your dates right away. If I had the good luck to live in a dorm, my father couldn't cross-examine all of them while I finish dressing and get myself downstairs. Even when I'm ready ahead of time, he manages to squeeze out as much information about them as he can, once he's shaken hands with one, and while we're standing there looking for our exit line.

He likes Alan right away.

After dinner is over, while Alan and I go for a walk, Alan says, "I really like your family. Did they like me, do you think?"

"I know they did."

But my mother never once threw her head back and laughed, the way she used to when Sunny was at the table, never said, oh, *you!* to Alan, like someone trying hard not to love his teasing—no one ever teased her but Sunny.

He'd tell her she looked like Princess Di (maybe . . . a little) and he'd often exclaim, you've made my day, darlin'! when he'd taste her special fried chicken. My father calls her Kate or Mama, and he can't eat anything fried because of the cholesterol, but they've been rocking together on our front porch through twenty years of marriage, and he *does* have a profession: law. He's a judge.

Oh, is he a judge!

Sunny, he said once when Sunny alluded to a future with me, every Friday noon Marybeth's mother comes down to my office and we go out to lunch. It's a ritual with us: I get to show her off to my colleagues, and we stroll over to the hotel, enjoy an old-fashioned, have the special-of-the-day, and set aside that time just for us. . . . I hope someday my daughter will be going down to her own husband's place of business to do the exact same thing.

Later Sunny said, He wasn't kidding, was he?

Him? I said. Kid? I said.

It was a week to the day that Sunny asked me to marry him. We were just graduated from high school. I was already planning my courses at the university when Sunny got wind of a job in Santa Monica, running a shop called Sun & Surf. Sunny'd moved from California when his folks broke up. His mom brought him back to Greenville, where she waited table in his grandfather's diner. . . . I never knew what Sunny's father did for a living, but my father, who spent a lot of time trying to worm it out of Sunny, said it sounded as though he was a "common laborer." Can't he be just a laborer? I said. Does he have to be a common one?

Marybeth, said my father, I'm just looking out for you. I like the boy. He's a nice boy. But we're talking here about the whole picture. . . . Does Sunny ever mention college?

I want to go to college, I told Sunny.

You can go out on the coast somewhere.

How? Daddy won't pay for it if we get married.
We'll figure out something.
It's too vague, Sunny, and too soon.
What's vague about it?
Don't *you* want to go to college, Sunny? Don't *you* want a profession?

Sunny said he couldn't believe I felt the way my father did, in the letter he left with my mother for me. He said the Navy was his best bet, and at least he'd be on water. He didn't say anything about waiting for him, or writing—nothing about the future. I'd said some other things that last night together, after he'd made fun of my father's talk about my parents' Friday-noon ritual. They don't even touch, he'd said: I've never once seen them touch, or heard them use affectionate names, or laugh together. So she shows up at his office once a week—big deal! . . . Honey, we've got a love that'd like to bust through the roof! You don't want to just settle for something like they did! They settled!

They love each other, I argued back, it just doesn't show.
. . . Sunny said that was like plastic over wood, and love should splinter, crack, and burn!

You know how it is when someone criticizes your family, even when you might have thought and said the same things. You strike out when you hear it from another mouth, say things you don't mean, or you do, and wouldn't have said under any other circumstances.

I said, at least my father could always take care of my mother! At least he'd made something of himself, and she could be proud of him! That's good enough for me, I said. I knew from the hurt look in Sunny's eyes he was hearing that he wasn't.

"Seventy-four percent of American adults are interested in professional football," Alan says as we walk along under the stars. "Eighty-seven percent of men and sixty-three percent of women."

I can hear Sunny's voice saying blah blah blah blah blah blah blah!

"Alan," I say, "what kind of office does an advertising man have?"

"Mine's going to be in New York City, and there'll be a thick rug on the floor, and a view of the whole Manhattan skyline from the windows. Do you like New York, Marybeth?"

"Anyplace but here!" I answer. "I'd like to get out of the South! I'd like to live near an ocean." I was picturing Sunny coming in on a big wave out in California. "I'd like to always be tanned."

Alan shakes his head. "That's out of style now. The ozone layer and all. White skin is in. No one wants a tan anymore."

When we get to the curb, Alan puts his hand under my arm and remarks, "You smell good. What perfume is that?"

"I don't remember what I put on." I was thinking of nights with Sunny we'd walk down this street with our arms wrapped around each other, and Sunny'd say, let's name our kids. Say we have four, two girls and two boys. You get to name a boy and a girl.

Alan lets go of my arm when we get across the street.

"I like the fact you're majoring in cconomics," he says. "You could go into investment banking. New York is where *you* want to go too."

"Sure, New York," I say. "That's for me."

Next weekend I have a date with John. Premed. Chunky. Beautiful smile. On the porch he tells my father, "I'll take good care of her. Don't worry."

"What are you going to specialize in?" My father gets one last question in as we are heading down the steps.

"Pediatrics, sir," and John grins and grabs my hand as we walk to his white Pontiac.

My mother is sitting in the wicker rocker on the porch, waving at us as we take off.

"Nice people," John says.

We drive to the SAE house with the top down, the moon just rising. "Your family reminds me of mine," he says. "Your mom so warm and welcoming, and your dad all concerned about me. . . . My father's that way about my kid sister when boys come to take her out. I don't have a lot of time to date, so I like dating someone whose family I can meet. You can tell a lot about a girl by her folks."

"They never touch," I tell him. "I mean, not openly."

"Like mine. You watch mine and you wonder how two kids got born."

We look at each other and laugh.

I like him. His wit, his good manners, his dancing, even his "shop talk" about his premed courses. He is a good listener, too, questioning me about what I'm studying, my ideas; he is the perfect date.

"Did you have a good time, sweetheart?" my mother asks.

"So-so." I tell the truth.

"In that case I hate to tell you what's on the hall table."

It's an overnight letter from Western Union. Short and sweet.

ARRIVING TOMORROW NIGHT. HAVE PROFESSION AND HIGH HOPES. LOVE,

HAROLD.

"He's coming back, isn't he?" Mom says.

I show it to her.

"You like him, Mom, so why did you hate to tell me about this?"

"I like him a lot, but I don't think your father's ever going to resign himself to Sunny, even if he does call himself Harold."

"He has a profession, he says!" I am dancing around the room, hugging the letter. "He has high hopes!"

"I think he's the same old Sunny, honey, and I think it's just going to be more heartbreak. Oh, I *do* like him. Truly I do. But you started seeing Alan and John. You took a step away from Sunny."

"Just give him a chance, Mom."

"Give who a chance?" my father's voice.

He is coming into the living room in his robe and pajamas.

"Harold!" I exclaim. "Just give Harold a chance!"

"We used to chant 'Give peace a chance,' when I was in college," my father says, "and I'd say Sunny having a chance is like peace having a chance. Peace being what it is, and Sunny being what he is, no chance will do much to change things. Won't last. . . . Now, John is a young man I really warm to. Did you have a good time with John?"

"He was the perfect date," I answer.

"You said it was a so-so time," says my mother.

"Maybe I'm not into perfection."

When I meet the little plane that flies from Charlotte to Greenville, I can see Sunny getting off first, lugging his duffel bag, dressed in his Navy uniform, hurrying through the rain, tan as anything, tall, and grinning even before he can spot me in the small crowd.

He has a box of candy—"Not for you, my love," he says, "it's for your mama." Then he kisses me, hugs me, hangs on hard and whispers, "Let's name our kids. Say we've got six, all boys, first one's Harold junior. We could call him Harry."

There is no way I can get him to talk about his profession on the way home in my father's Buick. He says he is going to tell me at the same time he tells my folks, that all we are going to talk about on the way there is how soon I can transfer to the university near the base. He has three more

years in the Navy and an application for reduced tuition for
Navy wives, providing I still love him the way he loves me,
do I? . . . *Yes?* Okay!

He says, "Park the car somewhere fast before we go
straight home, because we've got to get the fire burning
lower, or we'll scorch your loved ones." Here's a place.

My father growls, "One *hour* getting back here from the
airport, was the traffic *that* bad on a weeknight? We thought
you'd had an accident. . . ." And my mother purrs,
"Guess what's cooking?"

"Fried chicken!" Harold cries, sounding like the same
old Sunny. "Darlin', you have made my day! Love you and
want some huggin' from my one and only!"

"Oh *you!*" my mother says.

It does not take my father long to start in; he starts in at
the same time he picks up his fork.

"What's this about a profession, Sunny? Harold?"

"Yes, sir, I am a professional man now."

"You're becoming a professional sailor, is that it?"

"No, sir. I'm leaving the Navy eventually, but thanks to
the Navy, I now have a profession that suits me."

"Which is?"

"I'm an underwater welder."

"Let's eat before we get into all this," says my mother,
fast.

"You're a *what?*"

"An underwater welder."

My father begins to sputter about Alan, who is going into
advertising, and John, the aspiring baby doctor, those are
professions, but what kind of . . . what kind of . . .

And my mother is passing the gravy, passing the cran-
berry relish, the biscuits, keeping her hands flying between
the table and Sunny.

"Where will you, where will . . ." my father again, and if

he ever finishes the sentence, I don't know. For I am seeing Sunny see me. I am seeing him be true to me and to himself. Perhaps my father wants to ask where will you do this, where will your office be, for my father is one to think in terms of a man's workplace.

But I am drifting in my thoughts to future Fridays, traditional and loving, donning a wet suit for a rendezvous in the deep blue sea. Keeping my date with that warm fish I married.

M. E. KERR

M. E. Kerr is just one of several pseudonyms that belong to Marijane Meaker, who was born in Auburn, New York, and is now a resident of East Hampton on Long Island.

Her earliest and best-known novel for teenagers, *Dinky Hocker Shoots Smack!*, is about an overweight girl who "overdoses" on food to compensate for the lack of attention from her parents. In addition to being named one of the Best Children's Books of 1972 by *School Library Journal*, it was made into an ABC-TV "Afterschool Special."

Many of her novels—such as *The Son of Someone Famous; If I Love You, Am I Trapped Forever?; Is That You, Miss Blue?; What I Really Think of You; Him She Loves?* and *I Stay Near You*—have more intricate plots and are peopled by more unusual characters than those found in many other young adult novels. Her most unusual characters are found in *Little Little:* a beautiful seventeen-year-old girl who is only three feet, three inches tall and her boyfriend, Sydney Cinnamon, another little person who plays "The Roach" in a TV pest-control commercial.

M. E. Kerr's two most important novels for teenagers are *Gentlehands* and *Night Kites*, both of which were named Best Books for Young Adults by the American Library Association. *Gentlehands* begins as a summer romance between two mismatched teenagers and slowly unfolds as a hunt for an ex-Nazi war criminal. *Night Kites* concerns the relationship that develops between Erick Rudd and a free-spirited girl and then shifts to the family problems that occur when everyone learns that Erick's older brother has acquired AIDS.

Her most recent creation is a series of mystery/detective novels featuring John Fell, who uses some of his late father's detective techniques for getting himself out of trouble. *Fell*, the first book in that series, is followed by *Fell Back*.

Kerr's own zany teenage adventures and the models for some of her adolescent characters are described in her autobiography, *Me, Me, Me, Me, Me.*

In addition to editing the two predecessors of this book, *Sixteen: Short Stories by Outstanding Writers for Young Adults* and *Visions: Nineteen Short Stories by Outstanding Writers for Young Adults*, DONALD R. GALLO has also written *Presenting Richard Peck* and is the editor of the 1985 edition of *Books for You*. He is a former editor of the *Connecticut English Journal* and past president of the Assembly on Literature for Adolescents of the NCTE (ALAN). A former junior high school English teacher and reading specialist, Gallo lives in West Hartford, Connecticut, and is a professor of English at Central Connecticut State University, where he teaches courses in writing and in literature for young adults.

5C
Cor